OUT OF THE WILDERNESS

OTHER FIVE STAR WESTERNS
BY MAX BRAND:

Stolen Gold (1999); *The Geraldi Trail* (1999); *Timber Line* (1999); *The Gold Trail* (1999); *Gunman's Goal* (2000); *The Overland Kid* (2000); *The Masterman* (2000); *The Outlaw Redeemer* (2000); *The Peril Trek* (2000); *The Bright Face of Danger* (2000); *Don Diablo* (2001); *The Welding Quirt* (2001); *The Tyrant* (2001); *The House of Gold* (2001); *The Lone Rider* (2002); *Crusader* (2002); *Smoking Guns* (2002); *Jokers Extra Wild* (2002); *Flaming Fortune* (2003); *Blue Kingdom* (2003); *The Runaways* (2003); *Peter Blue* (2003); *The Golden Cat* (2004); *The Range Finder* (2004); *Mountain Storms* (2004); *Hawks and Eagles* (2004); *Trouble's Messenger* (2005); *Bad Man's Gulch* (2005); *Twisted Bars* (2005); *The Crystal Game* (2005); *Dogs of the Captain* (2006); *Red Rock's Secret* (2006); *Wheel of Fortune* (2006); *Treasure Well* (2006); *Acres of Unrest* (2007); *Rifle Pass* (2007); *Melody and Cordoba* (2007); *Outlaws From Afar* (2007); *Rancher's Legacy* (2008); *The Good Badman* (2008); *Love of Danger* (2008); *Nine Lives* (2008); *Silver Trail* (2009); *The Quest* (2009); *Mountain Made* (2009); *Black Thunder* (2009); *Iron Dust* (2010); *The Black Muldoon* (2010); *The Lightning Runner* (2010); *Legend of the Golden Coyote* (2010); *Sky Blue* (2011); *Outcast Breed* (2011); *Train's Trust* (2011); *The Red Well* (2011); *Son of an Outlaw* (2012); *Lightning of Gold* (2012); *Comanche* (2012); *Gunfighters in Hell* (2012); *Red Hawk's Trail* (2013); *Sun and Sand* (2013); *The Double Rider* (2013); *Stagecoach* (2013); *The Wolf and the Man* (2014)

OUT OF THE WILDERNESS

A WESTERN STORY

MAX BRAND®

FIVE STAR

A part of Gale, Cengage Learning

GALE
CENGAGE Learning®

Farmington Hills, Mich • San Francisco • New York • Waterville, Maine
Meriden, Conn • Mason, Ohio • Chicago

GALE
CENGAGE Learning

LIBRARY OF CONGRESS CATALOGING-IN-PUBLICATION DATA

Brand, Max, 1892–1944
    Out of the wilderness : a western story / Max Brand. — First edition.
        pages ; cm
    ISBN 978-1-4328-2848-6 (hardcover) — ISBN 1-4328-2848-7 (hardcover)
        1. Ranchers—Fiction. I. Title.
PS3511.A87O76 2015
813'.52—dc23   2014031316

First Edition. First Printing: January 2015
Published in conjunction with Golden West Literary Agency
Find us on Facebook– https://www.facebook.com/FiveStarCengage
Visit our website– http://www.gale.cengage.com/fivestar/
Contact Five Star™ Publishing at FiveStar@cengage.com

Printed in the United States of America
1 2 3 4 5 6 7 19 18 17 16 15

ADDITIONAL COPYRIGHT INFORMATION

★ ★ ★ ★ ★

PART I

★ ★ ★ ★ ★

CHAPTER ONE

Of course, a forced sale is always a painful thing. Dunstan felt wicked about it, partly because he knew that he had bought the Morgan place for about thirty percent of its real value, and partly because he knew that Morgan had not deserved to lose it. That is, he knew in his heart that bad luck had beaten the doctor more than anything else. That was the very reason that Peter Dunstan put on his grimmest face, and, for the ride to the Morgan place that morning, he selected the toughest and the meanest horse in his string. He had a good string of horses, all with high strains of breeding, but that good blood was crossed with common, old mustang stock. Peter Dunstan liked horses of that ilk—fine-standing fellows with a good deal of devil tucked away in their hearts.

This morning, he had a black-legged gray beneath his saddle. The gelding fought him for a full ten minutes before he would straighten out and take the road. Peter Dunstan let him go like the wind, then, and Dunstan's men followed in the rear.

They were accustomed to following their master at some distance. Not that they were men who would willingly take the dust of another. Indeed, Peter Dunstan had hand-picked them for just the opposite reason. All his hands were selected because they knew horses, and knew cattle, and understood that a horse exists only to be ridden and that a cow exists only to be turned into so many pounds of beef. Besides this, each was a good fighting man. With knife, gun, or fist, there was not a man in the group, from the little red-headed man who rode aslant, to the big solidly seated fellow with black hair, who could not hold his own ninety-nine out of a hundred times. These cowpunchers stayed with Dunstan in spite of the fact that they had to take hard work and hard usage from him. They stayed with him because, except for the one master, they were free men.

Peter Dunstan liked to rule his men as an overlord, and he did not want them to be subservient to any other person than himself. The sheriff wanted no nastier job than to try to get one of the Dunstan outfit, because the first hand that crossed his was not that of the guilty man but Dunstan's own. If there were long hours and poor feed on the Dunstan Ranch, it was a consolation to know that the boss had long hours and poor feed himself. If every man there had had cause to understand that Dunstan, in spite of his forty-five years, was his master— whether with fist or with gun—there was a deeper satisfaction in the knowledge that Peter Dunstan would fight *for* them even more readily than he would fight with them.

They willingly allowed Peter Dunstan to ride first, and all those fierce men took his dust on the way to the Morgan place. They were as happy as their master. They knew that on this day he was about to take over the big valley farm. They knew that when that farm was taken over, it would be redeemed from the plow and turned back into open range. Dunstan knew horses and cattle and men. As for the seasons for plowing, sowing, and reaping, he cared nothing about them. He would let in the open range upon the fenced fields. Therefore these hardy men rejoiced in their own strength and in the strength of their master.

Dunstan had not chosen the gray gelding in vain. The nervous, powerful brute had plunged and shied and bucked all the way across the dusty hills. His rider was in a fighting humor when he arrived at his destination—just the sort of a humor that he needed to face the doctor. Yet, when he encountered Dr.

Henry Morgan, he saw that he had built up a savage spirit in vain.

The doctor did not intend to make any faces over the affair. He had played a big game in this effort to dry farm so much territory. He had lost a great amount of money and time. Yet, after his failure, he would not whine. He met the man who had paid him $3 in cash for $10 in value with a smile.

"Now, Mister Dunstan," he said, "I'll take you into my office and show you my plans. I'm glad that you came early. I had hoped that you would be over yesterday, but there is still time before I have to ride for the train. Before I go, I can put you in mind of everything that I wanted to do, here in the valley."

"You mean," Peter Dunstan said, "in farming?"

"I mean that, of course."

"Why, then," said the rancher, "I'll tell you how it is. I've got a lot of respect for you, Doctor Morgan, but for the thing that you've been trying to do out here, I have to tell you bluntly that I don't give a hang." He thrust out his square jaw. He would much prefer to make a fight out of the transaction.

The doctor merely sighed and shook his head with a smile. "I was afraid that it would be that way," he said. "I had hoped that the man who took over this place would inherit my own ambitions with it. But I see that cannot be, and the plows and the harrows and the rest must go to rust."

Dunstan grunted, and his swift eye ran over the farmhouse. Trimmings, trimmings, trimmings everywhere. What a man needed was a roof to sleep and eat under. What call was there for the shade trees that spread their green branches near the house, watered at such expense? What was the need of the great verandah? Why the spreading lawn, tended and clipped and watered by so much time and money and labor? Wherefore the screen of climbing vines that twisted up the sides of the house and fell toward the ground again in tender showers?

11

That active eye of his instantly stripped away these ines-sentials, and already, in spirit, he saw the dust clouds arising at the very foot of the walls of the house. He saw the hitching rack where the ponies of his cowpunchers should be tethered conveniently beside the door. It would not take long for their sharp hoofs to trample the neglected lawn to powder.

Perhaps Dr. Morgan saw something of this in the hawk-like gaze of his companion. He said: "Well, at least you'll be interested in the hay press. You need winter feed, Dunstan."

"Aye, there's sense to that. Come along then, Morgan, if you will, and show me the press. Though I suppose that I could find out about it for myself."

The doctor called for his horse, and a little sad-eyed Negro brought it—no steed with limbs of brass and soul of fire, but a gently ambling veteran mare. Once she had known the glories of the fox hunt. Now she was content with the retired life of the quiet country.

As the doctor mounted, Dunstan said: "What will that mare mean to me, Morgan?"

"Nothing," said the doctor. "She's to go with me."

"Go with you!" the rancher cried. "Why, man, she's twenty if she's a day. Will you pay for her shipment all the way East?"

"She's twenty," the doctor said, and patted the neck of the mare fondly, "and I pray that she'll live to see thirty, too. Molly and I have lived through too much together. I wouldn't be without her."

"Every man," Peter Dunstan commented, "to his taste."

"Exactly," the doctor said, and turned his fine head a little away. "Yonder in the southeast quarter-section," he picked up, "is the press at work now, doing up the last of the stacks. Good oats and barley in that hay. You'll have a chance to see more of the quality of it before it's all in the bales."

"Sowed barley and sowed oats!" exclaimed Dunstan. "But

12

what sense is there in such fodder? A cow will not thank you for it, at least, not in language that you can understand. She won't put on many extra pounds of fat."

The doctor changed the subject. He pointed to a small corral that they were passing. "There's a prize winner," he said. "That big Durham bull has a pedigree that a duke could envy. The list is longer than my arm."

"But why the corral?" asked the rancher.

"Oh, he needs hand tending and hand feeding, and all the rest. Grooming is as important to him as it is to feed him, almost."

"Bah!" exclaimed Peter Dunstan. "Where do you find men who'll do that sort of work? My boys would never lay a currycomb on the back of a bull. But they might dress him down with a quirt. Eh, boys?"

The subdued laughter of the Dunstan hands was like the looming of distant thunder.

"Have him out," the rancher said, "and let him take care of himself in the open, will you?"

"Man, man!" the doctor cried. "You don't mean that. He'll be horned to death by the first wild devil of a bull that he meets on your range."

Dunstan turned toward the other a grave face with speaking eyes. He was not accustomed to hearing his orders questioned in the presence of his hands. He waved them on to execute his orders, saying to the doctor: "He'll learn to care and fend for himself, or else he'll die. That's the way that I have with my men, and that's the way that I have with cow and horse. I find that it prospers the breed in the long run."

The doctor shook his head. "He's not meant for it," he said. "He's not trained for it. A ton of fat and good nature. Look at his sleepy eyes. He doesn't need that ring through his nose. I could lead him about with my bare hand . . . I've done it."

"But perhaps," the rancher said, "when he has to work for himself, that ton of fat and bone will turn into a ton of bone and muscle. Perhaps he'll wake up. Do I want sleeping blood like that in my calves? No, sir, I want a heart of fire. That makes the stuff that will not have to be corralled and fed all through the winter. Look at the fat fool. He won't leave even when the bars are down. Whip him out, 'punchers!"

They whipped him out, readily enough. With their quirts cracking and cutting at his rump, he was sent lumbering over the next hill and away toward the open.

The doctor watched him go with a dying dream in his eyes. The ribbons that that bull had won were delights that had haunted his sleep for many a night. He said nothing, and led the way on toward the hay press.

It stood in a hollow beside the butt end of a great stack of hay. A hundred-and-fifty-ton stack that monster pile had once been, and still in what remained standing there were forty solid tons of fine feed. Beside the loose hay stood the neatly squared and growing stack of the bales, flaring in the bright sun like cubes of pale, polished amber.

They could distinguish these things, but not the minute details, for the whole scene was obscured with a mist of dust, ever rising, as the fork dragged fresh sections of the stack toward the feeding platform, as the fork horse plodded out or sluggishly back, or where the beater rose and fell in the box, or most of all where the four power horses trotted in their jerky circle.

"Bale!" shouted the power driver.

The bale-roller leaped for the dog house under the feed platform. He snatched his bar and jammed open the heavy door. As it swung wide he caught at the wire heads that the wire-puncher shoved through from the farther side of the box.

"A good bale-roller," said the doctor, "ought to take the wire off the last hook. He ought to be waiting for it . . . you see?"

Sure enough, the bale-roller had gripped the last wire the instant the wire-puncher's needle slid through. The wire was tied with a single twisting grip of the gloved left hand.

"Tied!" yelled the bale-roller.

He caught his hook from the nail above his head and sank it in the top of the bale as the power team lurched ahead, and the heavy beater rose. He jerked the bale out, turned, and "broke" it across his knee—with his right hand. With his kit, he slammed the door shut, disengaged the hook, and with it pulled home the locking bar—all of this before the beater could rise a scant few feet, and the feeder push down the first slug of the new bale.

"Aye," the rancher said, "all very good. But where d'you get the men that will do this sort of dog's work?"

"From dawn to dark," the doctor said, "but they get as high as seven dollars a day for it."

"You could pay my men," said the rancher, "seven dollars an hour, but they wouldn't make themselves slaves for that. Slaves to a master, or slaves to money, what difference does it make? The fellows in my outfit want to be free men."

He said this a little louder than he had spoken before, because there was no reason why his men should not hear the noble sentiment that he had just spoken in their behalf. They did hear, as they nodded, self-satisfied.

"Aye," Peter Dunstan said, "and now I can see the sort of men that have to be hired for this work. Dead men . . . sleeping men . . . like the fat bull that you kept in the corral, Morgan. Look yonder. It makes me yawn."

"Why," said the doctor, "he seems a very well set-up fellow."

"What does the body count!" Dunstan cried. "It's the heart of fire, man . . . the heart of fire. It isn't the show horse that wins the race. It's the broken-kneed cripple, perhaps, if he has

15

wings in his mind and a heart of fire. And that poor devil yonder . . . why, he doesn't live, he sleeps. There's more life in the eye of a dead fish than in his eye."

"I am sorry you think that," Dr. Morgan said. "Because I want to talk to you about that very boy. You remember that I said I should ask you to keep one of my men?"

"It was written into the bill of sale," said the rancher. "But I hope, Morgan, that you won't wish on me a joke like that . . . a dead lump like that."

"I'm sorry," said Morgan, "but that's the very man."

CHAPTER TWO

At this, the rancher shrugged his shoulders ever so slightly, as one who said: "This burden shall not gall me very long."

It seemed that the doctor read his mind, for he added: "I shall want to ask you to give me your word on it, my friend."

Here Dunstan rebelled. He was not the most scrupulous man in the world, though more so than many gave him credit for being. It could truly be said that he was one whose naked word was a more strongly binding power than another man's bond. Now, he said in resistance: "Look here, Morgan, you know me and you know my men . . . because you've lived in the same county with us for quite a spell. But still you don't know us well enough. You would never want to send a man like that along with us. Or is he only a boy, Morgan?" He said this hopefully.

"I don't know," said Morgan. "Sometimes I think that he's a case of arrested development, and that someday he'll take the next step and really grow up. Then again . . . I'm forced to feel that he's just simple. He's twenty-three, Dunstan."

"Twenty-three," Dunstan said with a groan. "And still leading a power horse up and down along one track all the day long. What a job for a grown man. Why, I was running a ranch at that age . . . you had a degree . . . we were our full selves, except for the lines in our faces and the toughness in our heads. Here's a man of that age just leading a horse up and down all the day long."

"I'll freely admit that it's bad, and very, very bad," Morgan

17

said. "But there's a story behind this affair. You must understand that this lad's mother and father both worked for my family most of their lives. When the mother died, she begged me to take care of the boy. Now, Dunstan, I'd be glad to take him back to the city with me, since I've lost my hold on the country, but I really believe that his one chance for getting back to normal is in the country. In the city, he sits like a block of wood all the day long. Nothing interests him. But in the country, he *has* interests. Queer ones . . . mostly animals. Shall I tell you about him?"

"If I've got to have him," the rancher said darkly, "and if I've got to keep him rolled up in cotton batting and out of the way of harm among my fighting men, you'd better tell me everything that you can."

"He spent most of his life in the city, as I was telling you . . . just stolid . . . only waking up for flashes. I tried to have him taught reading and writing, for instance. I was interested in the case. I got in an expert. And the expert teacher and psychologist worked like mad for three months. Well, the boy learned nothing . . . nothing, Dunstan, and to this day, he can't write his name."

Dunstan threw up his hands. "It's a good deal to wish on a man," he said. "Can he feed himself?"

"Oh, aye. He can do that and more."

"He'll work, at least," said the rancher, "and I may be able to find some fool job like turning the handle of a grindstone for him to do all day long."

"He'd never do it," said the doctor. "Oh, he'd never do that. He was three years here on the farm before he found work that he would do."

"In fact," said Dunstan in irritation, "you're turning over to me a plain case of charity."

The doctor was a mild man, as has been pointed out. But he

was not a man without spirit, and now he answered: "No, Dunstan. I'm not a fool. I would never ask you to work for nothing."

It was said in such a tone that the rancher felt as if a whip had fallen upon him, but not a lash that he could resent, because it had fallen upon his heart only.

"Very well," he said, "then I'm to keep a hay press running, so that this fellow can have a job like this to his liking? But go on, Morgan, and tell me all about the idiot."

The last word made the doctor wince in turn, but he continued gravely: "Very well. The teacher, as I told you, gave up in despair. He said that Sandy was not a fool, but simply asleep above the eyes, if you know what I mean by that."

"I suppose I do. After looking at his eyes, I suppose that I *do* understand what you mean."

"I got the boy here to the West with me, and he's developed a great deal in the past dozen years, since I have been here. So that I can tell you that he will not be a case of charity for you. He cannot do many things well, but he has a talent for handling certain animals. If there's a need of any hard shooting that you and your men can't manage to handle, you can turn the job over to Sandy. He'll turn the trick for you."

For all the apparent carelessness of the doctor, he had put his heel upon a very tender spot in Dunstan's honor, and he knew it.

"As for the hard shooting," Dunstan said, "I suppose that if there is anything that I can't handle, one of my men will be able to do it."

The doctor answered calmly: "Isn't there a cattle-killing grizzly that has been living on your cows for two or three years . . . and always on your own range, man? Are you leaving him there for fun, or is it because you *want* him to stay?"

Peter Dunstan grew hot in the face. "You are meaning that the idiot could bag the old devil who's been eating my cows?"

"I mean that."

"I have a thousand dollars," Dunstan said, "that say you are wrong."

"My friend," said the doctor, "I bet now and then, but never on a sure thing. If you send the boy after the bear, he'll get it. You take my word for it."

Dunstan was very loath to do so. There were a great many questions that he wished to ask, but he refrained, because there was something in the face of the doctor that said plainly that he meant what he had said.

"Very well," said the rancher, "if he can turn that trick for me, I'll admit that he has earned his board for a year or two. What else can he do, my friend?"

"If you have some bad-acting horseflesh on your ranch . . . and I believe that you like them that way . . . he *may* be able to tame the outlaws. If he takes a fancy to them, I mean."

"*If* he takes a fancy to them? He'll never take a fancy to any of the bad actors up my way," declared Dunstan.

"That's to be found out. I'll tell you this . . . I took him to town with me to see a circus, and in the circus one feature was a wild horse with a standing offer of a hundred dollars to any 'puncher who could stay on its back for five minutes. In this section of the country, you know there are plenty of the boys to take up a bet like that and call it easy money if they get off with sound bones. That horse was a devil, however. It tossed those 'punchers as fast as they could get into the saddle. Big Sandy, yonder, was delighted . . . not with the riding, but with the meanness of that horse. He begged me to buy the brute, and when I asked him why, he said that he would soon tame it. I bought the horse and brought it on to the farm at the end of three lassoes and with hobbles on its legs. When I got it out here, I turned it over to Sandy. He had it put in a big corral by itself, then he started to work on it. How, I never could tell, unless it was by fascination. It was about two weeks before he led that horse up to the front door by the *mane!*"

"The devil!" the startled Dunstan cried.

"And the day after that, he was riding the horse across the fields, sitting bareback on it. I saw that the youngster had power over horses, after that. When the bad horse fell and broke two of its legs, I thought that Sandy would die of grief. He would actually go to sit and mourn at the spot where it had been shot. I finally offered him another horse to take its place, but he wouldn't listen to me until Cristobal Mendez came by with a roan demon of a mare. . . ."

"I saw that man-eater," the rancher said, nodding.

"When Sandy saw that mare, he took a great fancy to her, and begged me to buy her. I remembered what he had done before, and I got her from Mendez for ten dollars. He was tired of venturing his head behind her heels."

"The devil," Dunstan muttered. "And did he actually do anything with that wild mare?"

"Look at the fork horse again," the doctor said, grinning.

The rancher looked, and, behold, the animal that big Sandy led up and down through the dust was a sleek roan mare.

CHAPTER THREE

The curiosity of Peter Dunstan was like the curiosity of a lion, in so much that where his eye traveled, his paw was apt to strike. Now that he had decided that this youth was worthy of more investigation, he touched his gelding with the spur and, at a bound, it placed him beside young Sandy Sweyn. The roan mare was at that moment in the act of advancing, and dragging the fork with its little load of hay out of the stack. Dunstan rode straight into the path of the horse and raised his hand. The horse stopped. The forker on the bench of the great stack looked agape at the rider who had dared to halt the fork horse, and the feeder paused on his empty table with the pitchfork raised, cursing the delay in a dust-roughened voice. All had to stop. The power driver had to reach for the rarely touched reins and jerk his team to a halt. The bale-roller could sit down on the weighing scales, and the wire-puncher could take time to roll and really enjoy the smoke of another cigarette.

All of this because Peter Dunstan chose that particular moment for asking a few questions. Morgan grew a little flushed. Then he remembered that the baling outfit was no longer his, and that it was practically in the hands of Peter Dunstan. He shrugged his shoulders and wondered. He wondered at the effrontery of the rancher, and he wondered at the way in which the balers of the crew took this interruption.

If he himself, who had introduced them into this section of the country, where their wages had been so fat for these many months, had held up their work for even a moment, they would have forgotten everything except that they were losing seventeen or eighteen cents a ton per man. When Peter Dunstan stopped the entire press and all the crew, that crew straightway seemed to take it for granted that there was nothing extraordinary in what the rancher had done. They merely made sure that it was indeed one of the working world, and not some mere idler who had come here out of foolish curiosity.

They took positions of easy rest and waited until it should be the good pleasure of Peter Dunstan to permit them to continue their labors. It wasn't from fear of Dunstan and all his fighting men, because men who labor up to a certain point of weariness and might cannot be bothered with such a trifling emotion as fear.

At any rate, there was Peter Dunstan sitting on his dancing, trembling gelding, looking down upon the roan mare. As he had said, he had heard much of her, and he found that she was worthy of all the talk. Those squared quarters of hers, viewed from behind, seemed to promise the bulk of a draft horse, and the depth of her girth would have done honor to a truck horse. She had other points to redeem her from massive sluggishness. It was easy to understand, how she could drag the heavy, creaking fork up and down, tearing out great bunches of wedged hay with enormous effort. When one studied the finely sloped shoulders, the length of the neck, and the tapered sweep of the legs, it was still easier to understand what legend told of her.

She had the speed of the eagle, and the endurance of the very wind that the eagle sails on. As for the soul of a witch that had been bestowed upon her, there was an ample foreshadowing of it from the little, restless, fiery eye that gleamed brightly at the rancher.

It made a silly picture—the harnessing of this glorious charger to such a menial task. She was of a mold that might have carried armored men to battle. Aye, and in need she could have carried a heavyweight hunter to many a kill behind the hounds, even over the fastest galloping country. Yet here she was, plodding back and forth, coated with dust, with only this Sandy Sweyn to control her devilish soul.

Peter Dunstan was amazed to the very roots of his soul. He did not believe in miracles. He had seen that gallant rider and horsebreaker, Jack Lamone, after Jack had been battered to worthlessness by this she-devil of a horse. Yet here she had given herself up to slavery at the bidding of a half-wit.

"Take her away again," Peter Dunstan said, and reined his gelding back from the path.

The youth did not speak. He merely put a hand against the broad hip of the roan. At this, with suddenly pricking ears, she leaned into the collar, and the fork with its great load of tangled, matted hay went dancing lightly over the rough surface of the stack, and then swung up and dumped at the feeding table. Once more the life of the hay-baler commenced with huge groanings and clamors.

Peter Dunstan watched the movement of that fork load on top of the stack, but he gave it only a glance, for his fullest attention was riveted upon the mare and the long, light, swinging stride with which she walked away under the burden.

Bitter envy took hold upon his heart. He was willing to work for his money and he was willing to spend his money for the thing that he wanted. Just at that moment he knew he was looking upon a thing that money could not buy. If he separated the youth from the mare, he would be committing a crime; it was the foreshadowing of the crime that darkened the heart and the face of Peter Dunstan.

He saw the fork tripped—the load of hay dropped with a jar upon the feed table—and Sandy Sweyn commenced to back up the roan. It was a different matter from her forward progress.

She had pricked her ears willingly enough, as though she did not at all mind the struggle of the lift. To back up—that was a thing that went against her grain. Back went the short, sharp ears, with a quiver of malice and hatred. She shook her head, and she switched her tail nervously.

Dunstan began to feel anxious. Assuredly had he stood in that place behind the famous heels of that man-killer, he would have jumped for safety. Not so the half-wit. He simply jerked impatiently at the singletree. He said not a word. It did not even occur to him, apparently, to touch the reins that were festooned about his neck, but he strained back upon the singletree in silence

Peter Dunstan observed two things. The first was a great shock of surprise to him—for the roan mare, after a brief instant of hesitation, did indeed begin to back up, obedient to that pressure—not with the lounging, sloppy step of a work horse, but a neat, precise, high leg action. She backed as straight as a string, and as fast and light as the forker could gather in the spare length of rope before he dragged the fork back upon the stack.

This was all very strange to Dunstan. For it was affording, in the most simple manner, the surest proof that the half-wit had fully conquered the great mare. And yet this was not the most remarkable matter that the rancher had observed. For the sleeves of Sandy Sweyn were no longer than his brown elbows. When he pulled back upon the singletree, Dunstan had observed that upon the forearm of the fork-horse driver an intricate tangle of twisting muscles leaped into view. Now Sandy Sweyn leaned dreamily against the side of the mare; she leaned a little against him, and the relaxed arm of Sandy Sweyn looked not merely large, but soft and round with fat. Dunstan had seen, and he knew that it was not fat at all. By the forearm you will tell the man. It was not the mere bulk and the sinewy

development of that forearm that interested the rancher; it was
even more the taper formation, which suggested an incredible
strength of upper arm and shoulder and back. There were only
some five feet and eleven inches of Sandy Sweyn, but the
rancher on his second guess shrewdly suspected that he carried
well over two hundred pounds of muscle. A burden, in fact, that
needed the mighty frame of such a horse as the roan to carry
him fast and far.

Dunstan rode closer and he looked down at Sandy's hand. It
was as he had suspected. That hand was not squared and
blunted by much labor; it was as tapered and graceful as the
hand of any gentleman of leisure who has never gripped a
heavier tool than a golf club. No, that miracle of strength that
had been revealed to Dunstan upon the arm of Sandy Sweyn
was not the power that is the result of honest labor, long
performed. It was a mere gift of Nature.

A sudden anger burned in the heart of Dunstan. Ah, how
cruelly unlucky it was that this simple creature should have
been endowed with the might of a Hercules, a power to which
even the stout and famous right arm of Peter Dunstan was like
the power of a child, and that this boy should have been
endowed with the singular ability to rule even such a dreadful
malefactor as the roan mare, Cleo. And then to blur and spoil
the splendid picture, that he should be a half-wit! Dunstan
could have used those gifts.

Then he lost all conscience. It was not right that to this
strong-handed idiot such a treasure as the glorious mare should
be entrusted. It was not right by any means. She was fitted to
bear upon her back a ruler of men—such a one as Peter Dunstan himself, and his two hundred pounds of fighting strength.
Peter decided to take her from Sandy Sweyn—not by force. He
would not be guilty of such an act—but by deception.

"Sandy," he said, "what will you take for the roan?"

Sandy Sweyn looked up to him out of vague eyes. They were a strange color, and they gave the strangeness to the face of the youth, Peter Dunstan decided. For the rest, he was a handsome fellow, though, perhaps, his features were a little too heavily and grossly made. The hair of Sandy Sweyn was tawny in hue, and his eyes were tawny, also—the color of a lion's mane. Such a color in eyes Peter Dunstan had never seen before except in the dazzled eye of an owl.

He waited a long moment for an answer, but when it came it shocked him.

"I don't know," Sandy Sweyn said, "but I suppose that I'd take a faster horse for the roan . . . if I can get one."

"Ah," Dunstan said. "You don't really love the mare, then?"

"I like her pretty well," Sandy Sweyn said, and he ran his mighty fingers through the mane of Cleo, "but I suppose that I would like a faster horse better."

CHAPTER FOUR

As Dunstan felt that he would be able to close the bargain, he felt an eye upon him. When he looked up, he saw that it was the doctor, studying him with greatest attention. Peter Dunstan flinched, as though he had been caught in the commission of a most unworthy act. He rode back to Dr. Morgan.

"Of all the half-wits that I've ever seen," he said, "this fellow is the queerest."

"Perhaps," Dr. Morgan said, "he is. But for my part, I've never been able to make up my mind as to whether he's a half-wit . . . or whether he has the real sense, and I'm the fool."

The rancher did not like mysteries. He felt that matters that he could not instantly understand were almost immoral. He frowned now upon the doctor. "I'd like to know what you mean by that," he said.

"Why," replied the doctor, "it's really hard for me to explain, except in a general way. But you have heard a good deal of talk, now and then, about the primitive man . . . the abysmal brutes?"

"Oh," the rancher said, "I see what you mean. Well, I suppose that you may be right, in a way. I am able to imagine that the cave dwellers may have been like that fellow. He's born just a thousand years or so after his time . . . or maybe a million years, Doctor."

The doctor nodded. "That's one way of looking at it," he said. "That's the idea that got into my head after I had known him only a few years. But lately I've been considering the other side of the question . . . the opposite side."

"And what do you mean by that?"

"That he may have been born about a million years *ahead* of his time."

The rancher started in the saddle. "You mean that the human race will go backward toward the brute type again?"

"No, I'm an optimist. I think that we'll always slowly advance . . . until the human race freezes to death . . . unless it has found a way of transplanting itself to some warmer, planet by that time. But I wonder if this Sandy Sweyn isn't a type of what we are going to be as we climb the ladder?"

The rancher struck one hand heavily into the other. "Now, look here, old-timer," he said. "I'm a simple fellow, and I don't pretend to know a lot of things that are just ABC to you. But I hate to fool around with stuff that may be nonsense. Are you calling this half-wit a step toward a perfect man?"

"I don't want to be mysterious," the doctor said, "but frankly I'm talking about an idea that only is half out of the shadow in my own mind. I mean . . . this fellow who appears like a half-wit to us might be a most tremendous person if he ever were to have a chance to develop himself. Well, how is a man developed? How did you and I get our education? By playing and talking with other boys of our own age, and so growing up to have what we call good sense. This Sandy Sweyn has never found people of his own kind."

"Because, of course," the rancher said, "most of his kind are sent to institutions where they're not apt to do themselves any harm."

"Do you think that?" the doctor asked. "Ah, well. Perhaps you are right. But the other idea sticks in my crop. That boy needs conversation that you and I and other people can't give him. He's a mute because there is no one to understand him . . . except animals."

"Confound it, Morgan, that is too much, unless you intend it as a joke."

"Wait till you have a better chance to know him. You'll see what a considerable distance he is from being a fool."

"Aye," the rancher said, "I'm going to study him. But first of all I want to buy that mare of his."

"He won't sell her."

"Why, man, that shows that you really don't know him. He has said already that he'll give her up for a faster horse, if I can find one for him." There was triumph in the tone of the rancher.

The doctor flushed a little. As a matter of fact, he had expended a great deal of patience and self-control upon the rancher. Now he was near the end of his string. He answered calmly: "I'd like to wager that you won't find a horse very soon to beat Cleo."

"Nonsense," answered Peter Dunstan. "She's a fine brute, but too heavy to move fast. I have a dozen ponies who could step right past her."

"Do you think so? Well, Dunstan, I'll bet you that you haven't a single *one* that can outrun her."

It was time for Dunstan to flush—and he turned a dark and dangerous red.

"Do you mean to say, Doctor Morgan, that you think this gelding I'm on couldn't walk away from the mare?"

"I mean just that."

"And you'd bet on it?"

"I shall be breaking my rule, if I do, for I never bet on a sure thing."

If there was one vanity that stood near to the heart of Peter Dunstan it was the breed of horses that he had introduced upon his ranch. Except for racing thoroughbreds he was of the opinion that no stock of horses in the world could beat his own. Of all the horses that he had ever owned, the gray gelding had the fleetest foot. When he heard the doctor, therefore, casting aspersion upon the gelding in such a confident manner, the very hair of Dunstan stirred upon his scalp.

"A sure thing, Doctor," he said sarcastically, "is the sort of a matter that a fellow will put *real* money on."

"Dunstan, I don't like to rob you."

The rancher broke out with a huge oath. "Man, man," he cried, "if you're fool enough to back the roan against this flyer, I have five hundred dollars to say that I'll win!"

"Do you mean that?" the doctor asked stiffly.

"As the boys used to say . . . put up or shut up."

"Dunstan," the doctor said, turning pale with anger, "I tell you that I have seen the mare run and therefore I have an advantage over you."

"Bah!" Dunstan hissed. "And I've heard the stories about her when she was running wild. But I tell you, man, that she weighs close to thirteen hundred pounds . . . or even more. No brute of that weight can really move with a horse like the one under my saddle. When a wild horse is chased, there's no rider, no saddle, no cinches, no bridle and bit to bother it. That's why the mare baffled the hunters for so long. Besides, she's a tricky fiend. You can see that in her eye, quickly enough. Don't tell me, Morgan, that she could move in the same flight with the running type."

The doctor exclaimed: "I tell you that mare will walk away from your gelding! And if you want to bet on it make it five hundred or five thousand. I don't care which. Five thousand would teach you a lesson."

That talk was just a shade franker than any that the rancher had listened to since he became a known man in the West. His fighting jaw thrust out ominously.

"Do you mean that you would put up five thousand dollars on the race, Doctor?"

"My checkbook is in my pocket. Shall I write my check?"

Dunstan answered: "I'd just as soon tell you that I'm carrying *my* checkbook, also. If you don't mind, we'll leave the checks with one of the boys as stakeholder. . . ."

In another moment two brown hands were scratching away at narrow, colored strips of paper. Then the two checks were in the hand of Shorty. His blue eyes blazed when he heard the terms of the bet. He asked with an almost moaning eagerness whether there were any other people on the Morgan place who would back the roan with hard cash.

Oh, yes, there were plenty. All the crew of the hay press, said the doctor, would be willing to bet their shirts on her ability to beat the gelding thoroughly. The doctor was right. The instant that the rumor of the race reached the hay-press crew, the baling operations stopped at once, and the crew swarmed out to make sure that the race was indeed to take place.

All was not ready, however, when the doctor and the rancher had decided upon the contest. There still remained another party to the contract. At first he seemed to raise insuperable difficulties. That was Sandy Sweyn.

He had fallen to work the instant that the hay press stopped in its operations. With a hard-twisted wisp of hay he was rubbing down the roan assiduously. As the living dust cloud in which she had been walking cleared away, her coat could be seen to glimmer and then to shine like a burnished metal under the swift and powerful strokes of Sandy.

The rancher, observing her anew, felt a sudden sinking of the heart. He was aware, for the first time, of the reach of her legs, of the great bone with which they were finished off beneath knee and hock. Still, such was the massive bulk of haunch and shoulder that he was encouraged again almost at once. Looking at her up to the belly, with its clean line like the hull of a racing yacht, she appeared a true flyer. Above that point, she might almost have been a work horse. No, not quite so bad as that, for no work horse since the beginning of time ever had muscles so neatly outlined and so sleek. Such bulk and suggested speed combined had never been seen by the comprehending eye of Dunstan, unless it were in the single glimpse he had had of the naked forearm of Sandy Sweyn, when the latter had tugged at the singletree of the mare.

The doctor explained to the youth with care that he wished to have him ride the mare against the rancher's gelding. Sandy Sweyn listened, his eyes fixed not upon the doctor but upon the gelding with a strange blank look that filled the rancher already with horror and wonder and aversion.

"I dunno," Sandy said, "but I guess that I ain't gonna ride Cleo against a lame horse."

CHAPTER FIVE

The rancher stared, then shouted: "Lame horse? Lame nonsense! Doctor, you can't back out of the bet like this! The checks are posted, and I intend to collect. It will be a sound lesson to you. Stick to medicine and to dry farming, Doctor, but don't risk your valuable opinion on horseflesh, after this, and prepare to back it up with so much hard cash."

That was not a very rude speech, according to Peter Dunstan's standards of harsh and kind. Yet it made the doctor flush and toss his head, like a colt when the spur pricks, and it is conscious of no fault.

"It's not *my* remark," said the doctor. "It's Sandy Sweyn that says that."

"And what the devil does he know about this horse, when he sees it for the first time?"

"He's never wrong, Dunstan. I assure you that he knows what he's speaking about, or else he doesn't speak."

Dunstan, with the flaring vision of $5,000 at hand, could not restrain himself. It would be a stroke that would fatten his bank account on the one hand and give him a bit of excellent table talk the rest of his days, on the other. For both reasons the prospect was prized by Peter Dunstan.

He said, at last: "Look here, man, and see whether or not this is a crippled horse." He whirled the gelding away, raced it a few strides, and then swept it back again. "Did it limp? Did it falter?" shouted Peter Dunstan hotly from his cloud of dust.

Then he was aware of Sandy Sweyn approaching, with the unhitched roan mare following like a dog at his heels.

"He ain't gonna show up lame until he's rode hard and begins to bang the ground racing," Sandy Sweyn said. "This here is where he's gonna break down."

Raising his blank eyes to the face of the rancher, he pressed his forefinger deep into the muscular shoulder of the gelding. Beneath him, Dunstan felt a shudder of pain go through the body of the fine horse.

He glanced sharply down and into the dull eyes of the youth, trying to find his soul and perhaps a hidden cunning there. All he found was an impenetrable wall of mist.

"I'll try him again," Dunstan said. "I've ridden long enough to be able to tell a lame horse about as well as the next one."

And he carried the gelding off again in a brisk canter. However, the action of the rangy creature seemed perfection to him, and to all of them who stood by and watched, as well. Peter Dunstan came back more fixed in his purpose than ever.

"My horse is ready, man!" he called to the doctor as he swung to the ground. "I've posted my forfeit, and I've offered my horse. Now what will you do next?"

There was a clamor of noise around them where the hay balers were laying their bets with the cowpunchers of Dunstan's train. Big bets for them—$30—$50—$100—determined by whether a man had been unlucky and had to post his pay of the month to come, or had been more successful in his recent adventure at poker. In the midst of this confusion, Sandy Sweyn calmly protested that he would not race the mare against a lame horse.

"But," the doctor insisted, "he *wants* to risk the gelding."

"Has he asked his horse whether or not it wants to run?" Sandy Sweyn asked. "No, he ain't. Because you can see in the eye of that horse that he don't feel fast today."

Dunstan, leaving the gelding behind him, strode straight up to the half-wit and pointed a finger sternly in his face. "Look here," he said. "We've heard enough nonsense from you, Sandy. Now we're going to have this race run, and you're going to ride in it whether you want to or not. D'you hear me? Because from this time on, *I'm* your boss, Sandy. And you come to me for orders."

Sandy Sweyn looked in amazement from the tall form of the angry rancher to the saddened face of the doctor.

"You know," Dr. Morgan explained gently, "that I have to leave this place, Sandy. And you wouldn't be happy in the city where I am going to live. You couldn't take Cleo along with you, you know."

A dark understanding broke upon the face of Sandy. "I couldn't take Cleo?"

"No."

"Then I'd have to stay here, I suppose," Sandy Sweyn said. "But is *he* going to be my boss, then?" He pointed dubiously at Peter Dunstan.

"He owns this place, Sandy. And you like the place, don't you? You like the place and you know it. The people here understand you, and you understand them. So I thought it would be better for you to stay on here with Mister Dunstan. He will take care of you."

"If you mind your step, and do what you're told!" Peter Dunstan insisted loudly.

He did not believe in sentimentality, this Peter Dunstan. He believed in the facts of life, which to him were hard and stern matters that could not be winked at. He never wanted to shelter himself behind generalities or mask himself with soft speeches. His rough voice made the eyes of Sandy Sweyn widen and turn an appealing gaze upon the doctor.

The poor doctor looked only down upon the ground. He had

done all that he could for Sandy Sweyn, and he could not manage a better scheme of things for him. So he said gravely: "I think that you had better do as Mister Dunstan says, Sandy."

"Ah," Sandy said, sighing and looking with his blank eyes upon the rancher, "it don't seem to me like there is much but trouble lying ahead."

Then he turned to the mare and began to strip the harness from her back.

A saddle was quickly fitted to her. In the meantime, Dunstan was equally busy. If the roan had been performing brutally hard work in the dust beside the haystack, the gelding had just had a hard canter across the country, and Dunstan did not believe in throwing away any chances. It was not his style, for life is life, and money is money. Why should one be careless with it?

Straightway, he said to Shorty, the lightest in body and the toughest in soul of all who rode in his train: "Shorty, can you handle the big boy today?"

Shorty looked askance at the tall form of his master's horse. "I'll handle him or kill him," said the genial Shorty. "You leave him to me. Just shorten them stirrups a bit, will you?"

"I'll do that," Dunstan said, delighted, "and if you can ride him, Shorty, as I know you can, you get . . . an extra fifty, if you win."

For Dunstan was not needlessly generous. There is no law that compels a man to make large offers, you know. However, the mere honor of the task was enough to persuade Shorty. He tingled with pride to the roots of his very red hair as he strode with a swagger through his hardy companions.

"You soft-shelled suckers," the amiable Shorty said, "leave me be and gimme room."

They hardly begrudged him this speech—they were so entirely rejoiced to see a hundred and fifty pounds in the saddle on the gelding, instead of the two hundred at which Dunstan turned the beam.

The doctor, however, was amazed. "Why," he said, "I thought you were to do the riding yourself, man."

"Did you think that? Was there anything said about riders? Why, you can pick out any lightweight that you please, Doctor. And then double the bets, if you wish."

The right fist of the doctor doubled into an iron-hard knot, but he did not strike. Whether with hand or weapon, he knew that to engage with this bully would be simply to invite humiliation.

"The course then, Dunstan?" he said tersely.

"Around that black rock and back again, d'you think?"

The doctor allowed himself to smile. "That's nearly a mile and a half, man," he said, "and distance tells in favor of the lightly weighted horse, of course. Do you seriously suggest it, Dunstan? With seventy pounds less in the saddle than goes on Cleo?"

The nerve of the rancher was as steady as a wall of brass. Look for look he repaid the contemptuous smile of Dr. Morgan.

"Pick out another course, if you like," he said. "I've made my suggestion, but please yourself."

Dr. Morgan shook his head. "I don't think so," he said. "There's no use. I see that you've beaten me before the race begins. Why, man, you ought to know that nobody in the world can ride that roan devil except Sandy Sweyn, and Sandy weighs a full two hundred and twenty pounds. Aye, or a little bit more. But we'll have the pleasure of seeing how fast Cleo *can* run. Are you ready?"

"I'm ready."

"Just fire your pistol to give them the word. Sandy, it's to be around that black rock . . . the one with the three heads on it. Do you see?"

"I see."

"Ride hard . . . but not too hard, Sandy. You can't beat the gelding. But try not to be disgraced."

"Beat the gelding?" Sandy Sweyn said. "Why, there ain't no trouble about that. Even if he had four good legs under him, there wouldn't be no trouble about that. I'll catch him at the rock and I'll walk away from him coming back."

With one ear the rancher overheard the amazing confidence of this remark, but the greater portion of his attention was given to instructing his jockey. "Get the big boy going and keep him at it. Not too much of the spurs. He hates the spurs except when *I'm* using them, and then I *make* him like 'em. You can swing the quirt on him. It'll be good for him. Put a little spice in the loafer."

"I'll run his head off and make that plow horse sick in a quarter of a mile. The doctor is a nut to put a bet on a race like this," the gentle Shorty said. "Give us the signal to start, will you?"

CHAPTER SIX

The start was in line with the big derrick above the haystack, and the finish was to be at the same line. The spectators scattered themselves in various places of vantage, more particularly upon the top of the stack, on the table of the hay press, and one daring fellow—the roustabout of the baling crew—clambered out and sat on the swinging tip of the derrick's boom, to the envy and admiration of all of the rest.

In this manner, they got a view of the course from the moment that the rancher's gun exploded and the two darted off over the sunburned fields.

The yell that greeted that start was followed by a groan from the hay-press crew. They saw that their favorite was not only under the disadvantage of seventy pounds of extra weight, but also he was forced to run in going much worse than that of the gelding. That lithe racer, with the lighter burden of Shorty in the saddle, went lightly across the hay stubble, but the tremendously pounding hoofs of the roan broke through the crust and raised puffs of dust and clotted soil at every fling of his hoofs.

"We're beat . . . we're cheated!" said the bale-roller with a groan.

"Steady," answered Dr. Morgan. "Let's not whimper when we pay. They'd rather have us whine than take our money."

The faces of the hay-press men set like iron, while the doctor smiled almost benignantly down upon Peter Dunstan. Who could have guessed from the doctor's face that rage and scorn and regret were tearing his heart?

He managed to say amiably: "Cleo will beat your horse yet, Dunstan."

"Well," muttered the tall rancher, "I wouldn't believe that there was that much go in any horse of that cut . . . with as much weight on her back."

The doctor looked across the field carelessly. Then his heart leaped fairly into his throat. He had not more than pretended to stare after the two sweeping forms. Now what he saw was the gelding, stretched out true and straight in the height of his speed, with Shorty raised in the stirrups and bent forward along the neck of his mount, jockeying him along to take the full advantage of every effort that the fine animal made.

In the saddle of Cleo, the solid form of big Sandy Sweyn sat erect, as though he had no more than the most indifferent interest in this race. Yet the reaching nose of the big mare was upon the hip of the gelding, and she maintained her place fairly as they swept out of view behind the rock. Like a breeze, the memory of the doctor recalled to him the prediction of his jockey. *I'll catch him at the rock and walk away from him on the way back.*

This was a miracle, not a thing that any man could even pray for.

There was the utter silence of complete wonder from the watchers in the distance. There was the silence of despair in the heart of Shorty as he jerked the gelding short around the rock and headed him for the home goal.

The pounding monster had remained at his hip all the way to the rock, and a horrible dread was in Shorty that the promise of the half-wit to his old master would be performed. He straightened the gelding toward the haystack three quarters of a mile away. The quirt hissed and bit the flank of the gallant beast; in answer there was only a convulsive jerking of the body of the gelding—sure proof that the whip cut him, but that he could not answer with a greater burst of speed.

At that very moment, as the pride of all the Dunstan horses launched out at fullest speed, the monstrous roan mare drew up beside—a blue roan—like a gleaming blue shadow, with the red of polished granite shining through. The very ground shook under the beat of her hoofs, and she was gaining steadily. Then Sandy Sweyn leaned a little in the saddle, and, as he swayed forward, he seemed to make the great mare stumble into redoubled speed.

At every jump the distance between the two riders was jerked to a greater and to a greater stretch. Shorty, screaming like a soul in torment, yelled: "You fool! You fool! Are you gonna beat the horse and the bet of your own boss?"

The big man turned in the saddle, and Shorty had sight of a vague, uncomprehending face. No need to try this villainous temptation in a place where it would not even be understood. Shorty bowed his head with another groan and resigned himself to his fate—to come in eating the dust of this monstrous beast and his half-witted rider.

Still the great blue roan drifted farther and farther away. He knew horses, did Shorty, and with an anxious eye he waited to see her pounding in weariness in her stride—waited to see her head go up. Many and many a time, as he stood in the stands, with his bets placed, had Shorty seen the thoroughbreds come storming down the stretch. Many times he had seen the head of the spent horse jerk up and begin to bob like a cork in a wild-running stream. For that sign he waited now—or to see the mare bear out to one side or another.

There was not a hint of such a change. Suddenly Shorty knew definitely that there would *not* be such a change. There was an untapped well of incredible strength in her that had not yet been called upon. Sandy Sweyn sat, only slightly pitched forward in the saddle to break the wind of the galloping and to swing him with the swing of the mate. Yet with every drive of her massive haunches, she was running farther and farther away into the lead.

There was nothing left for Shorty but disgrace. Knowing his master, he knew that he would not receive any pleasant greeting when he came in on the losing horse. Neither would there be any cheer for him from his companions as they saw him ride their money into the pockets of the hay balers.

Just as that moment of bitterness swelled in the heart of Shorty, he saw the head of the gelding jerk high. At the same instant, there was a wrench and a horrible sinking of the body of the fine horse. He was halting and limping, a furlong from the finish line over which the great mare was soon bounding.

The yell of despair from the throats of his fellow cowpunchers was like a dirge to the ears of Shorty, and the shout of joy from the hay balers was a knife thrust of agony.

He slid from the saddle and walked gloomily on, leading the broken horse behind him. He would have been moved to the wildest curses, if there had not been something else that awakened a greater emotion than wrath and shame. That was a sense of superstitious awe.

For the shoulder in which the gelding had gone lame was the one in which the half-wit had declared that he had found a weakness before the race even so much as began. Into that shoulder he had thrust his forefinger, and had seemed to find an over-sensitive spot. Shorty found this too much for him. He walked in with a face that was a picture of silent and gloomy awe.

Into the uproar he walked. The checks had been handed over to the doctor. The balers had collected the cash of the cowboys. On the one side there was a wild rejoicing; on the other side there was a bitter gloom.

The laughter and the cursing died away on both sides, as the limping gelding hobbled in among them. What a picture between the dancing creature that had started in the race and this that hobbled home at the finish of it.

"If I had had a *real* rider . . . ," big Peter Dunstan said savagely.

Shorty turned upon him with murder in his eye. "If you'd've had the sense of a half-wit," he said, "you would never have started a cripple in a race like this."

Dunstan was a man of great passion, but there had never been a moment since his childhood when he had allowed a bad temper to decide his actions to his own harm. Now he merely looked Shorty steadily in the eye, and then he said: "You're pretty hot, Shorty, and I'm not going to talk to you now. You run along and try to raise enough wind to cool yourself."

He could afford to talk like that. If you have killed four men in your day, you don't have to worry about the manner in which your more gracious and gentle actions may be interpreted by a misunderstanding crowd of spectators. No one thought twice about this speech of the big boss, except to feel that it proved the good sense that he had often shown before.

Now, however, he turned to the limping gelding. He had lost through the disappointing running of that animal. That was not what hurt him so bitterly. The matter that cut him to the soul was that a half-witted boy had pointed out in this same gelding a flaw that his own experienced eye had not been able to see.

"Take that horse out and sink a chunk of lead through its brain, Harry," he said to one of the cowpunchers. "It'll never be any good to any other man. And it's cost me enough money by going lame *once*. I won't have it turn that trick on me again."

Harry took the reins—then paused to strip the saddle off the back of the tall horse, which stood with head hanging in weariness and in pain.

"Look here," said a voice from the distance, a drawling, slow, monotonous voice, "there *is* something that could be done for that shoulder."

They turned to find big Sandy Sweyn approaching—with the shadowy blue roan at his heels.

"Are you a doctor, son?" asked the big rancher sternly.

"Dunstan," broke in Dr. Morgan, "remember that if he has cost you five thousand today, he may be the saving of ten times that much to you later on. Don't throw him away."

CHAPTER SEVEN

As has been pointed out, Dunstan never allowed his bad temper to carry him away into any excesses of tongue or of deed that might result in an injury to his pocketbook. On this day, though a thousand curses were crowding up into his throat, he choked them back and dwelt upon Sandy Sweyn's blank face with less and less anger and more and more consideration.

Finally he said: "Now I'm going to turn this horse over to you, kid. If you know where the lameness is in that leg, I'll leave it to you to cure him of the limp, and do a good job of it, too."

After that, Peter Dunstan was busy riding about the place with Dr. Morgan and hearing from him the plans by which the good doctor had hoped to redeem a hundred acres here and five hundred there from the range to reduce them under the profitable sway of the plow. Dunstan had just enough kindness and diplomacy to listen to all of these explanations, and pretend to be gaining important knowledge through them. As a matter of fact, he was impatient and irritated. He did not want plowed ground, and he had never wanted it. As he rode, he was merely taking heed of the fences that he would break down to let in the wild, free life of the range again. Fences to Peter Dunstan were like a curse.

Scarcely had the doctor departed for the train before the first destructive orders were being given by Dunstan. He dictated them to his cowpunchers from the front porch of the doctor's house. While he gave the orders, the horse that he had taken

46

from one of his men after the laming of the gelding was pastured on the lawn. There it tore at the thick blue grass and stamped great trenches into the soft black earth. In ten seconds it had done such irreparable damage that only the complete remaking of the lawn would have been sufficient to eradicate them. Every time that the horse stamped, the heart of Peter Dunstan waxed more and more joyous. It was the sign that the new order had failed, and the old order had triumphed. Peter Dunstan was most distinctly a man of the old order.

For a fortnight he did not leave the new place. There was much to be done there—very much indeed, if he wished to have good pasture for his cows that winter. Every day he was in the saddle from morning until the night. Every night he sat up until after the middle hour, writing letters in a swift, bold, illegible hand, while the moths fluttered in white showers around his lamp and cast upon his letter paper the oily dust from their wings.

There was nothing but bitter hard labor in all of the changes that he had to initiate, but there was an infinite satisfaction to the rancher. He had one touch of amusement, too, three days after he arrived.

He was out with two of his men to supervise the construction of an artificial tank that might serve as a watering place for his cows. As they came over a hill, they heard the thunderous bellowing of two fighting bulls. Then they saw them in the hollow—one, the great red Durham of the doctor's breeding, already with flanks withering from famine, the other a hardy range bull, with a front, scarred by many a hard conflict of a similar nature. He could not, for a moment, endure the plunging weight of the red bull, however. Back he went, staggering, his knees sagging.

"He's going down and out," said one of Dunstan's men.

"Bah," said the rancher, "he's hardly started to fight. Wait till

he gets warmed up, and he'll make that hand-fed fatty grunt, I can tell you."

He was right. The range bull disengaged his horns, leaped to the side, and the red monster went floundering past. Before he could change the direction of his charge, the agile hero of the mountain desert had caught him full in the tender flank with ripping, goring horns.

One touch of that pepper was enough for the Durham. He fled for his life, bellowing twice as loud with pain and fear, as he had ever done with rage before. After him went the range bull, far fleeter of foot, and plowing up the crimson flanks of the Durham with repeated thrusts.

Peter Dunstan enjoyed the sight with a grim smile.

"Shall I drive 'em apart?" asked one of the men, as the pair disappeared over the next swell of the land.

"Let 'em go," replied the rancher. "If you save that fat fool of a prize bull today, he'll be butchered tomorrow. I wouldn't have such stock on my range, I tell you."

He went on, content. He only wished, in his heart of hearts, that he could have had the doctor at hand to see that combat and its result.

When the fortnight ended, and the rancher decided that it was time for him to hurry back to the home place, he came upon a most unpleasant spectacle. It was old Buck, the same range bull who had conquered the Durham on that other day— now lying on his side upon the plain, dead. He was terribly cut up, and the spot, where the horn of the victorious bull had plunged through his side and found the heart, was plainly visible.

"But what bull could have done it?" Dunstan asked. "Unless one of the youngsters got in a lucky crack at Buck, I can't explain it, because none of the old fellows is foolish enough to even lock horns with him. He's given a lesson to all of them."

Indeed, he was the lord and the patriarch of the Dunstan herds, and he had carved the fear of himself with dreadful horns on all the thousands of cattle that roamed upon that section of the range. The explanation was not far to seek. They had not ridden on a mile and a half before they came upon a mighty bull, sunk to the belly in the cool wallowing mud at the verge of a tank. The red of battle was not yet washed away from his front. His horns were painted from the war, and his sides were covered and criss-crossed by the black markings of wounds, recently received.

When he saw the riders, he backed from the mud and whirled upon them with the angry roar of a truly vicious bull. Lofty at the withers as a buffalo, ponderous of shoulder and of haunch, also, his eyes two balls of red fire, his flanks wrinkled, and his belly tucked up from the scant fare on which he had been living, who could have told that this was the great Durham bull of the doctor's breeding?

He charged them with a bellow of madness, and Peter Dunstan put spurs to his horse and rode away without a word. He did not like to have his predictions turn out so far from correct. Not one of the cowpunchers behind him dared to voice a comment. But when they came back to the ranch house they had quite an interesting story to tell.

However, Dunstan was in a quandary. He had announced before all his best men that the red Durham bull was a worthless thing and that he did not want it on his range. Now he had changed his mind, but could he afford to cast aside dignity and infallibility, with his cowpunchers realizing it? He would not have done so had it not been for the loss of the famous Buck. That was a grand bull, a perfect type for the range, according to Dunstan. He could not very well accept that loss without taking some steps to replace it. Here was the red bull, growing thinner and thinner with the passage of every day. He had proved the might of his limbs, the courage of his heart, and the readiness with which he could learn the lessons of battle. Still, he was starving to death. He had lived too long in reach of all the hay he could eat and cool water to drink. He could not forage for himself. The thought of that great red bull haunted Dunstan all the way back to the old ranch house.

He got there in the middle of afternoon and found, sitting on the corral fence, whittling, the bulky shoulders and the thoughtless face of Sandy Sweyn, his hat pushed far back on his head.

"Well!" cried the boss. "Is *that* all that you can find to do? Hasn't Steve sent you to do something?"

The half-wit raised his dull, handsome face, and shook his head.

It had been the rancher's idea of an easy job for the simple fellow to make him roustabout to his formidable cook. Steve McGuire's mulligan stew was famous across the width and up and down the length of the range. The length of his punching arm and the hardness of his fist were famous, also. It was never possible to keep an assistant with McGuire for more than a very short period, indeed. Surely it was more than wonderful if McGuire were not able to keep the half-wit busy from the dawn to the dark.

"No," Sandy Sweyn said, "he didn't seem to need me none."

"He didn't seem?" the rancher said. "Did you *ask* him?"

"Sure," Sandy Sweyn said with large and innocent eyes. "I asked him, and he said that he didn't need me."

"Did he tell you to come out here and sit on the fence like a scarecrow?"

Sandy Sweyn concentrated his faraway eyes in recollection. "He said that he didn't give a hang what I did," Sandy said, and then nodded, pleased with the flawless accuracy of his memory. "Yes, that's what he said."

"I'm going to ask Steve," the rancher declared, "and if you're lying, you'll regret it." He got to the kitchen door in two bounds of his spur-tortured horse. He flung himself from the saddle and quickly strode through the kitchen door.

"Hey!" yelled a giant voice. "What d'you mean by letting the dust in on this here coffee-cake, you long-legged shorthorn? Who asked you to step into this here kitchen, Dunstan?"

Peter Dunstan, abashed, closed the door hastily behind him, and watched the last of the dust that he had admitted settle on the surface of the twisted rolls of coffee-cake. There was never a breakfast without those cakes. It sweetened all the life on the ranch for Dunstan and his men.

He said mildly: "I only came to ask you, Steve, if you knew that your roustabout was sitting on the corral fence?"

CHAPTER EIGHT

With a glare Steve McGuire paused in his slicing of the coffee-cake, preparatory to strewing the sliced walnuts over its sticky surface.

"Is he setting on the fence?" McGuire said. "All I wish is that he was setting on the edge of a cliff, instead, and that there was a wind strong enough to blow him over the edge. All I wish is that there was a thousand-foot drop on the offside of that cliff, and that the rocks was hard below with just enough river to wash away the dust from the spot where he landed. Outside of that, there ain't much harm that I wish to him."

"He wouldn't work?" Dunstan asked. "Then there are ways of making him work!"

"Wouldn't?" the cook echoed. "Oh, he would work, well enough. He was plumb willing. But he *couldn't* work. Look yonder, I ask you, at what's left of the best cleaver that a butcher ever swung. How many steers and how many deer had I broke up with that cleaver? And now look at it." He took down from the wall a monstrous cleaver, larger and heavier than a woodsman's axe. Behold, all the biting edge had been stripped from the face of the tool.

"How the devil did *that* happen?" asked the rancher.

"I dunno," answered the cook sadly, turning the cleaver gloomily from side to side. "Look at the balance that it's got? And look at the make of it. That was the best German steel that was ever made. Why, you could stand all day long and bust up rocks with that cleaver, and it wouldn't even have its edge turned. I gave it to Sandy Sweyn to cut up a quarter of beef. He give two whacks. Then I hear a sort of a terrible pounding begin that made the house fair shake. I yells out . . . 'What are you doing?'

"He says . . . 'This here cleaver seems to be sort of broke.'

"I didn't believe that it was possible. I went in and I seen that he had smashed the edges of that cleaver like it was made of glass, not of steel at all. How he done it I dunno. But he ain't human. He's got the strength of ten mules locked up in that right arm of his and ten wild horses is in his left hand. And you never know, when you ask for something, if them twenty animals ain't gonna come a-ragin' out and trample right on over you."

The rancher took the cleaver, examined it, and passed it back, filled with wonder rather than with anger. He himself had swung that cleaver. He knew the strength of that steel. How dreadful, then, must have been the might of the man who had driven the cleaver with such force that it had shattered the entire edge upon the ox bone.

"You could let him do something that takes no sense, Steve," he suggested. "You could let him chop the wood for your fire for you. You're always saying that it takes half of your time for the chopping of the wood, you know."

Steve McGuire strode to the wall. He took down from it three axes. The handle of one was splintered to match wood. Another was broken across. The handle of the third was wrapped around and around with linen tape. Even so, the fracture was visible through the bandaging.

"All the finest kind of steel. You know the kind of axes that I've always made you buy for me, Dunstan. Them handles was the finest hickory that ever was grooved. I ain't no baby when it comes to the swinging of an axe. Not me! I've had the picking of those handles myself, and I know wood. But this fool . . . this blockhead, that you sent to me . . . he took them three axes of mine, and he went out to cut me up some wood. He cut me up two big armfuls mighty quick. I looked out through the window after he brought in the first armful, and I seen him working on that wood. It was all oak. All twisted and seasoned scrub oak, just one mite harder and meaner than iron is to work up, but the way that feller was swingin' that axe, he was just sinking it through that oak as though it was dough.

"I yelled out . . . 'Hey, don't bust that axe.' . . . because it scared me to see the way that he was sinking that axe as though it was soft white pine that he was handling. Well, sir, that yell of mine sort of startled him, and he gave that stroke extra hard. Smash went the handle. There it is now . . . the one that looks as though a lion had spent the afternoon chewing it up for fun. No, Mister Dunstan, I am not a very particular sort of a man, but I could put up with busted tools where I couldn't put up with bein' burned alive, and that's what pretty near happened."

Dunstan sat down in amazement and asked for fuller particulars and now some great black, burned patches on the floor were shown to him.

"I tell that fool to put some fresh wood in the fire. He does. But he gets a hold of a chunk of wood that he had cut with whiskers on it, and the whiskers make it so big that it won't fit into the stove. He turns around to me with the smoke pourin' out into the kitchen and spoilin' everything and he says . . . 'Steve, this here stick, it don't seem to fit very well.'

" 'You dunderhead,' I yells at him. 'Ain't you able to jam it in?'

" 'I'll do my best,' says he in that fool, mild way of his, and he does. That was what he done, too. He jammed it in. He give it a shove and there wasn't quite room. And then he braced one hand ag'in' the wall and he give the stick another shove, and this time, I can tell you that something moved. That stove buckled like a shell had exploded on the inside of it, and it comes down smash and leaves a lot of red-hot coals go rolling across on the floor.

"It was a terrible job. I got so choked with smoke that I couldn't do a thing, and had to go and hang my head out of the window to get some fresh air. While I was doing that, the house pretty near burned down. And it would've burned down, except that fool, he don't care what sort of air he has to breathe. He just out and clears up them burning sticks and tramples the sparks out, and then he helps me to set up the stove again . . . him doing wrong everything that I start to do right. Pretty soon I give him a yell and grabbed up a frying pan and slammed him with it. I thought that it would've brained him, but it was pretty near wore out, and it busted all to pieces. He just stood there, rubbing his head and looking at me sort of mild and surprised that way that he has. Then I told him to get out, and he got."

The rancher listened to this long narrative with wonder. "And then you couldn't find a thing for him to do?" he said finally.

"What could I find? If this here world was lined with steel, maybe there would be a place for him, or if we was sinking a shaft in quartzite with double jacks and extra strong drills, then he would come in pretty handy . . . if he could ever hit the drill on the head, without glancing it off and busting his own arms. Around a ranch, life is too dog-gone' delicate for a gent like him. What I would mostly like to know is how you got enough of a grouch ag'in' me to send me a dumbbell like that for a roustabout?"

Dunstan was too wise to remain there in conversation over such a dainty point. He merely added: "You told him to do what he pleased?"

"I did. And I meant it, and the man that don't like what I. . . ."

Dunstan waited for no more, but glided discreetly through

the door of the kitchen. He walked in thought back to the corral. He had his promise to the doctor in his mind, but to maintain on the ranch a youth who was incapable of service was a thought that goaded the rancher to the very heart. Waste—purest waste—and it was not upon such principles as these that his success in life had been based.

He stood, at last, before the stolid figure on the fence. "And what about the horse, Sandy?" he asked. "I suppose that the gelding is in his grave by this time. I suppose that after you got through taking care of him, he was about ready to feed the buzzards?"

"No," Sandy answered, "he ain't meant for the buzzards. Would you like to see him?"

"See him? Yes, where do you keep him?"

"Right here." He whistled a sharp, thin note that was answered by the beat of hoofs at once. From behind the shed, a horse came at a gallop. It was the gelding, with all the limp gone from his gallop, and the lame shoulder doing its full share of service without a perceptible flaw.

"Look out!" Dunstan cried, in even more alarm than wonder, as he saw the savage horse come straight up behind the half-wit. "Look out, Sandy, or he'll tear your head off. . . ."

"Why should he?" Sandy asked blandly. "Him and me are pretty good friends. "Ain't we, old-timer?" He stretched out his arm, and the long head and neck of the gelding were passed that moment beneath it. There he stood, with pricking ears and a happy light in his eyes that the rancher had never seen there before.

"Confound it," Peter Dunstan said, "how did you manage to tame that brute?"

"I'll tell you," Sandy said thoughtfully. "All he needed was somebody to talk to that he could understand. You see?"

"Talk to? You mean to say that he could understand you . . .

and you could understand him?"

"Oh, yes."

"What lingo did he speak?"

"Not words," Sandy explained. "But there is a different sort of a language for everything, you know. Only, you got to sort of open up your mind"—he made a wide gesture—"then, you sort of get in touch . . . you understand?"

The thin scream of a hawk floated down from above and slid coldly into the soul of Peter Dunstan in the pause that followed. He wanted to laugh but dared not.

"Do you understand that?" Dunstan as he pointed up.

"Sure," said Sandy Sweyn. "And he'll understand me." He placed both his thumbs in his mouth and then emitted a piercing, half-vocal whistle that tore through the air and drove up—until it seemed to strike the floating hawk like a bullet. In one swoop the preying bird sagged half the distance toward the earth, and then hung on what Peter Dunstan would have liked to call—a listening wing.

CHAPTER NINE

One might say that Dunstan found himself in a stupid position. He stood with mouth wide open, his face bearing a stricken look. When he glanced at Sandy Sweyn again, he saw that that young man had seemingly forgotten all about the hawk that he had whistled out of the sky. He was now rubbing the nose of the gelding with an affectionate hand. For the first time in Dunstan's life, there arose before his mind a strange premonition of events and things beyond all common seeing and all common hearing. Dunstan shut the door of his mind upon these uncanny emotions and mental hints.

"Saddle that gelding for me, Sandy," he said. "Saddle that gelding for me, because I'm going to try him out right now. It's not possible that he's cured so completely and so soon. Saddle him, and bring him to the door of the house. Then whistle to let me know that you're there."

With this, Peter Dunstan returned to the house. There he found Steve McGuire with a pan between his knees, into which he dropped potato after potato, as fast as his hands could slice away their brown covers and turn them to a crystal-shining white.

"Now, Steve," the rancher said, "I want you to tell me what that half-wit has been doing to cure the lame shoulder of the gelding?"

"What has he been doing?" Steve McGuire echoed with a frown. "All I know is that he went out, got an armful of weeds and stuff from the hills, came back, stewed them up in a wash boiler, and filled the house with an odor that hasn't washed out or aired out yet. And he's taken that stuff and used it to rub into the shoulder of the horse. It ought to've killed the poor brute or cured it. And if it's cured, it's because the nerves in its nose ain't sensitive none."

Dunstan sighed with relief. "There's no miracle about it, then," he said. "Just a simple matter of herbs."

McGuire sniffed loudly, then asked: "But where did he learn to doctor up animals like that?"

"From Doctor Morgan, of course," said Dunstan. But he did not believe what he said. "He gentled that crazy brute of a horse that I've been fighting every time I get on his back," Dunstan said.

"Would you call him a gentle horse now?" McGuire asked, putting his head to one side. "If you had seen him make a dive at me when I was coming back from the barn with a hatful of eggs the other day, you wouldn't be saying that he was gentled none. No, sir. He made a pass at me with his teeth just as I was driving through the bars of the fence and he pretty near tore out the seat of my trousers. I squashed a dozen eggs all over myself."

"*Bah!*" said Dunstan. "He has the horse so gentle that it comes running to his whistle. More like a confounded dog than anything else. I'm going to ride the horse now and see how he is."

"You're going to ride him now?" McGuire questioned. "Well, Dunstan, I'm telling you right here and now that that Sandy Sweyn ain't the kind that will ever do many useful things for other folks. The tricks that he turns might have some sort of use for himself, but not for no others. I'll bet you that you'll find that horse has got something wrong with him."

"Man," the rancher said, "haven't I seen him with my own

eyes, galloping as fast as he ever did in his life? A smoother action than he had the day that the roan mare with a ton of fool on her back was able to run away from him. I'll ride the gelding. You come and watch."

"Captain," McGuire said, "that's just the thing that I'm gonna do."

There was a wicked light in the eye of McGuire as he stepped to the door and peered at the gelding Sandy led up to the house. While Sandy stood at the head of the horse, Dunstan mounted with more ease than he had ever found possible on all of the occasions when he swung himself upon the back of the same animal in the past.

He had time to settle his feet in the stirrups and freshen the grip of his knees. If the ears of the gelding flickered back for an instant, they pricked forward again at once, for the hand of Sandy Sweyn was gently rubbing his velvety nose.

Sandy said: "He ain't feeling right, Mister Dunstan."

"Who told you that?" asked Dunstan.

"He ain't feeling right in his mind."

"About what?"

"About you," Sandy said.

"I'll mend that," Dunstan said. "Stand away from his head, will you?"

No sooner said than done. Sandy Sweyn stepped back to one side, and the gelding stepped the other way, and stepped into the air at the same time. He gave himself a twist around while he was off *terra firma*, such a violent twist that one of Dunstan's feet was disengaged from the stirrup. Before that foot could find its place again, the horse landed with all his force upon one stiffened foreleg. It happened that the side on which the leg came down was that on which Dunstan had already lost the stirrup.

He was a fine rider and in ordinary circumstances he would

have kept his seat in spite of such bucking. But the lost stirrup was against him. The force of gravity and the gelding worked in beautiful accord, and Peter Dunstan crashed to the ground.

His courage was not daunted. While he was flying through mid-air he was already yelling: "Stop him! Head him! Don't let him get away!" He rose with his face badly scratched, his shoulder almost dislocated, and a handful of sand sifting up and down between his shirt and his skin. Then he saw that there was no need to ride in pursuit of the gelding.

It stood with Sandy Sweyn as a sort of bulwark between it and the rancher, eying him with a bright, big-eyed curiosity over the shoulder of the half-wit.

Dunstan flung down his hat and kicked it farther away from him. "I'll ride that horse or break his neck . . . or let him break mine!" he shouted in a white heat.

For he had conquered that horse before, and it is intolerable even to dream that what we have once beaten cannot be controlled again. There is no war so fierce as that of a king against a rebellious conquest. The elder brother can never understand his younger brother for growing up, nor can he forgive him for it. Perfect confidence swelled the heart of Dunstan, moreover. If he had needed any spur, it would have been the calm remark of Steve McGuire from the kitchen door.

"I'd leave that horse strictly alone, boss. He ain't acting like he was at home to you."

Once more the rancher rushed and found himself in the saddle. He took a firm toe hold on the stirrups. A glittering devil shone from his eyes. "Let him go!" he shouted to Sandy Sweyn.

As Sandy Sweyn removed his hand from the bridle of the gelding, the same phenomenon was repeated. The mild, bright eyes of the gelding grew as wicked as those of his master. His head turned into a snaky, ominous thing. He left the earth as though he intended to live in air for a while. He did not fight in a foolish passion but with a wicked malice.

There are ways and ways by which a mustang deposits his rider on the desert, but perhaps one way is most certain of all— and that is to whirl while bucking. For as the rider swings dizzily in the saddle, he has to maintain his equilibrium, control his dizziness, and resist the whiplash snappings of his spinal column all at one and the same moment.

Dunstan was a fine rider, as has been said before, but he was mortal. Finally he swung far out to the side. At that very moment the gelding chose to buck jump in the opposite direction, checking his swing with a wonderful skill. It was as though the saddle had been snatched from beneath Dunstan. He was not slung from the saddle. He even seemed to hang for an instant in mid-air. He fell only a scant six feet, but that fall was solid and compact. He fell upon his side, rolled upon his back limply, and lay still with each fist clenched, but with his wide eyes blank.

Sandy Sweyn stood entranced in wonder. The yell of the cook did not rouse him. As the gelding ran to him again, he began to smooth the shining neck of the horse and murmur little, soothing, wordless sounds.

Steve McGuire, in the meantime, was busy fetching water. He drenched Peter Dunstan from head to foot. Still the rancher did not stir. He strove to lift his boss in his strong arms. But two hundred limp pounds are an almost impossible burden even for a strong man to manage, unless he knows the knack of it. McGuire was rather a master in the art of flooring men than in that of lifting them up again.

Strength of wits seemed to come to Sandy Sweyn at last. He advanced and brushed the cook lightly to one side. As McGuire explained afterward to a friend, it was as though a twisted bar of living steel—if such a thing can be imagined—had touched against him, with a mighty engine propelling it. Sandy stooped and picked up the fallen man, lightly. He advanced to the kitchen door. He shifted his burden, and supporting it in one arm, as a father might support a slender child, with his free hand he opened the door and so passed on into the house.

McGuire recovered his senses at last and showed the way to a bed. There the master of the ranch was laid.

A minute later he opened his eyes—closed them—and when they were opened again, they were lighted with full understanding of all that had passed. They rested upon Sandy's blank face for a long moment.

"There's a bull running amuck on my range, Sandy," he said. "A big, red Durham bull that used to belong to your friend, the doctor. Go out and bring it in. There's a ring already in its nose."

CHAPTER TEN

Making no comment, Sandy Sweyn turned in perfect good humor and left the house.

"How are you, chief?" said McGuire.

"Beaten," said the rancher, "plain beaten, Steve."

McGuire flushed. "If I had knowed that the horse was as plumb bad as all that. . . ."

That was the nearest that he could come to an apology. But Dunstan broke in: "Oh, I don't mean the horse."

Before McGuire could answer with a question, his eye fell upon a form beyond the window and he exclaimed: "Blast me, Dunstan, if the fool ain't starting out on foot!"

The reply of the rancher turned him to stone. "I knew he would," said Dunstan.

"Knew that he would?" McGuire cried. "Why, man, that there red bull has been tearing up the range. He killed the big. . . ."

"I know. I saw the body."

"He'll murder the boy, chief!"

"There'll be one fool less in the world," Dunstan said coldly. "No, what I'm after is to find out if this Sandy Sweyn is really just a man that has a sort of power over animals . . . or if he's really weird."

"Weird?" echoed McGuire.

"I mean that." He raised himself from the bed and sat down in a chair by the window. Apparently his mind was so intent on the problem that occupied it that he had quite forgotten his badly bruised body. "I used to hold that horse in the hollow of my hand, Steve."

"He was always a good deal of a handful," McGuire said. "But I've seen you make him like it."

"But today he was changed. He was like a crazy thing, Steve. Not crazy, either. He seemed to be fighting with brains. If a man's brain had the body of a horse to use, he might have fought something like that."

A little chill struck through the honest brain of Steve McGuire. "Chief, what're you driving at?"

Dunstan rolled a cigarette. "I hardly just know," he admitted. "But look here. We know that this Sweyn has done strange things with the roan and with the gelding. That may mean that he has only a trick with horses. And a good many people have been able to do something like that. But what is the biggest fool thing in the world? A bull, Steve. There's no sense to it at all, when it gets its temper up. That Durham has its temper up. Its sides are gashed, and the wounds not healed. It's made a kill, and it's the king of the range. Now, Steve, I tell you that if this half-wit can bring in the red bull, there *is* something weird about him . . . something so weird that I'll believe that he was able to put something into the mind of the gelding and show him how to pitch me on my head. We'll wait, and we'll see."

Steve McGuire was not mentally equipped to struggle with abstractions, and there was that in his soul that revolted against all that was supernatural. Yet he knew that his strong-minded employer was certainly more than hinting at the possibility of more than the earthly in Sandy Sweyn.

It put everything in a new light, and McGuire went out to the rear of the kitchen where, in a corner, he kept the three broken axes. That which had the handle broken to wiry match wood he picked up and considered with awful solemnity. Then, laying it down, he raised another memento of the axemanship of Sandy. This was a chunk of scrub oak, old and sun-seasoned, the grain twisted around and around, heavy as lead in spite of its dryness, and three inches in thickness. Yet there was only the one mark of the axe. It had gone through the limb with a single sway and left the surface of the wood as smoothly polished as though it had been burnished with much care and with long labor. McGuire ran the tips of his horny fingers carefully over this trinket. For a moment there rushed into his mind a shadowy-winged conviction that Dunstan was right, even without the further proof of the taming of any maddened bull. There was a sort of weird magic in this matter.

However, upon a more sober recasting of his thought, he recalled various significant details concerning Sandy Sweyn. He remembered the smooth, thick padding that rolled under the shirt of the youth like fat—except that it was not fat at all. He remembered, most of all—a thing once seen never to be forgotten—the singular naked forearm of Sandy Sweyn, the smooth roundness of it, the tapered exactness of its proportions, and all the myriads of coiled and twisting muscles that slid back and forth upon one another whenever the boy laid hold on any object.

Yes, there might be a sufficient explanation in the mere muscles of any feats of strength that he had performed—among which the light handling of the senseless body of the rancher was not the least miraculous to McGuire. As for the control of animals, doubtless these, too, could be explained away. Science was a queer thing. You never could tell what it would discover. Look at wireless telegraphy. That was a standing example with McGuire. Things might be mysterious on the face of them, but then there was always a reason. Only, there could not very well be any reason that would prevail over the red bull—unless it were the reason of strength superior to his own incalculable powers.

The more that the cook thought upon these matters, the more serious he became. When the cowpunchers came in from the field that night, he confided in them, seriously, that the boss had sent young Sandy out to bring in the bull—and had allowed the half-wit to proceed on foot.

Shorty said: "You're sort of fond of the kid, then?"

"Me?" McGuire said. "I don't care what comes of him . . . as long as he has a good fighting chance. But I'd like to see anybody get that. Even a snake. And if that kid don't come back, I surely. . . ."

They all agreed with him on this point. The chief had gone very far indeed in allowing a half-witted youngster to venture out on such a terrible expedition.

"Even with my best cutting horse under me," said Shorty, "I wouldn't want no part of the big bull's game. Not me! It would take three men and three horses to tire that big devil out and to bring him in."

The late afternoon sank into the amber evening; the amber turned to red gold; the red gold died to rose and crimson and orange and streaks of green. All of this turned to softly colored dusk, and dusk waned to twilight, and then across the pure face of the night the last small stars drew down in droves and in clusters. Still there was no sign of Sandy Sweyn.

Shorty rose in the bunkhouse and looked through the open window. He said: "I am gonna wait until mornin'. And if the kid ain't come in by that time, I'm gonna ride to town. And if the sheriff wants a posse to bring in the boss of this here ranch, I'm gonna be the first volunteer." He turned upon his heel and stood in the doorway with his thumbs hooked in his belt. Then he said to the open and solemn face of the night: "Not that I give a hang about that fool-faced kid. But there's really such a thing in this wide world as a truly square deal. . . ."

He left that thought unfinished. Because, in truth, it did not need any great amount of finishing. The rest made not a comment. The lantern was put out, some half hour later, and the first snore was making its trembling beginning, when another deep voice spoke out of the dark in a rumble.

"And me, I'm gonna ride right in at your side, Shorty, old-timer. There ain't nobody has got a right to act like a king. Not in this here country. Not in this here century."

Let no one think that Peter Dunstan did not realize very well just what was passing in the minds of his men. In the middle of the night, his sleepless mind tormented him to such a point that he rose, in spite of his aching body, and went out to the corral where his own saddle string was kept by itself, because he would not have his high-blooded horses mixed with others. A $1,000 blooded horse can be spoiled by a kick as easily as any $50 mustang.

He chose an easy-gaited brown mare. Since there was no one to see and comment, he could make this concession to his aching bones and to his bruised muscles. He saddled that horse and rode forth through the night, straight toward the spot at which he had seen the red bull the same day. Because, to his thinking, it was unlikely that the bull, untrained in the ways of the range, would wander far from the same spot, where the water of the nearby tank would tempt him to remain.

As he rode, his doubts grew greater and greater. If it had not been that his wits had been almost shattered and his vanity racked to death by that fall from the back of the gelding, with two capable witnesses at hand to relate his defeat, he felt that he would never have been tempted to give the boy such impossible orders. There was shame in the heart of Peter Dunstan. He realized more and more clearly that even black magic would have recoiled from such a task. Because magic—the kind that works—has to have a mind to operate upon. And what is the mind of an infuriated bull? What is it other than an insensate fury?

He rode freely, and he rode fast, but the distance was long. On the way, the moon stepped above the eastern horizon line and looked him in the face. That slanting light turned the quiet face of the broad tank into a sheet of solid silver, when at last he came into sight of it. The next thing that he made out was the great black silhouette of the bull against that bright background.

He rode a little closer. There was something white on the dark of the ground, and a shadowy outline beneath the moon— the form of a man. The heart of Peter Dunstan seemed to stop in his breast. He reined his horse to a standstill. There lay the motionless form of a man, not ten feet from the grazing bull. The dead body of Sandy Sweyn, of course. Across the brain of the rancher swarmed sudden and frightful pictures. For the first time, keenly, he was aware of how much the honest respect of his neighbors and his men meant to him. Beside their respect and beyond it, there was the dreadful arm of the law. What would the law say to a case of this sort—where a poor half-witted youngster, a poor mental child was the victim?

At least, he would put a period to the bull's existence. At that instant the bull saw him, too. Up flashed his tail and down sank his head. He rushed thirty steps nearer, and paused to snort at the earth and send low, long billows of dust rolling away on either side. He stamped and pawed the earth with mighty strokes. In the meantime, giving the rancher all the time that he needed to draw his bead and make sure of his target with a perfect bead.

His trigger finger was already curling softly about the trigger. Death was not a tenth of a second away from the Durham bull, when a mild voice said, not far away: "Hello, who's there?"

The voice of Sandy Sweyn.

Or his ghost? a dreadful premonition in the soul of the rancher said. No, for yonder stood up Sandy himself against the silver of the lake beyond. Sandy in the living flesh, saying to the bull: "Steady, steady, boy. So, boy. So-o-o!"

Behold, he advanced to the side of the bull. He stood with one hand resting lightly upon the horns where the blood of the day's victim was still black and stiff.

"Hello, Mister Dunstan. It's a grand, bright night, ain't it? I stayed out here to sort of enjoy it. There ain't no breathing in a house, you know."

CHAPTER ELEVEN

In the gray of the morning, when the cowpunchers turned out from their bunks, they were aware of the big outline of their boss riding in toward the house. Shorty, himself, hailed Peter Dunstan.

"Has the half-wit turned up yet, Mister Dunstan?"

"The devil with the half-wit!" Dunstan bellowed. And he hastily rode on.

That was why five Colts were plied and looked to with care in the bunkhouse before the men went in to their breakfast. As they sat about the table, there was a hoarse roar from Steve McGuire. What he said was not instantly made out, but it caused a rush to the windows. There they saw one of the strangest spectacles that ever the eye of a good Westerner rested upon. They saw the giant Durham bull meandering slowly in, pausing to crop a bunch of grass of favorable appearance, from time to time. And some fifty yards ahead of him, strolling along with an equal unconcern, walked none other than young Sandy Sweyn.

No man spoke. It was a thing to be expressed only in muted curses. Who could find the right words to apply to such a picture?

To have said that the bull was following the man at heel like a dog would have been an absurdity, a thing never to be believed. Yet what else was happening, if this were not the fact? The great red bull at the rear of the youth passed toward one of the corrals and entered it with a strange meekness. They saw the bars put up. They saw a quantity of hay taken from the shed and pitched down in a corner for the hungry beast to feed upon. They saw Sandy then place his hand upon the top bar of the fence and vault over it with as much ease as though a great beat of wings were floating him across it.

What seemed, to some of them, strangest of all was that the hollow-sided bull, in spite of his famine, straightway left the hay and ran to the corral fence, pawing the ground into clouds of dust as he bellowed forth a thunderous call after Sandy. Sandy turned near the house and spoke a few words that had no sense at all, but that changed the restlessness of the big bull into perfect passivity.

The bull went back toward his hay, and Sandy entered the kitchen.

"He's promised to come back and see that brute again," somebody said.

The others glared askance at the speaker, for the same absurd idea had entered every brain, and a cowpuncher is not used to attributing brains to beef.

"Familiarity breeds contempt," says the crusty old proverb, and certainly the Westerner sees nothing but trouble on the hoof in the herds over which he watches. Yet here was a half-witted youngster who seemed to have discovered not brain only but soul also in a monstrous bull. Such a matter was not to be spoken of. It was a mystery to be stored away with one's religious experiences.

They heard Sandy in the kitchen asking the cook if he were too late for breakfast, and they heard big Steve McGuire grumblingly admit that he had something for the boy to eat. So Sandy came in and sat down at the table. He did not speak to them. The necessity of greetings at morning or at night was not obvious to Sandy. He sat down, and while the cook prepared his tin plate and poured his cup of coffee in the kitchen, Sandy leaned his chair back against the wall, and dropped his head upon his breast. He was asleep!

They knew some of his peculiarities already, and therefore they spoke out at once, freely and loudly, for they knew that nothing would rouse him from his slumber except some danger call, or the rattle of the plate as the cook placed it before him.

"Just the way that a tired dog will curl up and close his eyes and be off that minute," Dunstan declared, leaning his broad chin upon his fist while he scowled at the sleeper in study. "And yet," he went on, "he had his share of sleep last night. I went out there early this morning and found him lying down on the ground asleep, with this brute of a bull grazing near him . . . sort of keeping watch over him, you might say."

Another stunning blow for the cowpunchers. They stirred their coffee and stared gloomily at Sandy, who was tearing down a veil and giving them glimpses of a world at which they had never before so much as guessed.

"Now, take a look at him," said one of them. "All relaxed like a kid asleep . . . there ain't another growed-up man in the world that knows the secret of sleeping like that. What tired him out, then?"

Another suggested: "Using his brain to find the way to tame the red bull. That was the sort of an idea that would tire out any man, to get the solution of it, maybe. Hey, what's going on outside?"

This remark was called for by a wild outburst of neighing and squealing from the corrals. Big Peter Dunstan rose from the table and peered out of the window. The distant hubbub only caused Sandy to moan in his sleep. He did not raise his head. What Dunstan saw was a form like a pillar of blue morning mist shot through with the rose of dawn. It leaped the lofty corral fence and plunged on toward the house—the blue roan mare.

"It's Cleo," the rancher said in the same gloom. "She's coming, looking for her boss."

"Tell him," one of the ranch men said. "That fool horse is apt to kick down this old shack of a house, if she don't find him pretty soon."

So—Sandy was roused with a sharp word from the rancher. He awakened from the depth of his sleep as a dog awakens—the mere opening of his eyes opened his wits, also, to their full activity. He stood up, raised the window, and instantly the long neck and the glorious head of the mare were thrust through. With flaring nostrils she snorted at the others, then thrust her muzzle into the hand of her master.

He gave her a single word, and she went back contentedly and began to pick and choose in the grass that grew near the house. Then Sandy's plate came from the kitchen. It was not like the plates that had been given to the other men. They were mighty men, these cowboys of the Dunstan outfit, but when the cook supplied victuals to Sandy Sweyn, he discarded plates and brought in a great platter.

It was rough but useful food. All one end was heaped high with an enormous quantity of beans. On the central section fried potatoes were piled aloft, and next to these there was a mighty wedge of half-fried ham. To finish off the trencher there was half a pound of stale bread. For drink, there was the greater part of a quart of black lye, disguised by the name of coffee.

Quality was not essential to big Sandy Sweyn, but quantity was a prime requisite. Dunstan, who hated waste, was nevertheless not unwilling to feed a man who had turned a terrible menace on his range into a valuable piece of property quietly in hand in the corral near the house.

The other men wandered out toward the day's work, but Dunstan made pause in the kitchen. "What's that beef that I saw in the meat house, Steve?"

"A yearling that Buck got."

"That infernal bear. How did it happen?"

"I don't know. The same that usually happens. The boys was close enough to hear the bawl of the calf chopped off short in the middle by a blow that sounded like a whang on a bass drum. When they come up, Buck wasn't waiting for them, but there were his tracks leading away through the brush. And there was the calf, dead on the ground, with his ribs along one side smashed in flat."

"They didn't follow the trail?"

"What's the good?" McGuire asked. "They've follered his trail a hundred times and never got nothing out of it. Ain't you follered it ten times yourself, Dunstan?"

It is very bad for a man when he has no vent for healthy rage. Dunstan, striding back into the dining room, glared down at Sandy. He saw the eyes of the youth widen and his color alter a little. He half choked upon a great chunk of bread.

He was afraid of Dunstan. The rancher knew it, and rejoiced in it, as a woman rejoices when she has a strong man at her beck and call, without exactly knowing why. In his own arm Dunstan knew there was force enough to overmatch any man on his place. But in the terrible right hand of Sandy there was an incalculable power, and yet all of that power was the rancher's to command. In the frightened eyes of Sandy he looked with a wonder and a pleasure combined. If there were any clue to this mystery, it was that he had driven the doctor from the country. Sandy knew it, and Sandy had loved and reverenced the doctor. Therefore he regarded the rancher with a superstitious awe.

"Sandy," Dunstan said, "I have a job for you."

Gloom descended upon the features of Sandy Sweyn.

"It would be a job for anybody else," said the rancher, "but I think that you would like it. It's to go off by yourself for as long as you like, and bring me back a grizzly's hide."

The gloom lifted from the face of Sandy. "Oh," said Sandy, "I'll start after breakfast and a nap."

"You'll find my rifles in the front room," Dunstan advised. "And you can take the one that you like the best. Take your pick of saddles, too. And the roan will. . . ."

"Why," Sandy Sweyn said, "horses throw a scent farther than a man does. And a rifle is too heavy to carry."

Dunstan swallowed with some difficulty. "Are you going to spend the season trapping him, Sandy?" he asked.

"No," Sandy said. "This will shoot hard enough if you get close and hit the right spot." And he brought out an old-fashioned Colt and laid it on the table, where he regarded it for a long time with the most affectionate eyes.

"Come, come," Dunstan said. "You'd have to get right on top of him to kill a grizzly with a gun like that . . . or else you'd have to put a bullet through his eye."

"Well?" Sandy asked.

Dunstan said no more, but he took notice that, according to his speech, Sandy Sweyn took with him neither horse nor rifle when he left the house. Neither would he carry flour or bacon or any of the other necessities of camping.

"And why not?" Steve McGuire roared at him.

"It's a lot of weight," Sandy said in apology. "And if I got a pinch of salt along. . . ."

"You get along," McGuire said. "You're too weird to be right."

McGuire said afterward to the boss of the ranch: "There ain't gonna be no good come out of him. If he does you good by killing that bear, like I think that he's gonna do, he'll do you a bigger harm in some other way."

"How could he do me a harm?" asked the rancher. "Will you tell me that?"

"He tamed a horse for you already," the cook responded.

"And I'd think that you might've learned from that just how useful a gent like him can be. What use did you get from the horse, except to get slammed on the ground? Besides that, ain't he tapped you for five thousand dollars, or something like that?"

Dunstan groaned with the recollection. He said at last: "Nitroglycerin is a pretty dangerous explosive, but if we didn't have it, we couldn't make dynamite. This kid is a high explosive, too. I'm going to learn how to handle him."

"Bah!" said McGuire. "Put him in the prize ring, and let it go at that. Be his manager, and you'll make money out of him if you can ever get up his courage to the point of taking on a fight."

They watched Sandy amble leisurely across the top of the next hill and then disappear from view.

CHAPTER TWELVE

The direction in which Sandy Sweyn started off was that leading toward the spot where the yearling had been killed by the
great grizzly. When he had reached the spot of the killing, he
made no attempt to follow up the trail of the bruin. Instead, he
busied himself for some time with strangely minute details. He
regarded the trail, not to follow it, but to make out all of its
peculiarities—the length of the two hind paws and the length of
the front one, the twisted claw on the right hind foot, and the
broken claw on the right front foot, the average length of stride
as the bruin walked, as he ambled, and as he galloped at full
speed.

After this, Sandy lay down in a spot where the trees wove a
motley pattern of shadow above him, and he thought drowsily
upon the problem that lay before him until kind sleep closed his
eyes.

He slept until far into the afternoon, and when he wakened,
he was ready to work. Appetite did not bother him. Although
Sandy made vast assaults upon the larder when the spirit moved
him, he also cared not to eat more than once a day.

But what would be the dictates of the stomach of the great
bear? Roots, cattle killing, sheep raiding, the demolition of an
ant hill—indeed, almost anything might be to the point with a
bruin. What Sandy finally decided upon were the rich stores of
berries that could be found loading the bushes of the uplands.

In this direction he turned and made off, not in haste, but

with a long, stretching step that never varied. It carried him over, up, and down, rough and level, with an equal speed. There were five hours until sundown, and in the five hours he put behind him twenty-five miles—which, over that rough going, would have been a heavy whole day's march for any other man.

He slept again until midnight. Then he was up and marching until dawn.

Here he made his second halt. He had climbed out of the rolling brown hills. He had passed the foothills of the range. Now he was in a chilly region of pines, with great mountain heads going up about him and thronging in the sky, their shoulders partly veiled in the thin lawn of lodgepole pine, their black throats gleaming in the morning light, their heads now bald, now covered with magnificent white.

Here Sandy made a halt again. He knocked over a mountain grouse with a stone. No need to waste a bullet on the stupid, fearless bird. He had that and his cousin roasted for breakfast. Then he climbed into the biggest tree that he could find and surveyed the mountains more clearly, and especially the bottom of the valley.

It was just such a range as a bear might like. Fifty miles away were the cattle ranches, and the sheep ranges were nearer. His lordship could have beef or mutton when he so desired. Here was a valley where he could levy his tribute of honey and ants and of luscious, pale-white roots, among the damp shadows. Yonder was a stream, idling into little pools, beside which he could lie, and flick out the darting fish by the magic of either forepaw. On either hand, too, there were the uplands with their sparser growths of trees but their abundant covering of berry-laden bushes. Higher still were the serene heights where the forest dared not venture—where the summer was short, and where the winter came back to dwell every night—where the insects lived in mighty colonies.

It was a perfect realm for a grizzly. He lay between two stalwart ranges, and from these rampart walls he could look down upon undiscovered kingdoms on either hand, ruled over, no doubt, by monarchs like himself. Perhaps, at times, the tyrannical desire of the very strong came upon him, and he contemplated descents for the sake of conquest. But the descents were never made. There was too rich a soil here at home, too many familiar faces of things and events. Above all things, the bear, and the grizzly above all other bears, is an economist. He lives for the moment, like a base fellow, and has no more romance in his make-up than goes to the robbing of a wretched ant hill.

These were matters that Sandy took for granted. He had found, he knew, the real home of the king of the lower ranges. Unless the big fellow were really out on a cattle rampage to extend over a long period, it was much more than likely that after his recent kills he had returned to the uplands and to the fat berries that were turning stale there for want of his attention—turning stale by the tons and tons for lack of his regal presence.

From the topmost fork of the big tree, Sandy had regard for all of this. Then he climbed down and began to make a circuit of the valley. He had not gone four miles before he came on a trail. He could recognize it without stooping to make measurements. It was Buck who, exactly according to the predictions of Sandy, had returned, tired of his cattle raiding, to this more peaceful and congenial work of berrying.

Sandy took two steps, leaped, and caught a branch. Then he pitched himself up among the branches—looking like a madman, so rapidly did he work. Foot and hand were accomplishing only the objects that had been planned by the mind of Sandy, and so he went almost noiselessly up through the tree until, once more, he lay, precariously balanced, and studied the forest beneath him.

There were signs and signs to Sandy. The mist that hung upon his mind when other men were near him now lifted a little, and then a little more. He was like one awakening. His glance roved upward, where the eagle tipped and slid sidewise upon great, patient wings as it hung there at watch. He looked downward, where a red squirrel was already venturing down the trunk of the very tree up which he had climbed, going about its business again with the invincible impertinence of its race. Yonder, he saw a blue jay, dipping up and down among the trees, like a sea bird skimming the waves, scolding at a great rate.

It was so far away that it was only a flashing blue jewel in the morning sun, so far away that ears less marvelous than the ears of Sandy would have heard no sign of a sound. He heard, and he guessed at once what was up.

He climbed down the tree in a manner even stranger than his manner of ascent. As an eagle closes its wings and drops, stiff and straight, through the air, so Sandy stiffened his body and dropped down through the tree, only breaking the speed of his fall by an occasional grip on a branch as he passed. Even the monstrous strength of his arms was tried by those strains.

However, he was on the ground almost as suddenly as though he had descended at a single bound to it. Then he set forward across the forest, abandoning his ordinary walk and breaking into a run. What a speed was that of Sandy Sweyn when he chose to run! Long striding like that of a running horse, smoothly and swiftly he whipped along with a soundless step, or with only a rustle and a whisper among the grasses to betoken his passing.

He came to the place above which he had seen the blue jay flashing. Though he reached the spot, the blue jay was no longer there. It was a place where a great fallen trunk had been rolled over by the Herculean strength of the grizzly, which had then fed upon the worms and the insects that wriggled out at the touch of the strange day. For the stomach of the grizzly is truly omnivorous; nearly all that lives is welcome to his great paunch, particularly when he is lining his ribs with a blanket of fat against the long winter *siesta*.

The grizzly had finished his task at the log and gone on. Sandy only paused to try the weight of the tree with his own powerful arm. He could make it tremble through all its bulk, but he could not actually stir it.

After that, he could have followed the trail of the grizzly readily enough across the forest. It is not such a simple matter to follow my lord, the grizzly. Of all the brains that live in the wild, his is the most cunning, just as his paw and his jaw are among the most dreadful in strength. His scent is a keen one, but his power of hearing is a real miracle—almost like the ear of the owl.

Sandy did not choose to blunder along such a trail, and perhaps become presently the hunted instead of the hunter. For one can never tell what vagary will strike the brain of the grizzly. As he treks steadily along toward the berry beds, his mind may be crossed by the ravishing vision of a certain root patch in the hollow of the valley, or as he heads for the root patch, he may pause to follow a trail of busy ants.

Up another tree went Sandy, but he was hardly at its top when he saw what he wanted. It was not a hundred yards away that the air was turned into confusion. There was a whirlpool of disturbance, a visible movement of the thin air itself, rather than anything palpable. There were tiny specks in movement, and Sandy knew by old experience that this was the swarming of a hive of bees. The bear was on the trail of honey.

Once more Sandy dropped to the ground through the branches and started for the place ahead of him. He went with more care, since the distance was so short. This time he traveled in a semicircle, so that he would come at the bees against the strong wind that was blowing, and so keep scent and sound of him, if possible, from the bear. As for eyes, the bear is not gifted extraordinarily with them. For that matter, there are no hawk eyes among four-footed creatures, no eyes, even, to match the dull eyes of man himself.

Sandy made his detour and slid through the pines until he had an unbroken view of a clearing, just before him, and in the clearing the outline of a monstrous grizzly reared against the trunk of a tree, busily tearing it open with his steel talons. Sandy stopped short in the midst of his next step, for he found that he was not the only watcher of the scene.

Just before him there was a great, shadowy figure, staring intently. Another grizzly was watching the theft of the hive.

CHAPTER THIRTEEN

They were both males, and this made the event doubly interesting to Sandy. He pressed himself close to the trunk of a tree and stood at gaze, perfectly confident that the two would presently be so absorbed in the doings of one another that he would not be heeded unless he actually shouted at their ears.

For grizzly males do not meet in this fashion unless there is an excellent reason for it. When they are young—yes, that is a different matter. A youngster may well wander onto a range, hoping that he will be able to make it his, only to meet with the rightful possessor on whose fishing streams and berry patches and rooteries he has been poaching. A few cuffs end the fray, and the youth scampers away to hunt for more peaceful hunting grounds, even though they be more barren ones as well. As for males, unless they be old and weak of wit, they do not venture into foreign estates except when dire calamities draw them away from their own kingdoms.

Of all of this, Sandy was a little better aware than anyone else in the world. Therefore, he fairly gaped at the two. He who stood up at the bee tree was not the object of his quest. The formidable Buck was equipped with certain defects in the claws, with which Sandy was familiar. This fellow at the bee tree was a dark-robed giant with whose paws nothing whatever could be found at fault. He, who squatted in the brush, therefore, a dirty cream-gray in color, must be the cattle killer.

The honey seeker was now furiously at work with the heart

of his problem. His powerful claws had already torn away bark and the outer and softer layers of the wood of that big tree. Although the core of the trunk was made of much sterner stuff, it also had to yield to the ripping claws and tearing teeth. Presently his whole body shaking with terrible greed, the big dark-robed fellow pressed closer to the tree and began to wolf down the masses of honey.

Buck raised himself a little in the shadow of the trees. Behind the veil of the brush, Sandy could almost feel his envy at this wonderful feast.

The bees, swarming in brown-and-amber-flashing armies, made wild assaults upon the big bear, but all in vain. Whether they lighted on face or tangles, coat or paws, he paid no attention to the myriad of their stings but continued to gorge himself.

Only when the main mass of the honey had been consumed, he drew out his head from the tree and made a few careless passes with his paws to beat away some of the legions of infuriated honey makers.

There was more to be done in that nest. There were the grubs and the last remnants of the wax and honey to be devoured. As for the choice in delicacies, no grizzly would very well know how to choose between a bit of honey and the same weight of honey-fed grub.

So he at the tree paid no heed to the stealthy progress of Buck at his rear. Buck was moving like the best of hunters. A grizzly has not quite the uncanny ability of the moose to move through heavy brush without a sound, but still six or seven hundred pounds of bear will be maneuvered with wonderful silence through crackling underbrush. Buck, on mischief bent, and for revenge, slid on like a shadow among shadows.

He came out to the exact rear of this intruder upon his lands, and stole forward, foot by foot. Sandy shifted his place to gain a nearer view. When he was drawing nearer to the dark stranger, one of the big feet of Buck snapped a small straw beneath him. Only the ghost of a sound, but it was enough to reach the electrically sensitive ears of the other even though they were partly muffled by the surrounding core of the tree. He jerked out his head.

However, Buck was instantly attacking. He leaped forward with a lightness wonderful in one of his bulk, reared, and struck like lightning with either forepaw. The weight of those blows would have torn the ribs out of a range bull, and, aimed at the head of the other grizzly, they knocked him flat.

He fell with a roll, however, and came to his feet as Buck rushed in to finish the fight with his teeth. Alas for too much eagerness. The dark-coated stranger was rearing as Buck rushed in, and the full weight of a driving forepaw landed on the snout of Sandy's quarry.

It was a solid stroke and stopped the charge of Buck as effectually as ever a well-aimed drive stopped a rushing pugilist in the ring. Buck, crumpling back on his hindquarters, came only half erect. Before he could gain his balance, the stranger was on him.

Nothing but the effect of the first surprise had enabled Buck to stand up to the other for even this length of time. If Buck himself had some six hundred pounds of durable weight and might, the stranger had a vital advantage of more than a hundred in weight. Besides, he was a good span of years younger. Youth had enabled him to recuperate quickly from the opening blows of his enemy. Youth now gave him the speed to lunge in, strangely like a human being, and grip the throat of Buck as the latter went down. What a grip was there!

There is no bear that will not prefer infinitely to do his battles with the marvelous cunning and might of his forepaws. But when it comes to the finishing touches, he has jaws unmatched in the whole range of the American wilderness. A very admirable pair of jaws was now clamped in the throat of Buck.

He struggled as well as he could. It was only chance that gave him a moment's respite. One of the forepaws of the stranger came close to his own choking, gaping mouth, and instantly his great teeth were clamped upon it. A roar of fury and pain—and the two were separated.

Once more they rushed together. Now a forepaw of the big dark bear dangled useless. He came off a bad second in the exchange of long-range blows, and so he pushed in close for the teeth again. The weight of his lunge was too much for Buck again. Down he went. Again the teeth of the stranger plunged into the throat.

Thirty seconds of writhing, gasping, and snarling, and then the body of Buck quivered and lay still. Grinding deep through fur and flesh, the blunt canines of the conqueror had found the life nerve and destroyed it. Never again would Buck wander down toward the cattle ranges to eat his fill.

One tentative blow of his unwounded paw was tried by the victor. When Buck made no response, there were no further insults. The victor ambled slowly away, pausing to shake himself now and then, and limping heavily as his weight came rolling onto his badly bitten paw. Until, at length, that paw was lifted altogether, and the big chap went awkwardly off on three legs.

A moment later, Sandy was busily at work on the job of skinning. First a long slit down the belly, and then one down each leg. After that there followed a session of cutting and tugging. It is a hard task for two skillful men to take the robe from a big bear. In the mighty arms of Sandy there resided a strength sufficient to do it all.

Three days later Peter Dunstan came in for his dinner and sat wearily at the head of the table in the ranch house, weary but happy. The bitter sun and the desert wind had been in his face all the day, but his eyes could squint the light away, and his skin had been weathered to the strength of leather. Therefore, he endured the fatigue willingly. Having ranged far and found his cattle in excellent condition, already proving the value of the new pastures that had been opened to them on the Morgan place, Dunstan was content. As he ate his supper in silence, a new vision formed before his eyes of a second purchase that he might be able to make soon. For the Gregor Ranch that adjoined Morgan's old holdings upon the farther side was in poor hands. Gregor himself had lost so much money that he must soon be willing to sell, and to sell very cheap, indeed.

Full of that thought, Dunstan was slow in opening his mail—a single letter in the handwriting of Dr. Morgan. There was another reason for that slowness. Now that Morgan was off the range, he was of no more interest to the cattleman than a fixed star of the very least magnitude.

My Dear Dunstan: I am sorry to learn that you have decided not to take advantage of the farming possibilities in your new acreage, but that is a matter of your own business and not mine. There is another matter in which I still retain an interest, and that is the person of young Sandy Sweyn. I am a thousand times obliged to you for taking care of him up to this point, according to your agreement.

When I returned to New York, I found that my affairs were in a much better condition than I had expected. A very lucky upward movement in some stocks has left me financially at ease, and therefore I am buying a place in Connecticut.

It is rather a wild section, and I think that Sandy would be perfectly at home here. He will be able to bring the roan with him. I enclose a check that will be enough to bring Sandy and Cleo, also. And besides, you will find enough in it to give Sandy a suit of Sunday clothes, and a little spending money from time to time.

May I trouble you to see that he buys the clothes and gets the necessary tickets? Once aboard the train a word to the conductor will be enough to assure the delivery of Sandy at my place.

In conclusion, I am sure that you have not found that your time with Sandy has been entirely wasted. I used to learn something from him every day. So much so, that I shall hate to look forward to a stay in the open country without Sandy along to act as eyes and ears to me.

Please let Sandy know the contents of this letter. I would ask you to let him read it, but reading is a long and bitter process for Sandy.

Faithfully yours,
Henry Morgan

The rancher read the letter through a second time, and with more care. The first image that formed in his brain was that of Sandy lying asleep on the ground with the great bull beside him. After all, there was a couple thousand dollars in cash value in that reclaimed bull, and if it had not been for Sandy, how would the great beast ever have been handled? Dunstan did not know.

He had just reached that point in his thoughts, when he heard the voice of the cook, roaring in the kitchen.

"Here's Sandy back . . . and he's got it!"

"Got what? The bear?"

There stood Sandy in the doorway with a great pile of bearskin rolled upon his shoulder, a crushing weight of green hide.

"Good heavens, Sandy!" the rancher cried. "Have you carried that far?"

"Oh, about seventy-five miles," Sandy said. "I thought that maybe you would like to have it."

Let a man like this go back to Dr. Henry Morgan? A man capable of such a feat as this?

Peter Dunstan stared intently at the blank face of the hunter, then with hasty fingers he tore the letter into small shreds.

CHAPTER FOURTEEN

Men west off the Rockies still place a very high value upon mere physical prowess. The result was that the roll of the bear's hide was weighed, green and heavy as it was, and when the poundage was known, two of Dunstan's cowpunchers were commissioned to follow the trail of Sandy Sweyn through the lowlands and into the hills. Even for horses, hard-ridden, that journey took nearly four days, though part of this was spent in worrying over the problems of the trail. When they returned to the ranch of Dunstan, they came with the tale of a superman's achievement. As Shorty put it: "Not even a horse could've done that job and packed that hide back so fast."

When the two came back, they found that trouble was in the air, for in the first place Dunstan had drawn from Sandy the true story of all that had happened in the little clearing among the pines. When he heard of the presence of a bear bigger and stronger than Buck, with a pelt twice as fine as the one that was now being cured, he was greatly excited. He would have had Sandy start at once in the pursuit of the second bear, but Sandy was strangely reluctant. When Dunstan pressed him, Sandy relapsed into a gloomy silence from which nothing at all could be gleaned.

So Peter Dunstan decided that Sandy must be handled with gloves. It was not that he was afflicted with any peculiar sympathy for Sandy, but rather because he now recognized in Sandy Sweyn a property of such value that the rancher began to feel that therein lay his most priceless single possession. Although he had had Sandy with him only a short time, the youngster had rendered most important services.

The destruction of the big bear could hardly be attributed to him, but he had been able to stalk it with such uncanny closeness that he watched the battle between the two from a box seat, so to speak. It was only reasonable to suppose that Sandy could have killed the brute whenever he chose. That bear had cost the ranch a thousand dollars' worth of labor and time in futile pursuit, a thousand dollars' worth of worry, and well more than a thousand dollars in actual loss of cattle. Then there was the matter of the red Durham bull. How many other matters might appear?

In a single season, such a matchless hunter as this might rid the Dunstan range of all his coyotes, wolves, bears, and mountain lions. What would not this be worth to one who lost as many from his calf crop as did Peter Dunstan every year? Therefore, when Sandy grew silent and morose, the rancher did not insist, but he said gloomily to the cook: "What the devil can be bothering him now?"

"I tell you," declared Steve McGuire, "that nobody is gonna get any good out of him. But he'll do more harm in the end than ever he done good. And you write me down in red for that, partner."

The rancher wrote him down in red, as a matter of fact. He came to his new decision about the big invading grizzly. He would himself dispense with the services of Sandy and would ride up and try to trail the big fellow.

He informed Sandy to that effect. Sandy's reply was a staggerer to Dunstan. He sat with a contorted brow for a long time. Then he said: "Look here, Mister Dunstan, it ain't right, it seems to me."

"What's not right?"

"To kill that bear," Sandy replied.

"Not right to kill that bear?" shouted the rancher. "And why not, Sandy?"

"I dunno that the bear has harmed you, has he?" Sandy asked hopefully.

"Why, he's living on my land, part of the time, and he's apt to come down and begin to live on cattle the same way that Buck did, and kill hundred-dollar steers for the sake of one meal, the way that Buck did. Isn't that a harm to me?"

This proposition was long seriously considered by Sandy. Finally he said: "The way it seems to me . . . he is a bear, and no man."

"You're a wise fellow, Sandy," the rancher said ironically. "He's a bear and not a man. I grant you that."

"And how could he know what pleases you and what don't please you? And was he made for the sake of pleasing you?"

"Maybe not," the rancher remarked, smiling with pity at this sort of logic. "But my rifle was not made for the sake of pleasing him, either."

This seemed a great point to Sandy, and he went away and digested the thought for an hour. When he came back, he had attacked the problem from a new angle. He said to big Dunstan: "If you was to knock down a man, would you hit him after he was down?"

"I suppose not."

"Well, that black grizzly has got a hurt forepaw. That paw is so bad hurt that he can't run very well to hide himself, and he can't very well manage to fight much for himself, either, can he?"

The patience of the rancher was ended. He exploded suddenly: "In the name of the devil, what are you talking about? What has this nonsense to do with my right to go out and shoot a bear on my own range . . . or a range right near to mine?"

The blank eyes of Sandy filled with trouble. "It's this way," he said. "The trouble is that the black fellow . . . he was working for you and for me, in a way, when he killed Buck, wasn't he?"

"Working for me?" shouted the rancher, infuriated and confused.

Sandy shrank back. Anger always bewildered and frightened him. "You wanted Buck killed . . . and you sent me to do it. When the black fellow killed Buck, he did my work for me, and the thing that you wanted done. Ain't that all true?"

"By accident!" Dunstan cried. "Do you think that a bear has a reasoning brain . . . or what *do* you think, Sandy?"

"I dunno," Sandy said with a sigh. "Only, it seems to me that it ain't hardly right for the black fellow to be killed like this."

"*Bah!*" Dunstan exclaimed. "You stay here behind. I'm riding up through the hills with a couple of the boys. It's a long time since I've dropped a bear . . . but inside of a week, Sandy, you'll see the hide of the big black boy stretched out yonder beside that of Buck."

As he turned away, it seemed to Dunstan that a voice murmured behind him: "But I only wonder . . . is it right?"

This chapter made a good story for Dunstan to confide to McGuire. But McGuire did not laugh at it.

"You see," he said, "that's the reason he's dangerous. He might just as well as not be thinking the way that a bear would think . . . or a horse would think . . . or a hawk would think. But I can do my swearing that he ain't the kind of a man to think the way that a man should think."

He said this so seriously that Peter Dunstan regarded his wise cook with some wonder. There seemed so much meaning in what McGuire had just said, that Dunstan had no desire to press him for a full answer. Instead, he gave his attention to the task of preparing for the hunt. He picked out Shorty and Doc

Lawrence, his two best trailers and surest shots. In their company he left the ranch that same afternoon.

There was little to do on the ranch at that particular season of the year. The other hands would be able to take care of the work during the next week. Surely the chase of the lamed bear, if all went well, would not require much more than a week.

They struck away merrily in the indicated direction, and all went so well that, the next morning, they were well into the uplands. That very evening, cutting in great circles for sign, they came upon the trail of the mighty stranger who limped with one forepaw, stepping constantly short with it. On that trail they gathered. All through the day it grew clearer and clearer before them, until they discovered, in the midafternoon, that another horseman was riding on the same trail. For the sign of his horse lay before them, wherever the ground was soft enough to show the impression of the hoofs.

They pressed on more eagerly than ever, but now they came to country so rough that the horses had to be abandoned to the care of Doc while Shorty and Dunstan, being expert mountaineers, went forward with rifles and small knapsacks.

In the rougher going, even with a wounded paw, the bear could make better time comparatively. Still they felt sure that no crippled beast could long keep away from them. They pressed on swiftly, steadily, drawing their belts tighter as the day grew older. In the gold of the late afternoon, Shorty pointed with a sudden shout. The rancher looked up, too late to see.

"The bear?" he cried.

"No, but a horse and man . . . a sort of a blue-looking horse . . . it must be the gent that's hunting the bear ahead of us!"

Yes, for the hoof prints that had disappeared as the rough going began, now started in once more. Though it seemed a miracle that horse and rider could make any time over such going. "Unless that horse has got a cross strain of mountain sheep in him," said Shorty.

All through the rest of the afternoon, they drew fresher and fresher upon the tracks. At the very end of the day they came to a crushing disappointment. The bear had crossed a natural bridge that spanned a narrow gorge. Then, turning, he must have ripped the top boulders away until he came to the keystone of the arch. In the bottom of the gorge lay the rubble of fallen stones. In front of the two hunters there was a dismal gap of twenty feet—more than either of them cared to risk by jumping.

"I've heard of wise bears and wise bears," Dunstan muttered, "but never of one like this lame devil, and I'm going to get him now or die trying. Why, Shorty, this bear is worth writing a book about, if he has the sense to do tricks like this."

Shorty shook his head solemnly. "Chief," he said, "no bear ever broke down that bridge. It was done by the gent that's riding ahead of us. He broke it down so that we couldn't get at the bear before him."

"Man, man!" the rancher cried, pointing to the junk heap of immense stones in the bottom of the ravine. "Is there any man you know of that could handle stones the size of them?"

"Aye," Shorty said, coloring a little. "There's one man. You know him, too."

CHAPTER FIFTEEN

It was true that Dunstan understood the meaning of Shorty perfectly, but he made no reference to his understanding. He merely gave his strength and agility and patience to climbing down the near wall of the ravine and ascending upon the farther side. This work consumed an hour's time and left them utterly spent. As they came to the edge of the cliff, on the farther side of the ravine, they heard the ringing report of a rifle before them.

"The young devil," Dunstan murmured. "He wouldn't let me kill that bear with my own gun . . . he had to. . . . And now we'll meet him coming back, carrying the hide."

They built a large fire to direct the lucky hunter ahead of them. But no Sandy Sweyn appeared.

The next morning they had not advanced a half mile on their way along the trail before they came upon a half-consumed carcass of a mountain sheep. It had been shot from the towering rocks above and had broken its bones to bits in the fall from the height. It had not been more than touched by the hunter. Around the body were the huge imprints of the paws of the bear, which they had been hunting so eagerly. It had evidently dined most heartily.

Peter Dunstan swore volubly. He avoided the eye of Shorty as they hurried on down the trail again, for each knew the thought of the other, and each felt that that thought was too ridiculous to be trusted in words.

Presently they came to a line of blazes. That thickly blazed trail led them to a tree from which a great section of the face had been chopped away, leaving a broad and very. fairly smooth white surface upon which certain letters had been inscribed in a great, painful, childishly sprawling hand: *I don't think that you shuld wory this bear no more. He ain't traubled you none.*

"It's Sandy," the rancher said. "And you were right, Shorty. But it's a hard thing to believe that a man would ride up here for the sake of working for a bear."

Shorty shook his head. "This Sandy Sweyn, he's different," he said. "I seen that when I seen the way that he rode on that roan mare. Because I could tell that he knew how to lighten his weight a whole lot. No, he's a pretty queer sort of a man, chief. I tell you, right now he's riding his horse right alongside of that bear . . . otherwise, his tracks would fall in a straight line right on top of the grizzly's tracks."

This conjecture might be wild, but, at least, there was the token upon the ground as they crossed a bit of soft mountain turf, where the imprints were clearly revealed. There was the trail of the bear and just beside it the more deeply driven hoof marks of the horse.

"It ain't natural, and it ain't right . . . but it's a fact," Shorty commented. "And there you can see it with your own eyes."

Dunstan stopped and swore a great oath. "I'm going to keep right after this trail," he said, "if it takes me the rest of my life. I'm going to have that bear's hide and claws. Do you hear me talk, Shorty?"

"I'd rather not, though," Shorty answered, "because I've got an idea that maybe you'll wish that you hadn't said that same thing."

They hurried on again, striding long and free.

"Because," big Peter Dunstan said, "you can see how it is. That bear doesn't have to stop to forage for himself. He's got a hunter with him, and that hunter kills his game for him. As for his lame paw . . . why, he seems to be able to bear up on that, well enough."

For these reasons, they worked fast and gave themselves no rest. The evening of the next day found them footsore, utterly exhausted, and very hungry. Just at the setting of the sun, they came upon a crooked pine tree on the side of the hill, with the face cut away as the other tree had been. Upon the white surface thus exposed there was written in that same labored and sprawling hand: *This bear can't go no farthur, but I ain't gonna let you come at him. Sandy Sweyn.*

"He's not going to *let* us?" Dunstan said. "Does the fool mean that he would actually . . . ?"

The next morning, when he prepared to start out on the trail, Shorty remained stubbornly in the camp. "Look here," he said. "I ain't a coward, I hope. But I ain't gonna get myself killed for the sake of any bear that was ever born. I don't value them hides so much as all of that, y'understand? And this Sandy Sweyn, he means business now. And when he means business, he shoots too straight to please me a little bit. I'm gonna stay put right here in the camp. You go ahead if you want to, I'll start out a little later and make myself a burying party."

Peter Dunstan was angered by this defection. But after all, Shorty was a proved man of worth. The rancher had to start on by himself, in a towering passion. Passion was not great enough in him to make him go without caution. He stole through the scattering forest of these highlands with all the skill that he could muster. He came, at length, to a region of bare rocks, with a stream trickling feebly down among them—a region where there was cover, to be sure, but not cover like that of the woods.

Pausing, Dunstan looked to the loading of his rifle. Behind

him in the camp, he had left a man who would be willing to testify that an open threat had been delivered on the free range to a hunter within his own rights in hunting down destructive game on whose head there was a bounty placed. If the opportunity favored him, and, if necessity demanded it, Dunstan was prepared to shoot and shoot to kill.

Had he not registered an oath that he would have the scalp of that bear, no matter what obstacles lay before him? If he returned from the mountains, baffled by a half-wit, what manner of story would not Shorty spread through the cow camps about a once respected master?

For the first time in his life, Dunstan actually went out on the man trail. He had worked his way for a scant fifty yards when something whistling and wickedly brief passed above his head. It was a sound heard and gone before he could be sure that it was approaching. He jerked up his head in haste and snatched his rifle to his shoulder.

There was nothing before him, but a bullet had just been fired over his head.

Yet Dunstan went slowly on, for he was a very brave man, and shame and anger were forcing him along, as well as a great reputation that needed to be upheld.

Thirty slow yards away he found the following charcoal legend scraped upon the face of a rock: *Dere Mr Dunstan, I ain't gonna kill you unles you make me. Sandy Sweyn.*

Peter Dunstan felt the cold perspiration roll down his forehead. He realized, now, that that bullet had not been an accidental miss. It had been merely a warning; the next one fired by this hidden marksman would certainly put a period to his life.

He did not hesitate an instant. He stood up, turned his back upon the forward trail and all the oaths that he had sworn to keep to it. He trudged slowly, with bent head, back to the fire where Shorty sat, quietly smoking.

Shorty stood up and nodded. "I knew that you'd use good sense, chief," he said.

His chief made no reply. They went slowly on the back trail toward the far distant point where they had left Doc with the horses. All through that day, hardly a word was spoken, man to man, except a monosyllable, here and there. When the darkness came, Dunstan dropped a buck, as it sprang from a little covert. That night the roasted venison loosened their tongues.

"Two miracles," said Dunstan. "How could he ride a horse through country like this? Second miracle . . . how could he tame that bear enough to travel with it . . . even granting that he's crazy enough to really want to save the bear . . . and not just to make me mad?"

"I dunno," Shorty said. "But I sort of wish, chief, that you hadn't drove him off into the hills like this."

"Drove him off?" the rancher shouted. "What are you talking about?"

"Man, man," Shorty said with the dignity of the self-assured, "didn't he bring you in the bear skin that you wanted? Why shouldn't you let a poor half-wit like him keep the other bear where it was till it got well . . . and then he would've gone out and killed that bear for you his own self . . . or led you right up where you could've got in your shot at it."

Dunstan, for some reason, could not answer. He felt that half of his repute had been torn from him, however. He suddenly found himself echoing the words of Steve McGuire: "Nobody will ever gain, in the end, by anything that this fellow Sandy Sweyn might do. He's nothing but bad luck, Shorty."

Shorty said after a time: "We're gonna hear a lot more about him, chief, since he's up here in the mountains. Suppose that some gents meet up with him that see that he's a half-wit and don't see that he's what we know . . . a gent with a murder in each of his hands, if he wants to use them. There's apt to be dead men in these parts, chief. And I hope that you ain't gonna be blamed for them."

Once again, Dunstan had nothing to say. He thought of the letter from Dr. Morgan, and, with all his heart, bitterly he wished that he had followed the instructions in that letter.

It was too late for that. There was nothing remaining for him to do except to ride back to his ranch and there face the old life with the new name and the bad name that he had made for himself. He cursed the day when his eyes had first fell on the blank eyes of Sandy Sweyn. And something told Peter Dunstan that the days of his strength and the days of his glory were nearly at an end. This was a foretaste of his fall.

As for Sandy Sweyn—no one saw him for a long time. But there was a wild tale repeated some time later in the mountain villages about a great, dark-coated grizzly bear who was seen at close hand, with what appeared to be a great cloth bandage wrapped around a forepaw. In the rear, behind the monster, followed a man. The wind blew from that shadowy form of a man to the bear, and yet the bear's hair-trigger nostrils gave it no warning—or else this one man of all the race it did not fear.

★ ★ ★ ★ ★

PART II

★ ★ ★ ★ ★

CHAPTER SIXTEEN

"*Palabras de la boca, piedras de la honda*," said Diego Mirandos, who was fond, like most Mexicans, of bringing in a pat proverb wherever the chance offered. He said this at a time when chance so framed affairs that never was a proverb more truly applied.

"Words of the mouth, stones of the sling," Diego Mirandos had said, and quite truly for, after all, words fly as far and strike as deep as stones from a sling. To the truth of this remark pretty Catalina Mirandos could not be expected to pay any heed. She was in a mighty passion. Standing on the verandah of the house, she looked across the garden that her own hands had helped to make beautiful in this strange land of the Americans, then she twisted her fingers together and shook her head in violence.

José Rézan stood before her. He was at the bottom of the steps, but he was so big, and she was so small that even at that disadvantage he seemed nearly as tall as she. He was Mexican as much as she. Yet some said that his was a Russian name. Certainly his hair was blond, and his skin was pale.

He had said: "I have ridden everywhere. I have searched everywhere. But the little devil of a horse . . . I cannot find her, Catalina. She has turned herself into a mist, and she has disappeared."

Catalina raised herself on her toes, answering in a voice of passion: "It is not true! You have not looked. You have given her away. You have sold her. You *have* sold her! Because my father does not wish me to ride her. But I will ride her . . . I will ride her. I shall find her and ride her. I do not care what may happen. I shall have her . . . she is mine. I love her! I own her . . . you gave her to me with your own hands. I will not *live* unless I have her. Do you hear me, stupid José?"

Poor José. He was so big, so strong, so calm in his bigness and in his strength, that he loved her all the more because she was so tremendously spoiled. Her father was a big man and a gentle one, also. For so many years he had poured out to Catalina all that her heart could desire so that it had grown impossible for her to endure a disappointment.

"I'll get her for you if I can, Catalina," big José said. "But you have to remember that we trapped her by accident, really. She was always more than half wild . . . a real little devil, dear Catalina."

"Do not call me dear. I am not dear . . . I am not yours!"

The eyes of José Rézan grew greater than ever with a sudden fear. "Consider, Catalina, that she will have gone back to the same wild herd from which she came, perhaps. But even if it takes hundreds of dollars, I shall send men to follow her and run her down, and catch her if they can."

"Run her down, starve her down, ruin her, break her spirit!" cried Catalina. "Do I want a diamond with the fire gone from it? No, no, no! I shall have my Elena . . . my Elena Blanca . . . my beautiful white one! I shall have her again. I shall have her without a hair changed. I shall see her just as she was. And if there is so much as a rope scald on one of her legs, I will not take her at all. I will not, I will not!"

José was paler than ever. His eyes rolled frantically from side to side, seeking for help. Finding nothing that could save him, he said: "It is only three days to the wedding. After we are married a little time, Catalina, I shall go myself. . . ."

"After we are married?" the little tyrant screamed. "No, but before! Before!"

"Ah, my dear," José said, "but can I catch Elena Blanca and bring her back to you all in three short days? Can I do that?"

"Three days or thirty days," Catalina Mirandos said. "What do I care? I love Elena Blanca. I must have her again. And I shall never marry any but the man who brings her back to me!"

José struck his big hands together. "Child, child . . . you must not say it. You have given me your word, and the priest knows it."

"I take my word back. I catch it back!" Catalina Mirandos cried. "I catch it back and keep it again and swear a new oath!"

"Catalina, you kill me with sorrow."

"Ah, but you do not care when *I* die. You do not care at all. It is only for your own huge self that you care. I lose my beautiful Elena, and it is nothing to you. My father told you to kill her, or to give her away, or to turn her loose . . . and you have done it."

"I swear. . . ."

"Do not be perjured. I would not believe your oath. But I swear. . . ."

Here a sudden and a heavy voice struck in from the side, the voice of her father, Diego Mirandos: "Do not swear, Catalina!"

This double opposition did not check her. It only served to increase her fury more and more. It made her so angry that she danced up and down, unable to speak a single word. The two big men stood aghast at her, staring earnestly at one another, each with a prayer in his eyes, as much as to say: "You, who are big and strong and wise, do something with her, because you see that I am helpless."

Why did they care so much? I think that if she had been all that she was and yet just a little larger, no one would have put up with such nonsense. But she was not more than two or three inches above five feet, and she seemed smaller because she seemed so childish; she seemed so childish because she was so small. Who can be seriously angry with a child?

107

Moreover, she was made in such a way that—how shall I speak of her to make you understand? She was made as a great, great artist would make a little toy. She was made with love and with tenderness and with most infinite care. If you could have seen the delicate olive of her hand, with the sun striking a flush through it, you would have thrilled with joy.

That is why the two men stood helplessly before her. Even as she stormed and raged, and even while they trembled, her voice was so musical that they almost smiled with pleasure, as you or I would have smiled, also. The wisest man in the world with the whitest beard, and the youngest boy with the most careless heart, seeing her would have said with one voice: "Oh, to have her now and forever!"

When her voice came back to her, she cried shrilly at them: "I swear that I shall never marry anyone, except the man that brings Elena Blanca back to me!"

Poor José Rézan. He shrank from her, and a thousand terrible possibilities rushed upon his mind.

It was at this moment that her father said solemnly: *"Palabras de la boca, piedras de la honda."*

With that solemn voice ringing in her ear, even little Catalina Mirandos understood, indeed, that the words she had spoken might be like the stones from a sling. Where would they fall, who would they strike? Or might they not return upon her?

Then, for fear lest they should see the terror in her eyes, she whirled around, raced into the house, and got to her room where the silks whispered and rustled about her, and the canary began suddenly to sing for joy at the sight of her. There she lay, curled up on a couch, and felt the beating of her heart that made all her body quiver, while she said to herself over and over: "Surely it cannot be such a terrible thing that I have said. What difference can they make . . . the words that poor little Catalina may speak?"

A minute later she had nearly forgotten that last scene, except for a guilty sense of pleasure because of the pain that she had given to big, honest José and to her father, *Don* Diego. After that, she was thinking of nothing but Elena Blanca once more, yearning for her.

You must consider that, in all the world of horses, there was only one made for Catalina. That was the white mare. She had been a bright vision of delight, enchanting the eyes of many a hunter and many a cowpuncher who had some dazzling glimpse of her as she fled away across the hills or stood like a frightened deer against a dark bank of the pine trees. Chance brought her into the hands of José, who gave her into the hands of the lady of his heart. With infinite labor, through weeks and weeks, that wild creature was tamed until Catalina could be trusted in the saddle on her back. It was a crimson saddle, all fretted over with silver, and there was a crimson bridle worked with shining gold. When they saw the little mare dance forth, they knew that all their work had been well rewarded. It was like a harmony of well-matched sounds, seeing the beauty of the girl and the beauty of Elena Blanca together.

As for Catalina, she knew that when she sat on the back of White Helen she was mounted, as it were, upon an enchanted horse, with the surety that she could ride forthright into the hearts of all men. Do you wonder that she should have cared so much about this—seeing that she was betrothed to marry the good José, so rich, so handsome and so strong? You wonder, only because you did not know Catalina.

Perhaps the wild oath that Catalina had spoken that day would never have been heard of again had it not been that another ear had listened, the ear of Rosa, the half-breed *moza*. In another moment she was at the stable door, whispering to her wild-faced son Filipo: "The kind God has prepared riches and happiness for you, Son. The *señorita* has sworn that she will marry only the man who brings back the white mare. Whose hand but yours tamed her and trained her? And who but you will find her trail and catch her again?"

"An oath is only a word," Filipo said, trembling at the thought of all that might be.

"Oh, fool, fool!" gasped out Rosa. "It is the oath of a Mirandos, and their word is sacred always."

Filipo did not wait. He started at once, on his fastest pony, with his best rawhide lariat coiled beside the saddle. There was fire in his heart, and the thought of the *señorita* was like a living breath from heaven. He rode straight through the village down the trail. It was only when he got to the farther side that he remembered a certain little house on the edge of the town where, for a certain price, a known man might buy forbidden liquor, and drink it in a circle of the discreet. He turned back and sat in the little house the rest of that day.

By the time that the evening came, there were others around him. The spirit of good fellowship carried the heart of Filipo upon the wings of a swallow. He was in such a heaven of content that it seemed a bitter wrong that the precious secret should remain in his hands, only. Therefore, he confided it to one, and then to another. Before the world was an hour older, the eavesdropping vixen rumor had seized on the tidings and was abroad—clattering out the story. For it was one made exactly after her liking; it did not need a single stitch of embroidery. The naked facts were enough to strike silence and wonder through the hearts of men.

Before the next morning, every soul in the village had heard. Before the next sunset, the word was gone across the mountains, running like liquid fire down every valley, from village to village, from ranch to ranch.

CHAPTER SEVENTEEN

There is nothing like competition to create excitement. If men eagerly run horses to see which will pass under the wire first, they run even more vigorously themselves the same honor. If the challenge had gone out to catch the white mare alone, it would have brought a great answer. When such a reward as the hand of the Mexican girl was added, there was hardly a cowpuncher, competent or incompetent, who did not raise his head. The newspaper got hold of the thing quickly enough. Half a dozen photographers slipped out to the house of *Don* Diego, and managed to get snapshots of the beauty before her father herded them away, promising that the next man to approach the place with such an infernal machine should have a thorough slating down with lead, placed in the spots where it would do the most good.

However, the mischief had been done much too thoroughly to be undone. There was the story, in the first place, which editors caught up on the run and printed in broad columns, under titles sometimes witty, and sometimes not. Afterward, when the pictures went the rounds, the tale was printed again, with much embroidery.

It was something more than the melodramatic hunger of a pretty girl for publicity. Everyone knew that the tale had gone abroad by accident. In addition, when the house and the lands of *Don* Diego were described, even the most conservative could tell that in this game there was something of greater value than there were pictures on the cards. Besides, a girl might have been offered for any other prize in the whole world and been considered either vainglorious or a fool. When she offered herself in exchange for the return of her horse—why, that was a different matter, by far, you may be sure. It touched the romantic sense of irresponsibility that runs in every human being, especially in every Westerner.

The pictures crowned it all. Those wicked photographers had been trained to their arts in devious ways. They had practiced themselves, according to their politics, in snapping the candidate for mayor and making him look like a jackass, or in snapping him to make him appear a philosopher and a philanthropist. They had been able to make old actresses appear to be young ones, and they had learned the secret of putting guilt or innocence upon the faces of accused men.

When it merely came to showing the grace and beauty of Catalina Mirandos, they were at their ease. They showed her swinging into the saddle on another horse, stepping from the door of the house, in the garden, startled and letting an armful of flowers drop to the ground.

The editors, rubbing their hands, printed the pictures one by one. On each day, in some manner, to justify the successive stories, they raked up new material—something about Diego Mirandos and the angle of Mexican politics that had made him move north of the Río Grande, or something about the famous white mare, which had been sighted and run here, and only sighted there—or something. Best of all, were the stories about the girl herself, this last entirely out of the imaginations of the editors. They really agreed upon one point only—which was that the lovely girl was the only human being in all the world who could ride the spirited mare. That to her touch the strength and fire of White Helen responded instantly, and she became as a lamb.

On the whole, it was what even a metropolitan paper, in the daily hunt for "human interest" would have accepted with open arms and open columns.

As for the thousands of strong men who were at all near to the region through which the mare was wandering, those who were unmarried saddled their best horses, and those who were married looked down impatiently and scowled at the left hands of their wives.

Here and there, in a thousand places, the written stories opened the hearts of men. Then came the pictures, and a thousand men sat up at rigid attention, saying: "This is the girl."

For they were all hunting, of course—children and old men, single and married. Back in the mind of each, there is lodged a hunger and a hope. So that many men, as they stared at the picture of the girl, said—"If only I were young."—or "If only I were free." But many more said—"I shall go and do my best."

To no one did the sight of the girl come with a greater shock than to Peter Dunstan, owner of the great Dunstan Ranch that, during the last years, had spread wider and wider, eating up the adjoining cattle places. It struck him like the surprise of a midnight attack. A sudden rush, a whispering of many rapid feet—and then the voices of triumph are sounding over the great fortress before it is well roused from the drowsy content of its impregnability. So it was with Peter Dunstan.

It was fifteen years since he had what could be termed a foolishly light thought. Back yonder in the days when he was no more than twenty-five, he was still in the habit of riding a little out of his path for the sake of fun or fighting, each of which he liked equally well. Now it was a different matter.

Fifteen years ago, he had happened to overhear an old rancher say: "There go the rags and tatters of the old Dunstan place. It'll be on the auction block in another six months if that young spender keeps up his work."

In his fierce heart, Dunstan swore that he would make the prophet eat his words. He fixed his keen eye on the dollar that can be made to roll to one's feet even through the alkali dust that the trampling herds raise on the mountain desert. Then he strode toward his goal with an irresistible might. Nothing could stay him.

He went, not by sudden leaps and bounds. For five years, he accumulated stock, borrowed money, and bided his time. Then he sold when the market was at a peak, cleared a great profit, watched a neighbor foolishly wait until the peak was passed— and scooped in that neighboring place at the sale that followed.

For another five years he toiled, cut corners sharply, did the work of five men, and gathered a flock of devil-may-care cowpunchers. He drove them like pirates, underfed and overworked them. At the end of the five-year struggle, he sold again, and gained a return more enormous than before.

He was thirty-five, then. He had no money in the bank, but his credit was based on a foundation stronger than rock—of multiplying herds and spreading lands. The first ten years were the bitterest. After that, his fortune rolled on under its own headway. He had tried men to rely on; he had established rigid policies that often saved him the expense and pain of thought.

From thirty-five to forty he felt the taste of power, ranker and ranker in his throat, like a strong liquor. The more he drank of it, the sterner grew his soul, and the more his appetite raged. Now, at forty, he was an established figure on the range. Bankers knew him; other cattlemen looked up to him.

If men did not love him for himself, they loved him for the cause that he represented. He was one of the representatives of a class that grew smaller in numbers from year to year—the lovers of freedom, the independent cattleman. He looked like an older type. Men said that he was a generation after his proper time, when the range had been owned and manipulated by giants like himself.

Now, at the beginning of his fullest prime, with his mind occupied by the leaping visions of the greater things that lay at his hand, at a moment when he had relaxed on a visit to town just long enough to glance over an evening paper, his eye caught on a pretty face.

A picture actress . . . or a divorcee, thought Peter Dunstan. Then his swiftly moving glance entered the tangle of words.

Ten minutes later he had made up his mind that there was nothing that really mattered, after all, so much as the establishment of a home—a family. He formed his plan on the spot. The others had failed in spite of the numbers that they had employed—like the rich lumberman from Montana, who had come down with twenty men and whole trains of fleet horses to capture the white mare. Peter Dunstan did not intend to work with numbers. He intended to use only one person. That was one whose skill was without a duplicate in all the world.

CHAPTER EIGHTEEN

On the very day on which Peter Dunstan set forth, a rumor came in that Elena Blanca was caught. So many other rumors of the same effect had been circulated before, that no one took this seriously. Yet the truth was that on this day, the lariat, darting from the hand of big José Rézan, had swished dangerously close to the head of the mare. Had she not been shod with air and muscled with watch springs that day, she would have been entangled in the meshes of the rope. However, she whirled, and with a frightened squeal fled away like a white arrow across the sun-faded hills of the mountain desert. So the goal remained free for Peter Dunstan's attempt.

He took with him, of all of his band of hard riders and trained cowpunchers, only the redoubtable retainer, Shorty. For, except the cook, Steve McGuire, Shorty was the only one of the band who had ever dared to speak his free mind in the presence of his chief. Like all tyrants, Peter Dunstan valued an independent mind as much as he hated it.

They rode north. They crossed the belt of the sun-scorched desert. They crossed the region of the scrub cedar and lodgepole pines. They rode on north, where the trees grew thicker and bigger. Then they entered upon a region of plentiful rainfall. Here they began to make their inquiries.

Shorty said, scratching his red head: "This here is the sort of a country that you'll be sure to find him in. There ain't any doubt but that he likes a country where there's trees and water, because in them parts he'll find the animals."

"And the birds," Peter Dunstan said.

Shorty turned sharply about in the saddle and peered at his companion. "Birds," he said in a gasping voice, "birds, too?"

"Birds, too," Dunstan said with the calm of superior knowledge.

"Aye," Shorty said, after he had considered this tiding for a time. "Anything that ain't got human speech, I suppose."

So they came to a little crossroads town, and Shorty asked the blacksmith, who sat upon his rusting anvil, if there had been any sight in that region of a man who rode a blue horse and lived in the woods.

"A blue horse?" the blacksmith said. "Might you have been drinking, partner?"

"All right," Shorty said to his chief not deigning to answer this remark. "He ain't been around here."

They journeyed on, a wild, rough way, sometimes finding a ranch house or a little town to stay in at night, sometimes never coming to shelter, but sleeping out in the raw mountain winds, with the naked stars close and bright above their heads. Wherever they went, they asked the same question: "Have you seen a gent around these parts, riding on a blue horse? A blue mare?"

And everywhere, they were met with gaping mouths and staring eyes and no information.

"But," Dunstan said, "it begins to seem to me that we'll never find him. He may have had the claws of a mountain lion ripping through his innards before this, Shorty."

"Him?" Shorty said. "Nope, he ain't the kind that'll ever die by no wild animal. No varmint will ever sink a tooth into him, I guess."

"Aye," Dunstan said, "that seems likely, too. But why haven't we heard some word of him, then? He's strange enough, and different enough to be known pretty widely. I should think that anybody who had ever seen him would never stop talking about him."

"Look at the boys right there at home on our own ranch," Shorty said, who had worked on the place for so long that he looked upon it with an air of possession. "Look at them. We've had him right there among us. And et at the same table with him. We've rode with him and watched him. And we've seen him in action. But what have the boys got to say? Sure, they're thinking about him a whole lot, but they don't talk, and they won't talk. Why? Because when you run up ag'in' something so plumb out of the ordinary, so different from the way other folks are and act, you don't want to talk. You just set and think it over, till a chill runs up your spine. Ain't you felt that way, chief, when you thought about him before?"

Peter Dunstan had to nod. It was true. The rider of the blue horse was not a man to be talked of in a chatty fashion.

They came, in the bleak evening of a windy day, with the gale whipping volleys of rain against the roofs, upon the sight of the little village where a stream of lumber wagons crossed another stream of wagons from the nearest silver mine. The village had come into existence as a way station and a depot, where supplies for the neighboring ranchers could be stored. Into this straggling place they rode, putting up at the one-story hotel.

Because they were tired, and because they were beginning to despair of success, they delayed their inquiries until supper had been finished. Then Peter Dunstan said, as usual: "Have any of you fellows seen a man riding a blue horse in these parts?"

There was the usual blank silence, but, before the voices of wonder could break in and ask what was meant, a man said sharply from the foot of his table, lowering his coffee cup with a click: "What might *you* know about a gent with a blue horse?"

"I'm asking you if he's been seen," Dunstan said.

"Might you be a friend of his?" the other asked with gathering wrath masked under a gentle voice.

"No," Dunstan said truthfully enough.

"Well," said the other, letting his anger break through restraint, "next to layin' my hands on that ornery, good-for-nothin' sneak, I'd like nothin' better than to get hold of any friend of his and bust him in two and see what there is so funny on the insides of him."

"I see," Dunstan said, nodding, "that you know the man that I'm after."

Here the chorus of questions from the others at the table broke in: "A man on a blue horse? A *blue* horse? Who ever heard of such a thing?"

"Why," exclaimed the angry man at the foot of the table, "you all have seen a blue roan? But this here is bluer than that. A blue roan, right enough, but more the color of a shadow in the belly of a valley, betwixt afternoon and evening, if you get what I mean. A right fine-looking horse. If it hadn't been for the speed of it, I would've got up close enough to sink a chunk of lead in his back while he was running away from me."

"What might he have of done?" Shorty asked.

The stranger broke into a violent torrent of oaths. "What might he *not* have done!" he roared. "But the main part of it is that he's a plain horse thief! Here I was out disciplining a right mean four-year-old gray gelding. The damned horse laid me on my back and knocked most of the wind out of me, when I climbed into the saddle on him. But I had him on a long rope, tied to a tree. So I got up and dragged him up closer to the tree trunk with that rope and snubbed him up right short. Then I got hold of my quirt and give him a good lambasting."

There were nods and grunts of assent.

"And just then, as I stepped back to give myself a breath of air and sort of wipe my face, in comes a gent riding on a big blue roan mare . . . kind of a heavy-looking horse, like she could've pulled her share in a plow team, you might say, but finished off extra strong and slender in the lower legs. Below the knees, she looked like a real racer, and for all I know maybe she *is* a racer, that he stole from somewheres. The gent that was riding her, didn't look like nothing in particular. Just stupid. He had the face of a man and the eye of a kid that ain't never gonna grow up. He sits there looking at the gelding sort of sad, with his head to one side.

" 'What might you be wanting, stranger?' I says when he don't offer to speak up none.

" 'I was only thinking,' he says.

" 'About what?' says I.

" 'That it ain't the beating that'll do the gray any good.'

"I sort of looked at him.

" 'What *would* do him good?' I says.

" 'A mite of talking to, maybe,' he says.

" 'Step up,' I says, 'and try your hand on him. I ain't stopping you none.'

"Well, he slid off his mare and didn't bother to throw the reins, even. She followed him along and stood right behind him, all of the time. He went up to the head of the gray, and when the gray begun to prance and dance, damn me if this blank-faced young feller didn't just stand there holding out his hand to him, talking so soft and low that I couldn't make out what he was saying to the gelding."

Shorty broke in with conviction: "Aye, that's the man, and that's his way."

"This sort of talk," went on the stranger, "seemed to surprise the horse, after a while. He begun to stamp and step nearer, and then jump back as far as the rope would let him. The young chap, he just stood. It seemed like he just stood there for half an hour. Just when I was about to yell out that there wasn't any more use in making a fool out of himself like that and wasting my own time . . . just when I was about to holler that out, what should I see but that gelding come a step closer and stick out his nose and snuff at the hand of the gent. Then he give a shudder and jumped back. But he come in again, and in a minute there was that young gent stroking the neck of that horse.

"The gelding had never done nothing but want to eat every man that he ever seen . . . now he seemed tickled almost to death . . . and he kept his ears up and acted all around like he had just met one of the old folks from home . . . y'understand what I mean? Then the big young chap . . . he looked bigger and more solid . . . he got into the saddle, and he rode the horse up and down, and got him used to the pull of the bit, teaching him how to rein across the neck. He done it just as easy as I'm talking now.

"When he got down, I said . . . 'Why, you got that horse gentled already, and if you want a job, son, I've got some more mustangs of the same mean breed to home, and you can try out your hand on them.'

" 'No,' he says, 'all I would like is you to take it easy with this horse and not beat him no more.'

"And he rode off through the trees. Well, I walked right up and jumped into the saddle of the gelding, because I figured that the battle was all over. But it wasn't. I hadn't no more than touched him with my spurs than that horse, which had seemed so gentle, tried to hit the center of the sky. It missed, but it heaved me right in the same general direction. When I come down, I landed on my head."

The stranger paused to rub his neck in affectionate commiseration of the shock that it had endured.

He went on: "When I come to, I dressed that fool horse down and led him home. The next day I had it out with him again. That night I had a note shoved under my front door, reading

121

like this . . . *'Please don't beat the gray horse no more, because it don't do no good.'*

"That only made me mad, of course. I gave it the same medicine the next day. Because who wouldn't kill a horse sooner than to be beat by it? What good is a damned outlaw horse, I ask you? I dressed him down proper, and the next morning when I went out to find him, he was gone.

"Finally, I guessed what had happened. I hunted around till I found his trail. Sure enough, there was two horses there that had made that trail. I saddled my best pony and lit out. I had a glimpse of the gray and the blue as they went into the trees, and I lit out after them. But the gray was a fast devil, and the blue, even carrying the load of this gent, still faster. So they both faded out on me, and I done nothing but pump lead into the air for a mile, without coming into real shooting distance."

CHAPTER NINETEEN

When the stranger had finished this most odd narration that was attended by the others with the most breathless interest, one or two heads were shaken. Big Peter Dunstan at once put the seal of his approval upon the story.

"It's exactly the sort of a thing that I would've expected him to do," he said, "and that's just the reason that I would like to get hold of him. How long ago did you have him at your place?"

"Three weeks," said the other, "and he's a long distance away from my ranch, now. I hunted for him, and there ain't been a shadow of a sign of him."

"That don't mean a lot," Shorty said. "He's the kind that can make his sign fade out mighty quick, if he feels that way about it. The danger that he ain't able to dodge is a new kind of danger, as far as I know. Give us the layout of your home place, and we'll start hunting for him . . . because we know some of his ways."

The stranger seemed to have small faith, indeed, in their ability to locate his man for him, but such an invitation so freely expressed could not be at once refused. Therefore he laid out for them the straightest route toward his own neighborhood.

"But you won't find him," he concluded. "It ain't possible. Me and my friends give the place a pretty good combing to find him, and we didn't raise nothing at all."

This was discouraging enough, but before they went to bed that night, Shorty pointed out: "He wouldn't be living the way that other folks would be living, and they couldn't look for him by the signs that they would be looking for other folks. First thing to do is to see if that neighborhood looks likely for him. If it does, then we'll try to raise him."

Early the next morning, they took to the saddle and were soon on their way. That day and the next, till nearly noon, they traveled, until they came to the crest of a narrow range of mountains. Still north and west from this, they looked down upon a wide sweep of forest, cut by the shining length of many a stream. Here, there was a pool, and there, a long and narrow lake. Trees were everywhere, only falling back now and again, from some patch of bright green meadow, set like a jewel among the shadows of the trees—the field of grass that had grown up around the site of some vanished lake.

All of this, small with distance and clear under the noonday sun, they could see as distinctly as though they had taken a fine picture and held it at arm's length.

"It's the right place," Shorty said with emphasis.

"You talk as sure," Dunstan said, "as though you knew what was going on inside of the head of the kid, Shorty. What makes you so almighty confident that you're right?"

"I'll tell you," Shorty said. "Right from the very first, I've had an idea that I could feel something of what he was thinking. That day that he beat me . . . riding the roan horse and me carrying your money . . . well, right on that day, it seemed to me that as he come whizzing up behind me, gaining every jump, I could feel a sort of pity coming out of his mind, y'understand? Like he hardly wanted to beat me, because I was riding so hard. And when he come by me, damned if I wasn't right, because he was looking across at me and shaking his head. That was when he was rounding the rock at the end of the run."

"Well," said the rancher, "if you can guess what goes on inside of his head, you beat me, Shorty. But you were always a sort of a queer one yourself. How d'you think that we can go about catching this wild man, now that we've come to the place."

"This is the right place," Shorty assured. "And you can lay to that. What more would he like? Here's plenty of water for him to do his fishing in. And here's plenty of trees. There'll be bear and beaver, and bees and bugs and birds, too, since you say that he likes them. Them waters have got kingfishers and fish hawks hanging over them, you can bet. And if them cliffs across the way ain't got a few nests of eagles on them, I'm a fool. No, sir, this is the place for him. And most of all because there ain't any houses near. No houses between this here range and the next, so far as I can see. Nothing but a tangle of trees and creeks, and what not. This trail ain't been worn none too smooth."

So ended Shorty, and his master looked at him with a touch of awe; it was not the first time that he had had to look at the little cowpuncher in this fashion. He allowed Shorty to lead the way as, instead of dipping down into this unknown region, they wound along the side of the ridge, and so across to more open cattle country, with a tiny huddle of houses in the distance—a range town that they reached in the dusk.

"And now what?" asked the rancher.

"When you go fishing," Shorty said, "you find a likely look-ing stream and then you get a hook, and then you get your bait. Yonder is the sort of a place that the fish we want would like. And you and me are the hook. Now you go to get us the bait."

"Bait?" echoed Peter Dunstan.

"Yes," Shorty said. "What is the most noise-makingest thing that there is on four feet?"

"A calf," the rancher said.

Shorty shook his head. "I got to admit," he said, "that when a calf wants its maw, it gets to working a fine pair of lungs, but you take it at a little distance, and the bawling of a calf sort of melts into things in general. It ain't hardly no more than the

125

roar of a waterfall. What we want, is a noise that'll travel through your ears right down to your backbone."

The rancher nodded. "I've got the thing for you," he said. "A dog. Not a grown dog, nor yet a little puppy, but one about six months old, used to one home. Put that in a strange place, and it'll make a noise nobody within five miles can sleep through."

"You got your uses, Dunstan," the cowpuncher said, grinning. "Now and then, the things that you think of come in pretty handy, I got to admit. But now the next thing that I want is to find that same pup."

They found it readily at hand. In the very hotel where they stopped was a happy family of sheep dogs. A mother and four puppies not five months old—all legs and clumsiness, but with bright, warm eyes that told of growing mischief and wisdom, hand in hand. The purchase was made with $2.

The next morning, Shorty was busy at the blacksmith's.

"I want a collar," he said, "that can't be broke. An iron collar forged right so it'll fit the neck of this here dog, partner. One made out of a good kind of steel, that nothing but a steel saw or a good file will get through . . . and that none too quick. Y'understand? Then I want a chain of the same style. A chain strong enough to hold a horse, friend."

The thing was done, and no questions asked. In the West, strangeness in a stranger is taken for granted. The collar was made, and the chain was linked to it.

With the collar on the dog, and the chain fastened into the ring of the collar, the two men started on their ride. It was not a pleasant ride. For whoever has taken an untrained puppy away from his old home will understand that noise is the element by which they live.

All this while, though he understood nothing of all of these preparations, Dunstan said not a word. Due to his wonder, his admiration for Shorty rose with every step of the journey.

They continued straight on into the woods until they reached a narrow clearing, with the glint of the nearest brook shining at them through the trunks of the trees. There Shorty made a halt. It was near the evening of the day. At once he fastened the dog to the trunk of a strong tree, hammering down the locking link with a heavy stone until it would have taken a cold chisel to pry it open again. After that, they retired—but not unaccompanied. The wild wailings of the dog followed them until Dunstan wanted to hurry on, and leave the sound far sunk from hearing behind them.

Shorty would not hurry. He stopped in the very first shelter, sitting down to smoke a cigarette, while the horses cropped the grass, or jerked up their heads to listen to new notes in the crying of the dog.

"Suppose," Dunstan said, "that something comes along and takes a notion to have dog meat for dinner."

"We got to chance it," Shorty said.

"Besides," said Dunstan, "what the devil good can you get out of . . . ?"

He stopped. The last cry of the dog had turned into an almost human scream of pain and of terror. Then there was heavy silence. Even the horses understood and crowded closer together.

The two men rode back as fast as the crowding trees would permit them to go. When they came to the spot, they found only a splotch of crimson on the collar and a dabbling on the chain. The dog had been torn away and carried off. On an open, naked patch of forest mold, there was the vast imprint of a mountain lion's foot.

Dunstan did not shudder, but his upper lip curled. "This is the devil, Shorty," he said. "And why did you do it, man?"

"I'm going back for another of the pups in the morning," Shorty declared. "Can you stand for it?"

"Get me the kid," Dunstan said, "and you can kill half the dogs in the world. But it sort of leaves a stain on the whole business."

"Well," Shorty said, "this ain't my party . . . it's yours."

Which, after all, was true. Not a word of objection came from Dunstan when his cowpuncher rode back toward the village in the early dawn of the next day. Not a word of protest came from him when the puppy was staked out in another clearing, deeper within the forest.

Once more the two men retired. This time, they passed only the nearest fringe of the forest and then paused to wait for results.

CHAPTER TWENTY

The wailing of that sheep dog was a terrible thing. It rose and died and rose again, soaring across the evening and the forest. Shorty shuddered, but Dunstan, having once resigned himself to the necessity of the cruelty, paid not the slightest heed to the agony in that puppy's voice.

Then, far through the woods, they heard the long note of a mountain lion—no doubt the same that had answered the cry of the dog on the evening before and found a dainty tidbit waiting on the chain, helpless to flee away. The note came again, nearer, and so pitched was the hunting voice of the great beast of prey that the men could not be sure from which direction it floated toward them. A fugitive from the voice of terror might as well have run into the mouth of the danger as fled away from it.

Shorty said: "I'll get closer and take a shot at the varmint, if he shows himself."

"Sit still," Dunstan said. "A dog is only a dog. I don't know what you intend to gain for me by letting the pup howl. But, after all, a dog is only a dog."

Shorty had to sit still and contain himself, with a mighty effort, while the voice of the hunter sounded again, close at hand. Apparently there was not long lease of life for the puppy, and the last cry of the puma brought a wild lament from the sheep dog. Shorty clapped his hands over his ears. At that very moment a gun cracked in the trees nearby; the death yell of the puma followed. Shorty leaped up and gripped the shoulder of his companion in the greatest excitement.

"It's him," Shorty said. "I knew that I'd fetch him if he was in hearing of the yapping of that pup. It's him. Now, Dunstan, if you want him, you get close enough to see him catch that dog."

Peter Dunstan's turn had come to shiver with excitement. He slipped to the edge of the little clearing on the farther side of which the dog was tethered. Crouching there in the shadows, he waited, his eyes accustomed to the dim light and probing the darkness alertly.

There was unbroken silence. The sheep dog, wearied out, or as though knowing that the sound of the gun and the death cry of the mountain lion signified the approach of a friend, stood motionlessly, erect, head high, with only a slight wagging of his tail in a pleasurable anticipation.

Though Peter Dunstan was an old hunter and a good one, yet he heard not a whisper approach. He did not have the slightest idea that another person was near him until the puppy broke into a frantic whine of delight. Then Dunstan saw the youngster throwing himself in wild joy on the shadow of a man that emerged from the woods.

A dim and furtive shadow of a man it was. With a mere gesture—or at least Dunstan could hear no voice—this stealthy stranger reduced the dog to silence. The soft clinking of the chain told that the man was working to release the puppy.

Now, Dunstan had done his share of fighting in his time, but it seemed to him that the danger of stepping forth into that clearing was greater than the danger of facing any leveled gun. He even thought of covering the other with his rifle before he ventured forth. This he could not decide upon. For in that faint light in the woods, it seemed to Dunstan that he would be facing hopeless odds if the other should attempt to attack him. It would be like facing a royal tiger, felt Dunstan, a tiger that uses a gun and sees in the dark.

So he merely called out: "Sandy! Sandy Sweyn!"

The form of the man vanished. Perhaps it was a backward leap into the surrounding trees that whisked him from sight. But the thing happened so suddenly and so noiselessly that the blood rushed into the head of Dunstan; it was as though he had looked upon a miracle.

He stepped out into the open. There was no rustling among the brush, but he felt the withdrawal of the other to a greater distance, a swift and smooth withdrawal.

"Sandy!" he called frantically. "Sandy, I mean you no harm. I swear I mean you no harm, Sandy." Still, though he heard nothing, he felt the withdrawal of the other. "Sandy, Sandy!" he called. "Come back, Sandy, and you'll have something worthwhile!"

There was a pause, and Dunstan, cursing softly to himself, stared about into the shadows. The sheep dog made a tentative step forward, and then strained frantically in the direction in which the stranger had disappeared. Dunstan cursed the dog and its whining. With the oath still on his lips, he looked up, and he was aware of the shadow of a man, standing just within the trees. He took heart again, and said in his most amiable tones: "Are you there, Sandy?"

"I s'pose that I'm here," Sandy Sweyn answered. "And what might you want?"

"I want a word with you, Sandy."

"Is that your dog?" Sandy asked suddenly.

"Yes," Dunstan responded.

"I would make you a trade," Sandy said.

"A trade?" Dunstan said, seizing upon the first opportunity to open up the conversation. "Why, son, what is it that you want, that I have?"

"Yonder," Sandy Sweyn said, "there is a lion lyin' dead. I

would give you the skin of that, Mister Dunstan."

"Why, man, that's kind of you. What do you want to trade it for?"

"That dog, Mister Dunstan. I have sort of taken a hankering after that dog. Would you make the trade. *Hist,* boy!"

The sheep dog had begun to leap frantically toward the man in the shadows, but the soft hiss of Sandy made the puppy drop to the ground and lie there, motionless, waiting and watching the new master.

There was something in the dog that made the man come slowly, stealthily forth. He was walking over dried leaves and twigs, it seemed to Dunstan, and yet this uncanny forester moved without a sound. He came closer to the puppy and stretched a hand toward him. That youngster instantly was up, mute with the greatness of its joy, licking the fingers of Sandy Sweyn. Dunstan saw that he had a great power placed in his hands.

Just why any man should yearn after a dog like this—too young and untrained to be of vital use—was a great mystery to Dunstan. He himself would not have given $5 for half a dozen such creatures. But be that as it might, it was certain that the cunning of Shorty had devised a bait for Sandy Sweyn that had not only brought the strange fellow to hand, but which was still drawing him.

Dunstan said: "Why, Sandy, I don't want to disappoint you. I'd *like* to give you what you want. But this dog . . . you understand how a man will come to love a dog, Sandy, even when he hasn't had him very long?"

He could see the head of Sandy nodding. That was just the sort of a thing that the odd brain of Sandy could comprehend.

"Aye," said Sandy, "I can see what you mean. And if I got to love a thing, well, I couldn't hardly give it up, I suppose."

"But," Dunstan said, "we might as well sit down and talk the thing over. And I have in mind another sort of a trade, Sandy. I would like to trade a horse for that dog."

Sandy started. "You mean that I'm to trade Cleo for the dog?" he said with a sort of horror.

"Trade in the blue mare?" Dunstan said, laughing. "Oh, no. The horse that I want is a little thing. She would never carry your weight, Sandy, for half a day. A pretty thing, though. A little white mare."

"And how would I buy her, though?"

"Not buy her, but catch her, because she's running wild."

"Ah," Sandy said with a sigh of relief, "that's a different sort of a thing. I guess that maybe we could manage that."

"Good, Sandy. I'm very glad that you see the point that I'm making. You get the dog, you see, to keep as long as he lives. And then you get me the little mare."

"But how big might she be?"

"Oh, a little thing. An inch, or maybe two inches under fifteen hands."

"Aye," Sandy said. "I would not be wanting her, I suppose. And where might she be found?"

"I'll tell you all about that. Shall we sit down and talk it over?" He struck a match as he spoke, touched it to a bunch of grass at his feet and scattered a handful of twigs over it. From that small beginning, the flame spread in another moment to a comfortable fire. Then Sandy Sweyn sat down beside his companion, on a log.

Dunstan took careful note of him. He looked his height less than ever—seemed more fat of neck and shoulder than before— but Dunstan knew from of old that what seemed fat was the most flexible and leathery muscle. Sandy Sweyn was merely coming into his full strength of early manhood. He was dressed in a leather coat, much torn by long wear and rough usage. His hat was simply a shapeless thing that had once been black felt, now green with time and sun. His shoes having given out, he had replaced them with clumsily homemade moccasins. There was a revolver at his hip and a rifle under his arm. He looked to Dunstan much more like a vagabond than a hunter.

In all of these details, he had altered a good deal, but his face was practically the same. A trifle thinner, perhaps, a trifle more brown, so that at the distance he gave an impression of greater alertness and intelligence. When he sat close to Dunstan on the log, the rancher could see that the sand-colored eyes were as they had ever been—empty, vague, and misted over with the obscurity of incomprehension.

The old riddle passed through the mind of Dunstan. Was this man idiot or seer, fool or wise man? He had no answer at hand. He felt, as he had always felt, that in part he was dealing with the mind of a child, and in part with the powers of a giant.

"Now," Dunstan said, "I may as well tell you that other men are hunting for this same mare."

"Ah, yes," Sandy said. "And yet they haven't caught her?"

"They haven't caught her. She is as fast as a streak of lightning. Faster, I suppose, than any horse on the range.

"Faster than Cleo?" Sandy asked in surprise.

"Faster than Cleo . . . when Cleo has to carry your weight on her back, I presume."

"Well, I'll have to find that out for myself." He leaned and plucked up a bush by the roots, a stout bush with great roots that thrust far down into the earth. Yet the effort of Sandy Sweyn had been no greater than a normal man would have had to make in order to pluck up a knot of bunch grass. He began to tear the bush apart. It was green and the wood was as tough leather. Under the remorseless hands of Sandy, it was shred to small strips, which he tossed on the fire. All of this he did not with a concentrated effort, but rather with an effect of an absent mind—as though he hardly knew what his hands were employed in.

"How far away is the place where she is running?"

"Out on the Condon Desert. Do you know that country?"

"I don't know it. How far?"

"Oh, a hundred miles from here."

"And if I catch the mare?"

"You bring her to me, Sandy."

"And then?"

There was a startled exclamation behind them, and Shorty leaped out of the shrubbery, where he had been hiding all this while, to guard his master from any dangerous effects from conversation with this strange child of nature.

"Look sharp!" gasped out Sandy. "There's a grizzly as big as a barn right at my heels!"

Chapter Twenty-One

Swinging his own rifle under the pit of his arm, Peter Dunstan said: "Throw a stone, and the big brute'll scamper away fast enough."

"He ain't that kind of a bear," objected Shorty. "He come for me like he knew all about menfolk and wanted to examine me for what kept me running. Y'understand? He came up like he meant business, and there . . . there he is now."

He pitched the butt of his rifle into the hollow of his shoulder at the same moment that a great black grizzly—or one so dark-coated that it actually seemed black in this dim firelight, reared from among the bushes and stood before them. An eight- or nine-hundred-pound monster such as had never before come into even the dreams of Dunstan or Shorty—old hunters though they were.

The giant greeted them with its vast paws folded on its stomach and a growl that seemed to fill the forest and far corners of the night.

In another instant, there would have been launched at its vitals two streams of lead from the high-power repeating rifles of the men had not the voice of Sandy Sweyn broken in with a harsh shout. It carried a note in it such as Dunstan had never heard before in the voice of any man. It seemed to shrivel up his strength. It made the hand that steadied his rifle shake like a dead leaf in the wind. There was an evident prohibition in the command that made the trigger finger turn numb and refuse to contract. He did not have to look at Shorty to know that his cowpuncher felt the same sensations.

Then, to Dunstan's utter confusion of soul and mind, Sandy Sweyn leaped between them and the bear—leaped in between with his arms outstretched.

"Don't shoot!" Sandy cried. "He'll do you no harm. Don't shoot, partners!"

He backed up as he spoke, until he came fairly within reach of the monster. Aye, and the two arms, each as thick as a beam, unfolded, extended, and seemed about to take Sandy in a bone-crushing hug. No, only one of them touched lightly on the shoulder of the man and stayed there.

Shorty, who recovered his wits first, after sight of this, whispered: "He's tamed a plumb wild grizzly."

"He'll do you not a mite of harm," Sandy said calmly. "He was just wandering around and seeing who my visitors might be. There's no trouble in him." With the flat of his hand, he smote the great, muscle-cushioned shoulder of the black giant.

Peter Dunstan cast an anxious glance over his shoulder. "Have you got any more pets hanging around, Sandy?" he asked. "Because my life insurance has run out, and I don't want to get into your family circle without being pretty well covered."

"There's no more to speak of," Sandy said as the black bear pitched to his feet, and then sat down, with the hand of his master resting on his shoulder. "But there's one mean one that don't get on with me very well. He's sort of offish." And he raised his two thumbs to his mouth and whistled a screeching note through them. For answer, there immediately came a harsh spitting close at hand.

"There he is," Sandy Sweyn murmured, and smiled, while a faint, malicious light gleamed for an instant in his eyes. "He's generally close by, but he don't like to show himself none. He hates to have your eye on him, you know." He called: "Come here, boy!"

Among the shadows, Dunstan saw two round, gleaming eyes. Then a bobcat crawled forth on his belly, lashing his flanks with his long tail. On the verge of the firelight he crouched, blinking.

"I ain't gonna torture him by bringing him closer," Sandy said. "He hates me and everybody else, except himself. He's a queer one. Run along, boy." He waved his hand, and the big cat was gone, while Dunstan and Shorty exchanged mute glances.

"But Jim, here," went on the man of the woods, "he's my regular family. I'm wondering, sort of, how he would get along with the dog. What might the dog's name be?"

"His name is Chris," answered Dunstan.

Sandy, with some difficulty, freed the chain from the place where it was fastened about the tree. Then he carried the dog in his arms and placed him between the forepaws of the great bear.

Jim curled back his paws from the cowering sheep dog and lowered his great head to sniff at the puppy. His lip curled. One champ of those jaws would break every bone in the dog's body. Still Jim forbore. While the other two men stood by in wonder, they saw Chris, under the ministering hands of Sandy, lift his own head a little and begin to thump the ground with his tail in a most conciliatory fashion. Big Jim finally heaved his bulk up and, with his head turned to the side, and his small pig-eyes glittering, left the clearing with a rumbling growl.

"Jealous," interpreted Sandy. "He's jealous, d'ye see? Even jealous of the cat. I never seen such a bear. Eight hundred pounds of foolishness, pretty near." He laughed and patted the head of Chris, who straightened and began to whine with pleasure, now that the grizzly was gone from sight. "He's a brave dog," Sandy commented. "You could see that, eh? Put his head right up, even with Jim leaning over him. I'll tell you, I'll have a time, though, getting Jim used to the pup. Might I have the dog before I get the mare, Mister Dunstan? To give him back, y'understand, if I don't catch her for you."

Dunstan shook his head. "Business is business, Sandy," he said. "You get the horse for me and deliver that horse to me right at the door of my ranch house. Then you'll get Chris, safe and sound. But if the horse dies while you were hunting for her, or if somebody else gets her first . . . why, Sandy, you have to admit that these things happen . . . you might be so attached to Chris, by that time, that you'd hate to give him up."

To this logic of the businessman, Sandy listened with his head bent to one side. "I suppose that you're right," he said at the last. "I don't seem to have any way of answering what you've just said. But I'll have that mare down at your place inside of a couple of weeks, or else I'll bust."

"Will you shake hands on that, Sandy?"

"Sure."

Their hands closed upon one another.

In his own section of the country, the strength of the grip of Peter Dunstan was almost proverbial. Yet, under the casual pressure of the fingers of Sandy, he felt the strength of his wrist and his hand give way, and his power failed him. His hand buckled under that enormous pressure, and, though he managed to maintain his smile, his face went white.

Sandy stepped back. He looked up—and a broad moon with a yellow-figured face was drifting up among the trees. "Why," he said uneasily, "I suppose that there ain't any time better than right now, for starting. So long." He turned instantly from the clearing.

As for the men that he left behind him, they sat down and stared rather helplessly at one another.

Peter Dunstan worked blood and feeling into his crushed right hand. "It was like taking hold of soft iron. You understand

139

what I mean? It began closing in on me . . . and closing in . . . and it got stronger and stronger. In another fifth of a second, I think that he would have been breaking the metacarpal bones. What a man!"

"A man?" Shorty said.

"You look sort of wild, Shorty."

"I was just thinking of something."

"And what's that?"

"How empty-looking his eyes are, mostly."

"Aye."

"But when he jumped in front of us . . . you remember? . . . his eyes were blazing like the eyes of that cat, when it sneaked up to the edge of the fire. And I thought . . . I couldn't help thinking. . . ." Shorty paused.

"Well?" Dunstan urged.

"I guess it was the same thought that you had, chief, for that matter. And I'll name it, too. I figured that if I was to turn loose some of the bullets right into his hide, while he stood there in front of us, that maybe I would be doing the world a good turn."

Dunstan nodded solemnly. "I had the same idea," he admitted. "Because it occurred to me that, if he should ever start and run amuck among other folks, he would smash up a dozen or two good men before he more than got warmed up. Someday, he'll make a killing that will make the worst things that Wild Bill ever did look like fifty cents."

Shorty paused in his task of stamping out the fire, to look up and nod. They said no more, but presently they went to their horses, mounted, and started out across the forest. If they had luck, they could get back to the village by midnight.

They threaded their way until they came to a more or less obliterated trail that wound along in the general direction that they wished to follow.

"What put the idea into your head . . . of baiting him with a yelling dog?" asked Dunstan.

"I dunno. I remembered him and the gelding at the ranch . . . and then the queer look in his eyes, as if he understood things that can't talk."

"Shorty, you got a great head. Isn't that a galloping horse that we hear?"

Suddenly, across the face of the hill that rolled out naked from the shadows of the forest, they saw a rider on a speeding horse—a great-striding animal that showed only for an instant, and then was gone.

"There he goes," whispered Peter Dunstan. "More luck to him. Damn his weird heart."

"Mind the dog!" called Shorty.

Chris was struggling forward with all his might, straining against the lariat by which he was being led along, vainly endeavoring to follow the fleeing rider through the night.

CHAPTER TWENTY-TWO

Up on the Condon Desert, the horse hunters were not so numerous as they had once been, for Elena Blanca had given her pursuers the slip so often that many of them had given up the chase. But others arrived. Where a dozen careless fellows started in the beginning, there now arrived professional strivers after forlorn hopes—calm-faced, desperate men. They were old and young. If you asked some grizzled veteran whether he really wanted to marry beautiful little *Señorita* Catalina, he would have shrugged his shoulders and grinned.

Of course, he did not want to marry her, but he wanted the money that, as all men knew, her father would be more than willing to pay to the lucky captor of the mare, to buy off the claims of the horse catcher to the hand of the girl.

Young and old, as the weeks passed, these hunters after the little white mare began to grow into a loose society, known to one another, carrying news of the new arrivals in the chase, and narrating the historic moments in the pursuit of Elena Blanca when some cunning snare had almost entangled her.

Of all the moments in that Iliad of horse adventure, none matched with one that happened in the fag-end of a long, hot day. For the two foremost pursuers of the mare combined their efforts to capture her, that day.

They were José Rézan and John Lucas.

It would have been difficult to select two men of types more opposite. José Rézan you have already seen—big, blond,

142

splendid in his beauty and in his strength. John Lucas came from somewhere in the Vermont mountains. He was made long and narrow, body and head. His thin face seemed to have been designed to cleave through the wind with the least resistance. His neck was like the crooked neck of a bird. There was nothing about him of a manly size except his arms and his legs. They were long and strong, and John Lucas added to their animal strength an animal quickness. He was like a big snake, just as José Rézan was like a big lion, tawny and grand.

These two came together. Each had appeared as a hero more than once in the epic hunt for the white mare. José Rézan suggested that they join forces to see if they might not compass her capture.

"But," John Lucas said, "suppose that we get her. Who'll be the lucky man?"

"You take the money," José Rézan suggested, "and I'll take the girl."

John Lucas thrust forward his long, lean chin. "I'll have the money *and* the girl," he said ominously.

"Very well," Rézan answered without bitterness and without fear. "We'll wait till we have Elena Blanca. After she's ours, then we'll fight for her, you and I . . . a good fair fight, eh?"

John Lucas thrust out his brown hand. "We'll make that a bargain," he said.

They gathered their best horses, employed the cleverest helpers that they could find, and laid their plans with such effect that during half a day they harried the beautiful white mare, driving her not fast enough to come up with her, but continually turning her toward points where fresh horses would be available to take up the labor

Twice, as she streamed through the heat of the afternoon with the sun burning on her silver body, it seemed to José Rézan that she must be theirs—and twice she found in her strong, wild heart an extra fund of energy, and drew away from the pursuit.

It was not until the golden time of the day, when the sun was low in the western sky, that magical moment on the desert when the period of rosy light has not yet quite begun and the white light of the stronger sun has ended, that Elena Blanca broke suddenly across the line of the pursuit. She struck off for the mouth of a ravine that pointed into the broader valley, with all one side of it painted with gold and all the other side clouded in purples. In vain John Lucas and big José Rézan offered their best riding and strove with quirt and spur to get a little more power into the legs of their horses. They simply had not the speed. To be sure, they had not run, either of them, a tithe of the distance that the white mare had covered on this day. On the other hand, she was not carrying the weight of a heavy man, or the gripping burden of a ponderous range saddle, equipped with two biting cinches that hugged belly and chest. Neither was she worried by spur and whip. She flew across the desert, urged by the vision before her of liberty and hounded by the dread of slavery behind.

She left them behind her with every stride. She was tired but still had an untapped store of nerve energy, and pride to call upon. It seemed to the despairing pursuers that she ran as freely and as freshly as she had that morning when the first sight of them sent her drifting away downwind.

She darted into the mouth of the ravine. Perhaps it was a blind alley into which she had dipped? They flogged their frantic horses, but there was no more speed in them. They could rock along all day and not mind the labor of the canter greatly, but to gallop a single mile behind Elena Blanca was a killing thing. They were spent; their heads were up; their hoofs beat hard upon the ground. The spring was out of their stride.

When they reached the mouth of the ravine, the two saw

White Helen running lightly far before, and making for the uplands. At that moment, as they were about to resign themselves to the inevitable and draw rein, out of the shadows of the western side of the valley there started a rider on a strong blue roan—a long-striding creature that plunged after Elena Blanca.

She met that challenge with a stout heart. She tossed her little head and, with pricking ears, drew upon her great soul for greater and greater speed. The speed was there to be drawn forth. She darted with wonderful beauty of gait straight up the valley, like a true blood horse when it answers the call of its jockey and fights down the home stretch.

Such speed as that would have blown her instantly out of the reach of the best horse that the two men had ridden in their strings that day. Yet they had a fine speedster in the lot. Seeing her running, they could only gape and marvel at her and see how infinitely she had been beyond them, really, even when she allowed them to press along at her heels.

That frantic galloping did not settle the issue in this instance. The rider on the blue horse was not distanced. He was not even put slightly to the test. At once the two wondering observers could see that the reaching stride of the blue roan was gradually swinging up on Elena Blanca at every stride.

Aye, she had done great running and long running on this day. Even when she was fresh and free, could she have withstood this challenge?

She had still more to call upon. She flattened her ears in her desperation. She pushed forward with a relentless earnestness. It was not enough, and the blue horse gained still more rapidly.

Then a rounding elbow of the valley wall came between the two leaders and the two behind. When the latter were in view again, they found that the blue horse ran literally almost side-by-side with the little white mare. She, with tossing, frantic head, strove to get more way, strove to shake off this cruel runner, and strove in vain.

John Lucas, drew rein suddenly, crying: "He's only playing with Elena! He's only playing with her, old son. We could ride all night, but we'd never see him capture her. He'll take the heart out of her first, and then he'll take her when she has no more spirit in her than a lamb."

The white mare and the great blue roan disappeared into the highlands, while the two pursuers remained in the lowlands, staring with a deep wonder in the direction in which they had disappeared.

"He could never have come up to her like that," vowed José Rézan, "if she had had her strength at the end of the day."

"I dunno," Lucas said. "She's tired, and she's run a good many tens of miles today. But still, I don't know. I wouldn't want to bet on how fast that blue horse could run, even with a heavy man like that in the saddle. It's got a stride made of rubber, that blue horse has. I never seen anything like the way it walked right up on Elena Blanca. I never seen nothing like it. I wouldn't've believed that even a thoroughbred race horse could've closed up on her like that. But it ain't just the running of the blue horse that has me wondering."

"What is it, then?" Rézan asked.

"What I wonder at, is how did the gent that's riding that horse know that Elena would be taking her run up this here cañon? How did he come to be waiting here so pat?"

José Rézan nodded. "Maybe," he said, "the rest of these cañons are all blind . . . no easy way through them to the mountains behind. And so he waited here, thinking that she would know. Because that little white devil of a mare, she knows a great deal more than we think."

"You can explain it," Lucas muttered, "but I say that it's

strange, and ain't likely. It's as though he could've read the mind of that horse, friend. And that's what I sort of believe."

Elena Blanca had reached the high broken lands toward which the ravine pointed. There, with coverts on every side, she felt a greater security. There was still no escape, for the rider on the blue roan mare kept close at her side. When she wheeled, the blue horse wheeled likewise. When she dodged, she could not put any distance between herself and the pursuer.

Despair began to steal the strength of the white mare, more than had her heroic running of this famous day. The golden time of the afternoon ended, and the clouds in the west were masses of red flame when Elena Blanca, at last, came to a halt and stood upon wide-braced legs, her head hanging low, the fire gone from her eyes.

She waited patiently for the rush of the victor, the shout of triumph, and the stinging burn of the deadly rope around her neck. There was no charge, no shout, no hiss of the rope above her head. Instead, she saw the man dismount and come toward her with gentle words, his hand outstretched. The great blue roan was following him, willingly, with pricked ears.

Elena Blanca tossed her head and started off at a rickety gallop. Presently the blue mare and her rider were at Elena Blanca's heels again. Elena turned and paused, and whinnied faintly, more in wonder than in terror and despair. Once more the stranger came toward her with a gentle voice and an extended hand.

CHAPTER TWENTY-THREE

The news traveled on wings, as a miracle accomplished. After all their labors, all their weeks and weeks of patient striving, here came a man who, in a single day, did what all their work had not been able to accomplish.

"But," John Lucas said to half a dozen of his peers, the gloomy José Rézan among the rest, "what does it all mean? It ain't as if he had come and run her down by himself. Here was me and José, yonder, that worked ourselves sick and burned up our best horseflesh. At the end of the day, when she couldn't no more than raise a gallop . . . but when that gallop was more than our horses could match . . . just as she's barely strong enough to run away from our horses, in comes this gent and pops a rope onto her, you might say. Now I say . . . who gets the real credit? Us that wore her down till one kid on a common range pony could've caught her, or him that happened to be handy at the right spot and the right time. I ask you?"

Of course their answer was what he wanted it to be.

The honor and the credit by right belonged to Rézan and to the formidable Lucas. As for this interloper, he was a mere thief in the night, who had slipped in between them and the proper reward of their labors.

"But," said one of the listeners, "what you gonna do about it?"

Lucas thrust out his lean jaw, the fighting jaw of a bull terrier.

"All I want to know is if I got the right," Lucas said, "because, if I've got the right, I'll manage the way, well enough." And he grinned and nodded to himself.

José Rézan called Lucas to one side. "You are going gunning for this man?" he asked.

"Why not?" Lucas responded. "I ain't stealing no chances from you. You can do the same, and I say that finder's keeper. And did you see the rest of the boys? They got the same idea. Look at Buck Chisholm, yonder, already saddling up his best horse. Where would *he* be going, I ask you? Why, he's going out to find this same gent . . . and that's all that there is to it. But I'll beat him out, or I'll eat my hat."

Eight good men and true, each with desperation in his heart, rode out across the mountain desert to find the trail of Sandy Sweyn. He was not particularly hard to find. There was only one difficulty that hampered them, and this was the speed with which Sandy rode south toward the ranch of big Peter Dunstan.

Buck Chisholm found the trail first. He swore, afterward, that he rode for a whole day, following it south, but only twice did he have a fleeting glimpse of the pair of horses and the rider in the distance.

John Lucas came within half a mile of them. And John Lucas swore, afterward, that he saw the blue roan carrying its master along at a rapid, sweeping trot, while the white mare idled before and behind; sometimes she would pause to crop at the bunch grass, where she could find it in random spots, sometimes she would frisk far ahead of the blue roan. Of one thing Lucas was certain—that there was no rope on the wild white mare. She ran at her own free will, and her free will was to remain close to the blue roan and the strange rider.

After that Lucas gave up the pursuit. "Because," he said, "there ain't nobody on the range that I'm properly afraid of, as you might say. But there's something spooky about this business and this here Sandy Sweyn, if it's really him that got the mare."

The news flew far and wide and far and wide. It came through the valleys, over the ragged heads of the mountains, and swung down softly into the valley where the house of *Don Diego* stood.

He called his daughter down into the windy patio, where the tall, gay hollyhocks nodded solemnly back and forth against the whitewashed wall.

"They have caught Elena," he said to her.

"It is José!" cried Catalina, her eyes firing with a soft hope.

"It is *not* José."

She grew blank.

"There is a young fellow with a dead eye and a blank face who lives alone in the woods . . . like a beast. He can talk to a horse better than he can talk to a man. He can make a dog understand him more easily than a man can understand him. His name is Sandy Sweyn. He has caught the mare, my dear."

Pretty Catalina grew white enough, now. Then she asked fiercely: "Is this man a half-wit?"

"Not even a quarter-wit, my dear."

"I shall not need to keep my promise, then."

"Do you think not, Catalina? Now listen to me, and write down my words in black in your heart of hearts. You have given an oath that a million men have heard of. You have sworn that you will marry the man who captures Elena Blanca and brings her to you. So it has become a question of something more than the honor of a silly girl. It has become a matter of the honor of Mirandos. My honor, child. And my honor has been flawless. By heavens, Catalina, you shall marry the first man to bring Elena Blanca to this house, or I shall turn you out like a beggar . . . with bare feet . . . to be laughed across the mountains. Do you believe me?"

She looked up into his face and found a terrible and calm decision there. For once in her life, Catalina could not answer. Deep in her heart, the very roots of speech were frozen. She turned away, stunned, and felt her way into the house again, and so up the stairs to her room.

It seemed to Catalina, when she was in her room again, that she was looking forth upon a world as empty as a polished brazen bowl.

It was not only in this direction that the news traveled. It swung far to the south. On an instant wing, it reached the town nearest to the ranch of big Peter Dunstan and sent a messenger carrying the rumor forth along the road toward the rancher's house.

Dunstan was heavily occupied, on that morning. One of his oldest and best cowpunchers, Macfarlane, had just come in with a ringing complaint.

"How long might I've been working for you, Dunstan?"

"Nine years, Mack."

"Am I reasonable or unreasonable?"

"Except when you've been hitting up the red-eye . . . mighty reasonable, Mack."

"And what have I got that's better than anything else?"

"Why, your old cutting horse, Sam, I suppose."

"Would you mind coming out and having a look at Sam, now?"

Dunstan stepped to the door, and yonder was Sam, an ugly-headed bay horse, hobbling from one bunch of dead grass to the next, with a great limp in his off foreleg.

"What the devil has done that, Mack?"

"Look yonder." With a savage face, Mack indicated a little heap of black and white curled up in the shadow of one of the big posts of the nearest corral.

"It's that new dog that you brung down from the north with

you, Dunstan. It's that Chris. He's been seen hounding old Sam around the corral, and finally he run that horse ag'in' a post . . . and there you see."

"I'm sorry, Mack. I'm terribly sorry."

"Sorry is one thing. But a sorry dog is what I want to see. A dead dog out yonder would be a heap of use to me, Dunstan."

"You want me to kill Chris?"

"What use might he be here?" Macfarlane asked savagely. "Or maybe you're gonna start drifting sheep on this here ranch?"

At this sarcastic proposal, even big Peter Dunstan winced. "I'll never run sheep on this place. You know that. But I'll tell you what I'll do, Mack. I'll tie up that dog till it gets a little sense. Only . . . I can't shoot it. I've got a use for it."

Macfarlane removed his hat and scratched his half-bald head. "If he runs that horse of mine ag'in," he said, "I blow for another bunkhouse, and I take my Sam along with me. Dogs is all right, in their place. But their place ain't never been in the running of horseflesh, and it ain't never gonna be. So long, chief."

Macfarlane retreated toward Sam and led the cutting horse back to the corral, while the rancher took young Chris by the collar and tied him with a strong length of new rope to a sapling beside the house.

He went back to his office to wade through a stack of bills with his checkbook beside him—a dreary task. His payments were always slow for the mere reason that he detested these clerical duties with all his soul. He had not removed more than the top of the pile when a sharp, mischievous barking sounded from the corrals. Rising to look out the window, he saw Chris, with a chewed-off rope end flying from his neck, in hot pursuit of Sam.

Poor Sam, crippled and staggering, dodged and kicked as well as he could. But the wisdom of old inherited craft was working in the brain of Chris, and he rounded Sam neatly into a corner, where the gelding made a frantic and vain endeavor to jump the fence. He merely crashed against the top bar and sprawled back again into the dust of the corral.

"Chris!" yelled Peter Dunstan. "Hey, Chris!"

Chris was far too delighted with his work to listen to any human voice. He circled Sam with a wild outburst of yapping.

"Chris! Will you hear me? Chris! I'll kill you, you fool . . . Chris!"

The gun came into the hand of Dunstan. It was not a carefully aimed shot. It was rather a random try, directed by chance. But poor Chris leaped high into the air and came down with a death screech, flat upon his side, and lay still.

Dunstan did not wait to go through the doorway. He swung himself through the big window and reached the spot in an instant. He knew even before he started that it was useless to make an examination. Something in the mere yell of the dog had been enough to tell him that its life went out with the last of its cry. When he reached Chris, the lolling tongue in the dust and the glazed eyes were an unnecessary proof.

Macfarlane, at that instant, came on a galloping horse around the corner of the barn. "Did I hear that dog yelping again at the heels of my Sam?" he shouted.

"The devil with you, and your horse. Take this dog, and bury him . . . and bury him deep . . . and don't let me hear another word out of you for a month." Then Dunstan turned upon his heel, and Macfarlane was too astonished and overawed to protest against the shameful burden that was thus thrust upon his shoulders. He knew his own value, and he knew that his employer knew it, also. It was as though the heavens had fallen upon Macfarlane's head.

Dunstan, as he strode gloomily back toward the house, saw a small dust cloud rising far down the road. "It's the news," he

153

said to his gloomily prophetic heart, "that the kid has taken Elena Blanca and is bringing her south to me. And me with the kid's payment lying yonder . . . dead as a doornail. Oh, to blazes with Macfarlane and his horse . . . and ropes that a fool dog can chew through."

So said the rancher to himself, even before the figure of the messenger could be descried through the dust cloud.

For once, his prophecy was true.

CHAPTER TWENTY-FOUR

When Peter Dunstan first heard that Elena Blanca was indeed taken, and that the captor, instead of traveling straight toward the home of *Don* Diego was coming south, he understood at once that in the mind of Sandy Sweyn there was no thought of claiming the girl for his. Sandy was coming to execute his half of the bargain and render the white mare and receive, in return, the little shepherd dog, Chris. Since the shepherd dog was dead, what other payment could be substituted? Money?

He thought again of the gloom of the evening in the forest, the dark bulk of Jim, the bear, and the snarling, skulking form of the bobcat. Money was not the stuff with which he could tempt Sandy Sweyn, but since he had taken such a liking to one dog, might he not accept another in its place?

Over that thought, Peter Dunstan lingered for a long time. He was too logical to be carried away by a first hope. It was not the mere fact that Chris was a dog that had interested Sandy Sweyn. There could not be any doubt that Sandy could have had a dozen dogs better than Chris, by far, if he chose to ask for them at any ranch house where the place was overrun by mongrels of one breed or another. No, what mattered to Sandy was that with his own hand he had killed the prowling mountain lion that had been drawn by the crying of the puppy. He had seen poor Chris cowering at the feet of the black-robed grizzly. That was what had moved the heart of the strange fellow. It was Chris, and Chris alone, that he would want.

What would he do, then, when he reached the ranch and found that Chris was not there to be given to him in payment for his work? Perhaps it would force into his mind for the first time the thought of going to the house of *Don* Diego Mirandos and asking there for the reward that, as the whole world knew, Catalina had offered to the captor of the white mare. That would be sheer ruin at once.

First of all, therefore, the rancher decided that he must get the white mare from Sandy as soon as he appeared with her. Then, while he put off Sandy with one excuse or another, he would head north and west toward the valley where *Don* Diego lived. If Sandy attempted to follow when he discovered the fraud—why, he must be prevented surely in one way or another. *In one way or another,* thought the rancher grimly, and fingered his revolver as the thought went home. He took out the picture of the girl and stared at it hungrily. Her beauty was his excuse, and a vague feeling that, get her how he could, all would be fair in the war for her.

Two things stood in his way. One was that it was known that the dog was dead. The other was that he was on his ranch where all men knew more or less about Sandy and Sandy's prowess. If he tried to gather among them two or three willing to confront Sandy in wrath, it would be a hard task to find them.

He made his decision on the spot. First of all, he went to find Macfarlane. He found him heaping up and trampling down the mound over the spot where he had buried poor little Chris. As Peter Dunstan looked on, something like remorse stirred in him, and a vague feeling of dread, lest the evil impulse that had destroyed the dog should bring unhappy consequences upon him in the future.

On the whole, Dunstan was as little given to remorse or to the pangs of conscience as any man in the world. He trampled on this tender gloom as Macfarlane was even then trampling upon the grave of the dead puppy.

"Mack," the rancher said, "there's nobody in the world that knows about the death of that pup except you and me. You understand?"

"Why, that's straight enough," answered the cowpuncher.

"And, just now, I don't want any others to know. You hear?"

"You don't want anybody else to know," Macfarlane repeated, scenting a mystery with quivering nostrils. "Well, I'll keep it dark enough, then."

"Here's the main point. I'm riding out and taking that dog along with me."

"You're riding out," Macfarlane said, to get his lesson firmly in mind, "and you're going to take the dog along with you. I get that. What's next?"

"There's nothing next, so far as any of the boys on the ranch are concerned. But somewhere inside of the next two or three days, Sandy Sweyn is going to come back here, riding his blue roan."

"Sandy back!" exclaimed Macfarlane, and his eyes opened a little.

"You don't like Sandy?" the rancher asked curiously.

"I don't like nothing that I ain't able to understand," the sullen cowpuncher said. "Why?"

"You're like me," agreed Dunstan. "You don't like anything that's too ghostly. I'm with you on that. But now, old son, the point of this yarn is that Sandy is going to have something else with him . . . and that something is going to be Elena Blanca, that all the fuss has been made about."

Macfarlane took off his hat and gaped at his employer. "The white mare," he said. "And then . . . the girl. . . ."

Dunstan held the eye of the other with a glance like a bar of iron.

"The girl is out of it," Dunstan said. "That boy is a half-wit, as you know."

"He's a half-wit, or worse. He's plain batty, by my way of thinking. But . . . are you dead sure?"

"I'm sure that he's got Elena Blanca. There's no doubt about that. He's coming down here to find me and turn that mare over to me."

"You lucky devil," the cowpuncher muttered. "You're the one that gets. . . ."

"And what he is going to ask for after he asks for me is the puppy. Do you get this?"

"Every word!" exclaimed Macfarlane. "That's why that dog was so important, eh? He was the pay that fool, Sweyn, got for bringing down that. . . ."

"You can do all the thinking that you want to, Mack," Dunstan said. "I can't keep you from it, and you're too smart not to think things out pretty straight. But do your thinking to yourself. I've got no time to explain things to you, or I would. The fact is that when he comes down here and asks about the dog, you are to tell him that I've gone off with Chris. Is that clear?"

"Yes. I've got that, right enough."

"And then if he says that he's brought the mare for me and wants to know where to find me . . . and the dog . . . you're to try to get him to leave the mare here with you. If he'll do it, you're to put a pair of ropes on her and put her in that high-fenced corral, and then mount one of the boys guard over her, night and day.

"Right. Because she means something to you."

"She does, of course. But perhaps Sandy won't want to turn her over to anyone other than myself. If you can't persuade him to part with Elena, then you'll have to tell him that I've gone . . . to Chorleywood."

"Chorleywood!" gasped out Macfarlane. "Chorleywood?"

"That's what I said, man. Chorleywood."

"Chief," the other gravely said, "you ain't forgot that the boys over that way don't look on you as being any uncle of theirs."

"I've not forgotten them any more than they've forgotten me," declared big Peter Dunstan. "But the thing for you to remember, Macfarlane, is just this . . . that I've gone to Chorleywood, and that I've taken the dog, Chris, along with me. When you remember that, you can stop working your brain. And for the boys here on the ranch, you don't know even that much. You only know that I've ridden off, and that I've taken the dog with me. One thing more, Mack, if this thing goes through smoothly, you're not going to lose anything by it. Here's a twenty to stick in your hip pocket. And there'll be a good deal more than that when the deal is all finished. So long, Mack."

Not waiting for any reply, he turned on his heel and strode away, with Macfarlane staring helplessly after him.

That one word had frozen his brain and made him incapable of thinking. All that he could see, at that moment, was a time five years before, when the rustlers and crooks at Chorleywood had dared to lay hand upon some of the cattle of the chief. The result had been a stern campaign. Dunstan had gathered all his cowhands. He brought in recruits at the handsome tune of $10 a day, and keep. With a little army of fifty, all told, he started for the outlaws without asking leave of the state. He did not need to ask leave. Three governors had admitted that Chorleywood was a sore spot on the political map; yet three governors had been unable to deal with the menace, from which a score, or more, of criminals had been in the habit of issuing forth at their pleasure and executing their schemes before they returned to their well-known hole-in-the-wall country.

The fifty hard riders of Peter Dunstan had labored during a whole month. It was their boast that they made Chorleywood too hot to hold the crooks. They lost two good fighters, and half a dozen were more or less badly wounded, and an uncounted number injured, carrying back with their column no fewer than four men upon each of whose heads there was a handsome reward placed by the state or by the federal government. It was said that the government had had to pay for Peter Dunstan's little hunting party, and had given him all his fun and a little surplus of cash besides.

Not only had he effectually broken up the gang for the moment, but he had well-nigh ruined their morale. For a long time hard-pressed criminals in distant parts of the country forgot to look toward Chorleywood as a haven of refuge.

However, five years on the borderline of the law is a long time. Before it had half lapsed, the old gathering of yeggs and bad ones of one sort or another commenced to reassemble. As they gathered, they made one eternal rule, that no matter where they trespassed, it must not be upon the lands of Peter Dunstan.

Having been burned once, they rightly feared the fire, but, following the same rule, was not Peter Dunstan a madman to venture his head in such society?

Chapter Twenty-Five

As a matter of fact, Peter Dunstan had not made up his mind on the spur of the moment. It was only after the most mature consideration that he had decided that he would have to go to Chorleywood. The impulse that drove him was not, excepting even his love of money and power, the greatest that had ever entered his life. It was the love of little Catalina Mirandos.

When he came in sight of the mountains of Chorleywood, like a mighty green ocean, with all the waves torn to jagged edges by the pressure of a gale, he paused in doubt. Yonder, he knew, were men who would ask for nothing better than to put a pistol to his head. At last, he drew from his pocket the newspaper clipping that contained the picture of pretty *Señorita* Mirandos. One sight of her face was enough to remove all his doubts.

He dismounted and looked to his horse. The way had been long and dusty, but the gelding had stood the labor well. Its head was still high, and its eye bright. If Dunstan had to ride for his life, the horse could give a good account of itself, beyond any reasonable doubt.

Next, he examined his weapons. Since in his methodical life he had never gone forth in the morning without seeing that his guns were in perfect condition, there was nothing to be done to rifle or revolver now—except that the trigger of the latter was half an ounce too heavy in the pull. This he remedied by working it back and forth a few times, so freeing it of some unseen particle of dust.

When all was ready, he swung himself back into the saddle and entered Chorleywood.

It was not like any of the surrounding country through which he was in the custom of riding every day of his life. Raised from the flat or the lower, rolling hills, these stiff crests caught the warm southern winds and distilled from them all the moisture that they carried. The mountains of Chorleywood were generally distinguishable from the distance—when the south wind blew—by the broad cap of vapors that continually rolled around the summits.

Where the lower lands nearby had only the brief seasonable rains to raise the new grass crops, Chorleywood was replenished with moisture all the year through. Peter Dunstan found himself riding under great evergreens, with a thick, soft matting of pine needles beneath. Where the trees ceased, green grass began.

He had not been here in five years, and then he had ridden with fifty fighting men at his back. There was a reason, therefore, in the care with which he proceeded. When he rounded a forest-clad shoulder of a steep mountainside and saw a little shack before him, he reined his horse sharply back into the shadows of the pines again. However, he had not come to avoid men, but to find them. This was as good a spot as any in which to begin. He sent the gelding forth again.

It was a most dilapidated shack. The little hut at the back, which might have served as a cattle or a horse shed once, had been pressed flat by time and neglect. For a building, that might stand for three generations in the dry air of the desert, would rot to shaky softness in three years of this frequent rain in summer, and brittle frost in the winter of the year. The house itself was not large enough for more than one room. When Dunstan came opposite the open door, he saw that this was all that it actually contained. Kitchen, bedroom, living room were here, all in one.

When he leaned from the saddle, and tapped the wall with the handle of his quirt—holding the whip in his left hand, as a natural precaution that left his gun hand free—no one answered.

He was relieved, for a moment. When he dismounted and stepped through the door, he saw that a fire burned in the stove and a kettle steamed upon it. There had been men in that room hardly a minute before. The air was still thick with the smoke from their pipes. Yonder was half a side of bacon, in the act of being turned into thick, white, gleaming slices.

His coming had frightened the inhabitants away. Certainly here was enough proof that he was in the center of Chorleywood, where every stranger was a danger to every other man. There was only one vital consolation—the men did not know him. Otherwise, they might have begun with rifle bullets at him. As it was, they were lying low, somewhere, watching him from the edge of the trees, striving to make out what manner of man he might be.

He set their doubts at rest in the most eloquent fashion known to a Westerner. He issued from the cabin once more, unsaddled and unbridled his horse, hobbled him, and turned him loose to graze. Then, carrying saddle and bridle, he reëntered the house and stood in the doorway, holding the bridle over his left arm. To men west of the Rockies, it is the age-old method of demanding hospitality. Where this custom commenced, few men could guess, but perhaps it was a hint of Indian lore, transmitted by long usage to the white inheritors of the land.

The response to this summons, delivered as it was by silent gestures only, was in keeping with the character of Chorleywood. Suddenly Dunstan was aware of a shadow standing nearby, at the corner of the house.

Yet he did not turn his head. He steeled himself with a great effort, though he was aware that another shadow had come up on the far side of the shack and stood at the opposite corner of the house.

"Well?" asked the man on his right suddenly.

Peter Dunstan allowed his head to turn slowly toward the speaker. He saw a low, broad-built fellow with a fat body and great shovel-shaped feet. His face was strangely pale and intellectual—in contrast to his body and the clothes in which that body was equipped.

"Well," Dunstan said, "how's things?"

"Slow," the fat man said, "but pretty easy. How's things with you, stranger?"

"Fast," Dunstan replied, "and not so easy."

A sudden smile flashed upon the face of the other. A smile of infinite understanding. He felt that he was recognizing a real blood brother in crime.

"What's your name?" he asked.

"Pete," said Dunstan.

"Aye, but what Pete? Denver Pete? Cheyenne Pete? Chi Pete, or what?"

"Tomorrow," Dunstan said, "maybe I'll be one kind or other of Pete, but tonight I'm just that."

The other nodded. "I'm Lawrie," he said. "And this is Mike."

Dunstan turned about and faced a villainous-looking rascal with a week's red beard like thick rust upon his face. Mike blinked his eyes at the stranger and nodded; there was no word said between them. Turning into the house, Dunstan put the seal upon his claim for hospitality by hanging his saddle by a stirrup from a peg on the wall and his bridle over the horn. After that, he lent his hand to the cooking. They were hungry, all three, and until they had finished frying bacon, and eating it between cold, thick slices of pone, washed down with coffee, black as night and strong as lye, there was no further talk.

When the meal was ended, and the claim of Dunstan upon the hospitality and friendship of the others thus established, Lawrie leaned across the rickety table and said: "Now, Pete, you've got us where you want us. We can't pull a knife or a gun on you when your back is turned, not unless we want the same thing to happen to us, the next time that we run for cover. So what's your name?"

Mike stared at Dunstan out of bleared eyes.

"My name," the guest said, "is Peter Dunstan." He sat back to watch the effect of the hurling of this bomb.

It made Mike stiffen in his place, with rapidly blinking eyes, but Lawrie sprang to his feet, with a gun leaping from cover faster than thought.

"You're Dunstan?" he exclaimed. "You're Dunstan?" Then, remembering how fast the laws of hospitality bound him, he thrust the revolver back into its holster. "And I might have drilled you clean while you stood in the door of the shack! I wanted to drill you, because I thought that there was a look about you that meant trouble. And now here you are . . . and safe from me."

Even the steady nerves of Dunstan were troubled by this violent outburst. "I've never met you before, Lawrie," he said. "How have I ever managed to step on your toes?"

"Five years ago I had a pal here in Chorleywood," Lawrie said, eying the other with a fixed malevolence. "And you and your gang did for him . . . as you'll be done for, before ever you see your way clear of the trees again."

"Will they be hot to get at me?' asked Dunstan.

The other grinned with concentrated satisfaction. "I don't need to use my own hands on you, or my own guns," he said. "I can keep clean out of it . . . except just to spread the word that you're here. Only . . . I'd like to know what sort of a fool you are to put your head right into the fire, like this."

"Would you?" Dunstan said steadily. "Then, I'll tell you. I put my head into the fire, partner. . . ."

"You're no partner of mine!"

"I came here to Chorleywood because I need help."

"And the boys here having been old chums of yours . . . and you having done such a lot for us . . . you know that you can get what you need out of us?" Lawrie asked sarcastically.

"I know," Dunstan said, "that I kept my hands off you until you began to bother my cows. And then I raised the devil for you. But after that, we've let each other alone. I know another thing. By doing me a good turn now, you boys can make a neat little haul in hard cash. You understand? When I need help, I'm willing to pay for it."

Lawrie nodded. He was fairly white with scorn and with rage. "Money'll buy anything," he said, "starting right in with man. So you're going to buy us?"

"I'll buy you afterward," Dunstan said. "But I'll fight you first. When you spread the news around that I'm here, tell the boys that, if any of them have a grudge against me that won't stand wear, I'm here to meet him fair and square. I've got a gun, and the other fellow will have a gun. We'll fight it out here in the clearing in front of your shack, until I finish them, one by one, or until one of them drops me. And that goes for you, Lawrie, along with the rest. If you ache for a fight to clear your conscience, I'm the last man in the world to make things hard and slow for you. There's lots of room outside, and we have our guns at our hips. Step out with me, Lawrie, if you want a square deal. If you down me, that's the end. If I down you, my friend, Mike, here, will take the word through Chorleywood that I'm here, and that I'm ready to pay."

He hesitated a long moment, seeing the hate flicker out of the cunning eyes of Lawrie, and cunning brighten them instead.

"You've had chuck in my house," Lawrie said, "and you ought to know that you're safe from me. But the other boys . . . there'll be some of them that'll take it in another way, your being here. I'm starting now, old-timer. And maybe you'll have new callers before sunset."

CHAPTER TWENTY-SIX

A man without fear is usually a man without sense, and no one could accuse the rancher of being a fool. It was a long and anxious time that he spent in the shack, in the company of Mike. He spent that time in talk—the talk of Mike, not his own. Finding himself with a celebrity, Mike was glad of an opportunity to unbosom himself of his thoughts and his deeds. That is the way of the lesser spirits. They expose their littleness and their crimes to the eyes of the discerning as though a passion for confession seized upon them when they were in the presence of the strong.

So it was with Mike. In the two hours that followed, he trailed his listener with him from a little Ohio town through a hundred scrapes and disgraces, up and down the Mississippi, through two state prisons, and finally into the far West, where reputations tarnish more slowly and are scoured clean more easily. Even here Mike was a known man—mean, cheap, vicious, dangerous, most of all to his friends, and only significant because of the rat-like venom and courage with which he fought when he was cornered.

"They've got me twice and got me good," Mike said, hunching his narrow shoulders up to his ears. "But they'll never get me again, so help me. Not while my gun will work . . . not while I got the wits to keep a last bullet for my own head. That reminds me of a time that a smart dick got onto my trail down in N'Orleans. He'd got himself a reputation by knocking a yegg by name of Sanderson on the head, while poor Sanderson was asleep in an empty boxcar. This dick gave Sanderson a fractured head what he died of afterward, in the hospital. You know . . . resisting arrest . . . but one of the hospital orderlies heard Sanderson tell the real truth before he went West. Well, when I heard that this dick was after me, I was down in a joint kept by a. . . ."

He stopped the easy flow of his narrative. Big Peter Dunstan had risen from the chunk of log that he was using as a stool. As he rose, he turned toward the door and brought out a Colt. He was wearing a broad, heavy felt hat, of a pearl gray in color—for fine hats were the one vanity that had entered the life of Dunstan. Unless horses were counted as vanities, also. This hat, caught over the muzzle of his Colt, he extended cautiously past the doorjamb—held it there for a moment—and then hastily withdrew it.

Mike, understanding, sneaked into a far corner of the shack and crouched there, grinning and shaking with expectancy like a drunkard eying a glass of whiskey that he has not the price to buy.

Dunstan, as he pushed the hat out a second time, received what he wanted—the bark of a revolver from the farther side of the clearing, and a sharp twitch that knocked the hat spinning from the Colt.

His eye was at the door in an instant. Yonder he saw a tall form rising from a screening bush with a yell of triumph. It was a long shot for even the best of Colts, but Dunstan risked it, with a quick snap shot. He saw the man in the brush run forward a blundering step or two, then fall heavily upon his face—down, but not dead. He lay yonder, twitching and then writhing convulsively.

"Lemme get to him," Mike said in a passion of commiseration. "I've been down just like that."

When he reached the door, he struck the arm of Dunstan, like a bar of iron, beating him back.

"He's got pals behind him," Dunstan said, "and we want to know just who they are."

Certainly the groaning of the wounded man in the clearing might have moved any torturer, but Dunstan was serene.

Presently a voice shouted: "Dunstan, give us a chance to help him, and we'll give you a chance to get away!"

Other voices broke in, in agreement.

"Who are you?" Dunstan shouted in answer.

"I'm Coudray."

That name was vaguely familiar to the ear of Dunstan. It was connected, by rumor, with sundry atrocities on the highway. It was not the most famous name in Chorleywood.

Dunstan answered in a ringing voice: "I'll talk to Simonides, and nobody else. If Simonides is not there, I'll take my chances with the rest of you, but if he's there, I'll dicker with him."

Simonides, the little Greek, had written himself large in the recent history of Chorleywood. Of all the criminals who had sought shelter there, he was far the most famous; of all who had dwelt there among the mountains and the evergreens, none had behind him so long a list of dead men, of wrecked bank safes, of prodigies of cunning and invention. He had risen to fame first as a great counterfeiter. He had gone on growing in importance after skillful detectives broke up his gang for manufacturing and pushing the queer. Now it was said that no man led a successful life of crime in the West except by the direction or the connivance of Simonides. Now a voice answered from the edge of the woods—a voice pitched just high enough to carry to Peter Dunstan without effort.

"Here I am, Dunstan. I'm Simonides. If you want my word for your safety, you'll have it."

"Simonides, I hear you. And I take you at your word. You

boys are free to take up the chap I winged. Hop to it!"

"All right, men!" called the calm, strong voice of Simonides. "Get to him!"

The numbers that responded sent a shiver down the back of Dunstan. For he knew that he had long been hated in Chorleywood, but he did not dream, really, that the power of his name could draw so many enemies about him, and so quickly. Now a full half dozen men hurried out from the covert of the trees toward their fallen comrade.

There were others as well, to say nothing of Simonides himself, who now stepped from the trees—a little man with a great, Napoleonic head. He wore an air of distinction; he stepped as one in authority. Peter Dunstan saw that he had made a ten-strike when he placed himself, more or less, in the hands of this formidable outlaw.

He came straight up to Dunstan and shook hands with him, saying: "I thought that I'd be looking at your dead face, Dunstan, when we all started for the shack, here. But perhaps we can patch things up pretty well. Tell me what's brought you here?"

Honesty, as Dunstan could very well see, was the usual policy of this arch criminal. His dissimulation he reserved for great events of death or of plunder. In his usual intercourse with other men, no matter what crude criminals they might be, he chose to be bluntly frank, hyper-honest.

"First," Dunstan said, "tell me who I dropped. He must be some important man."

"Why?"

"By the willingness of you all to make a bargain to save his hide."

"That means nothing at all," answered Simonides, turning his great, black, considerate eyes up to the face of the tall rancher. "When we're here in Chorleywood, we pretend to be

171

very fond of each other. But after all, there is *some* sense in this mutual devotion in Chorleywood. You save me when I'm in danger, then you can depend upon it that I shall try to save you.

"I have known yeggs who rode five hundred miles from Chorleywood to go to the help of a man they had never heard of before, simply because they knew that he was a fellow crook. You understand how it is . . . the romantic idea, something for nothing, the forlorn hope, the necessity that all of us have in believing in our virtues as individuals and even as a class . . . that's what creates the bonds between us rascals here in Chorleywood. Down in our more honest hearts, that so seldom influence our actions, we know that we are great liars and hypocrites."

It was in many ways the most astonishing speech that Dunstan had ever heard. He watched the speaker from the corner of his eyes. On the other hand he watched the crooks of Chorleywood tenderly caring for the wounded man, binding up his hurt, and then carrying him away on an improvised stretcher.

"Through the hip," Simonides said, nodding. "Very painful, that. I think I had rather be shot through the body, though that is painful enough."

He spoke with quiet authority, and well he might, for legend declared that Simonides had been blown almost to bits, one time or another in his exciting career by the bullets of the men of the law, or of rivals in his own profession.

"But," the rancher said, "who the devil might he be?"

"If you don't know his name, don't ask me," answered Simonides. "When he gets well, he'll come calling on you with a pair of guns, and you'll find out his name well enough, unless you die first. Now, Dunstan, what has brought you here?"

"Necessity," said Dunstan.

"*Bah!*" exclaimed the other. "Do you imagine that I thought you had come here for fun? Who do you want robbed or murdered, Dunstan?"

The latter started. "Robbed or murdered?" he echoed. "I don't want either." He checked himself abruptly. "That is to say. . . ."

"Good!" said the outlaw. "You may as well be perfectly honest from the start. What is it, man?"

"In the first place," Dunstan said, "I don't know how serious this affair may be. You understand me?"

"Very well. I'll use my imagination."

"In the second place, I want to find out how I can be useful to you before I ask you to be useful to me."

"Friend," Simonides said, "you are supposed to be our great enemy. If we could use your ranch as a second Chorleywood, when in a pinch, it would be worth ten thousand a year . . . to me alone."

"That is not enough," said the rancher.

The other whistled. "You are going to put up a high price?"

"I am."

"What is it, Dunstan?"

"Do I know you well enough to talk straight out?"

"You do," Simonides said. "I can be honest with you because I have not a thing to gain by lying to you. Go on and put your cards on the table."

"A poor half-wit youngster," Dunstan said, "is riding in this direction, I'm afraid, and bringing a horse toward my ranch. I won't go into all the details. I'll only tell you that with one man at my ranch, I've left word that I'm at Chorleywood. The half-wit will start in this direction after me. Now, Simonides, I have to have the horse that he is bringing along with him."

"I knew that you were fond of good horseflesh," said the outlaw, "but I didn't know that you were as fond as all of this. Go on, man . . . I'm interested."

"When the fellow comes here, I want that horse taken away

from him and turned over to me."

"Look here," Simonides said solemnly, "do you mean to say that you respect the law so much that you wouldn't dare to take away from a half-wit anything that you wanted?"

"Simonides," the other said, "you're a keen fellow. The law wouldn't hold me back. It's the fear of the half-wit that stops me."

"Fear of a half-wit!" cried Simonides.

"Exactly that. And, if you undertake this job . . . to get the horse and turn it over to me . . . I want you to understand in the first place, Simonides, that you have taken on a man-size job. I'm a fair hand with a gun. You're a much better one, perhaps. But if the two of us went out gunning for this simple-minded fellow, I'm afraid that the money would be on him, and not on us."

CHAPTER TWENTY-SEVEN

While Dunstan and Simonides stood in comfortable conversation in the clearing at Chorleywood, a strange apparition appeared before the blinking eyes of the two toughest and oldest cowpunchers on the Dunstan Ranch—namely Shorty and Macfarlane.

They had barely finished dragging a stupid cow out of the muddy margin of a tank, where she had mired down almost to her back. Turning, almost too weary to curse, Shorty cried out in a loud voice and pointed up the slope. Mack, looking in the same direction, saw only a thick dust cloud blown down the shallow draw. As the sand mist dissipated, he was aware of the brilliant figure of a white horse—a dazzlingly bright form, as though cut out of a rock crystal.

A moment later, he yelled to Shorty: "It's Elena Blanca! It's White Helen!"

"Ride to the right!" Shorty cried in a voice made husky with terrible excitement and suspense. "I'll go to the left, and if we can cut in behind her and turn her down onto the ranch. . . ."

For she was running freely down the draw, until she saw them and came to a stop—like a wild wolf, with a hoof raised and her head high. As she was at that instant, with the sun burning upon her, and the wind combing out the silver of her mane and tail, there was never in the world a creature more beautiful.

Yet even then, the nearer approach to them did not seem altogether to daunt her. She turned her head and whinnied softly—then she actually advanced toward them again, down the draw.

The cowpunchers were frozen in place and overcome with awe. Did they not know the tales with which the mountains were now filled, of how this wind-footed mare was instantly away at the first suspicion of the scent or sight of man? So much so, that even the most careful hunters had their view of her only through strong glasses in the distance?

The explanation was almost stranger than the fact. For now, above the farther side of the draw, there appeared Sandy Sweyn on the great blue roan. A dusty man on a dusty horse, like a poor attendant following a bright angel form—like a picture of labor following wearily after wild freedom.

"It's Sandy," Macfarlane said gloomily. "Just for a minute, I thought that you and me would have to shoot it out to see who had caught the mare. It's Sandy, and he ain't got her on a rope, even. Can you get over that?"

A call from Sandy, and the white mare whirled and darted back to his side. She looked no larger than a pony, as delicately lovely as any antelope, dancing along in the shadow of the great blue roan.

So Sandy Sweyn came down to the waiting pair. Sandy was not one to waste much time upon idle greetings. He merely wanted to know at once where he might find their master.

Shorty answered: "He rode off the other day, taking a dog along with him. . . ."

"Taking a dog along with him," Sandy said sadly.

Macfarlane waved Shorty back. "I've got to talk to this gent alone," he cautioned his friend. He rode up close to the blue mare until his mustang touched noses with her.

"Sandy," he said, "the chief left word that you was to leave Elena Blanca here and ride over to meet him . . . and get the dog from him."

Sandy nodded, saying: "I'll take her to a corral. . . ." He paused abruptly. "But suppose that Mister Dunstan won't believe that I've got her until he sees her . . . I'll have to ride clear back here with him . . . and I got to go north pretty quick. No, you tell me where to find him, and I'll take Elena Blanca along with me. Look at her, Mack. She's a pretty thing, ain't she?"

Macfarlane agreed with all his heart. Something kept him from trying to press the point and draw the mare from Sandy now and keep her at the ranch. He did not want to be inveigled into the war that was apt to follow between Dunstan and the half-wit.

"Go to Chorleywood, Sandy," he said. "You'll find that Dunstan is over there, some place. Ride to Chorleywood and look sharp around, and you'll find him. . . ."

"The dog . . . Chris . . . ," broke in Sandy, "how was he looking?"

"Pretty well," Macfarlane said tersely. "Pretty well, I suppose."

"It's a queer thing," Sandy said, "how a dog will sneak along and step right into your heart, that way. Before you can hardly tell what's happening. I've been missing that dog a pile ever since I last seen him. Which way lies Chorleywood from here?"

"Why, Sandy, you seen it every day while you was working here. There it is, north and east . . . that black smudge on the edge of the sky. D'you see?"

"I see it. I can make it by tomorrow morning."

"Easy. It ain't so far off as it looks."

"So long, Mack."

"So long, Sandy. But ain't you gonna stop in at the house and say hello to the boys and have a cup of coffee, even, before you start along?"

"I'll start along the way that I'm fixed right now. *Adiós.*"

He waved to Shorty in the distance, and, turning the blue roan, he sent her away at a free-swinging trot. It is at that gait that a horse will cover long distances with the least effort. As for the racking, jolting effects of the gait upon the rider, Sandy Sweyn showed that he had learned to sit the saddle without stirring, no matter how the hoofs of the blue roan pounded the earth. With the white mare running daintily beside him, he recrossed the draw.

Shorty and Macfarlane followed to the edge of the farther rise and, sitting in their saddles, watched him draw farther and farther away. Still, when they thought that he had disappeared, the sun would flash upon the silken flank of Elena Blanca and send an electric signal back to the watchers.

Shorty said slowly, at last: "Something says to me that there is gonna be something wrong when Sandy gets to the boss, wherever he might be."

Macfarlane, who knew all, started guiltily. "What makes you think that?"

"Because it ain't exactly right . . . that a gent should get a horse and a wife and a fortune . . . all for the sake of a dog that didn't cost him no more than two dollars and pretty little care. There'll be no good come out of that."

Macfarlane said nothing, but he agreed with all his soul.

Sandy Sweyn, in the meantime, had no thought for anything in the world except the strength and the truth of the blue mare, Cleo, carrying him swiftly toward his goal, the beauty and grace of Elena Blanca, sporting before him like a happy child—and before him, drawing him on, the desire to see the shepherd puppy, Chris.

Men and the thought of men rarely entered the brain of Sandy. He was far too busy in a world which he could understand far better, the world of beasts and of birds.

He camped early that evening, before he had entered a mile into the green margin of Chorleywood. There he set about getting his own meal. For provisions, he carried salt in a little leather sack—and a store of cartridges, for rifle and revolver. A rabbit and a squirrel were collected by two snap shots, before he had roved five minutes from the camping site beside a bright little stream. In a trice, he was back at the place, with a cheerful fire burning.

The squirrels, startled by the noise of the gun, even if they had not known that one of their own kind had been slaughtered, were hushed in the branches above him. Such silence did not please Sandy. While he turned the roasting meat on the wood spit above his fire, he raised his head from time to time, uttering little sharp chattering. Once he gave a cry that exactly imitated the noise of an angry squirrel, surprised by another in the harvesting of a rare prize, and ready to fight in its defense.

Presently he had his reward. Half a dozen squirrels slipped out on overhanging branches of the great trees about the spot and commenced to chatter down to him, or to one another, or to the curious blue jay that dipped in and out among the shadows, like a gay jewel.

The jay itself came down at last to a lower branch, and cocked its head to one side while Sandy uttered faint little pipings, imitating with incredible skill the murmurs of a wounded nestling fallen from the nest. The bright, cruel eyes of the jay wandered here and there, in search of the fallen one. At last it looked full at the man, rose with an angry squawk, and hung in the air above the top of the tallest pine. From this height, it seemed to see something behind it in the forest that drew his attention. For it slid through the air to a place where Sandy could no longer see it. Hovering there, it uttered a series of harsh cries. Then its strident voice rapidly grew dim as it flew away.

Before the last of its calls trailed away, Sandy had laid aside his roasting spit and caught up his rifle. He knew the ways of the jay, and how that most hated of birds hunts the helpless, haunting those who are strong enough to hunt for themselves. Yonder among the trees was something that had been dreadful enough to startle even the cool nerves of the blue jay. Sandy wanted to learn what it was.

With never so much as a whisper of noise, he melted into the forest, following through it, close to the bank of the stream until his ear, close to the ground, heard the faintest of noises. Hardly a noise, indeed, it was only the soft, soft rustle of pine needles when a heavy weight is brought gently down upon them. It was a weight like the falling foot of a hunting bear.

Prepared to stalk the keenest of all hunters, Sandy Sweyn turned aside and made for the spot from which he had heard the sound by a little semicircle that should bring him behind it. And he smiled to himself as he moved, for he had no doubt that it was a bear, indeed—perhaps some sage, old grizzly, bent on trailing down the scent from the campfire, and the delicious odor of the roasting meat.

True to the spot, as though he had had the most accurate means of estimating the distance, Sandy Sweyn came upon a narrow gap among the pines. Now he saw the hunter straight before him—not a bear, but an enemy indeed terrible enough to make the blue jay flutter screaming away across the trees. It was a crouched man, stealing forward foot by foot through the trees, his rifle in his hand.

CHAPTER TWENTY-EIGHT

The slow mind of Sandy turned heavily upon this important discovery. What bewildered him was the reason that could have induced the hunter to approach his camp fire with such consummate care and skill. There could not be a doubt in anyone's mind as to what lay in the clearing, just beyond the next barrier of the trees, for the smell of the wood smoke from Sandy's fire blew plainly across the woods. Now, as a pitch-filled twig caught the flames, there was a very distinct crackling. This stalking fellow, therefore, must know that it was a man who was yonder. What, except mischief, could make him wish to get to the spot with such secrecy?

He was a most expert hunter. Sandy, who had often marveled at the clumsiness of other men in the woods, was all the more amazed by the silken smoothness with which this adept made his way. Once—with a sharp turn of head and body, though soundless as ever—the hunter whirled and showed Sandy Sweyn an evil, suspicious face and two bright eyes bent upon the very thicket where Sandy was hidden.

There was no doubt in the mind of Sandy, now. He knew little of men and their ways. He knew enough of beasts to tell those that preyed from those that were preyed upon. Beyond the shadow of a doubt, this was one who lived upon the prey that he could capture.

It was the more exciting, then, to steal forward along his path. If the hunter was soft in his movements, those of Sandy

Sweyn's were like the mere trailing of a shadow. To the ear of owl or bear, the noises he made might have been intelligible enough, but to the human ear, they were nothings.

He gained fast. As the stranger came to the very edge of the clearing and began to straighten to his knees behind a comfortably wide pine trunk, which would give him shelter while he spied upon the place more deliberately, something caught on the butt of his rifle as he drew it up. Without turning his head, he increased the pressure a trifle to free it from the root that must have caught in it. He increased the pressure to a tug. Suddenly the rifle was flicked from his grasp. As he turned with a gasp, he saw Sandy Sweyn in the act of rising to his feet with a smile.

There was little real mockery in that smile, rather the natural amusement that Sandy felt on a trail thus followed to a successful ending. To the hunter, it was like a grimace of a fiend. He uttered a faint groan of terror and of rage and jerked the revolver from its holster on his right hip.

No doubt Sandy could have pulled the trigger of the rifle and sent a bullet plunging through the body of this enemy. Such a thing did not even occur to him. He cast the gun itself against the other. The shock of it made the revolver bullet go wide. When the Colt sent out its second shot, the grip of Sandy was on the gun hand of his foe. The revolver was twisted helplessly to the side.

By loosing his grip on the gun, the stranger managed to free his fingers from a grip that bruised his flesh like the steel of a machine. He drove his fist into the face of Sandy, but it was like striking a heavy India-rubber pad. It did not seem even to jar the head of the other. The next moment the grip of Sandy fell where the teeth of a fighting animal fall—upon the throat of his victim. There was no resistance. A single pressure, and the hunter hung limply, gasping with wide-opened mouth. Sandy trussed him under one arm and carried him out to the open light of the day in the clearing, beside the blazing fire. He put him down where the stranger could sit on a fallen log, while Sandy squatted on a rock and began to munch his roasted meat, all the while eying the other curiously from head to toe.

He saw the rising of a desperate hope in the eyes of this hunter, marking that there was no weapon leveled at him. Sandy shook his head to discourage flight.

"If you was to run away," he said, "I could run after you and catch you. Or, if I didn't feel like running, I could just stop you with this, d'you see?" He drew a revolver from his belt.

Though it seemed to the stranger that the weapon exploded without more than the most casual upward flash of the eyes of Sandy, yet so carefully was the bullet aimed that before the echoes of the explosion had finished, rushing away among the big trees, there was a rustling and light crashing above them. The limp body of a headless squirrel fell, with a loose thud, upon the bare ground of the clearing.

The hunter buttoned his leathered coat a little more securely around him. Then he shuddered. For, a tenth of a second before, he had actually been considering flight—flight from such a marksman as this. As well might a pigeon strive to flee from an eagle in the high regions of the sky, with cover dreary, dreary miles away. He fingered his terribly bruised throat and looked downward to the ground.

"What might you have against me?" asked Sweyn.

"Me?" muttered the other. "Nothing."

Sandy shook his head. For the first time he frowned. "What's your name?" he asked.

"My name is . . . Coudray," said the other, stiffening just a trifle as a man will do when he expects that his name will have some effect upon another.

The eyes of Sandy remained blank, except for the cloud of

his frown. "Coudray," he said, "it's not the truth, and I know it. You *have* got something against me. You were hunting me. I ain't smart, but I know you were hunting me."

Coudray attempted a smile. "It was only a joke," he said. "I smelled the wood smoke. And I thought that I'd sneak up and surprise the gent that built the fire. . . ."

Again the head of Sandy was shaken vigorously in denial. "I've seen a mountain lion hunting for fun," he said. "I've seen cubs stalking each other. And, also, I've seen them stalking because their bellies was empty and they wanted food. But you ain't hungry, Coudray, and I ain't ever harmed you none. But still, you was trying to get at me . . . to murder me, Coudray."

In all the forest of Chorleywood, next to Simonides himself, there was no one man with a reputation like that of Coudray. Whether for strength of hand or ferocity of courage or skill with weapons, he stood by himself, dreaded even by the fiercest of the outlawry. Now he shrank before the youth who watched him.

"Murder?" Coudray said. "What could I want to murder you for?"

"I dunno. I ask you that."

Perspiration poured down the face of Coudray. "Man," he said, "you're talking foolishness."

"I ain't bright, Coudray, but I know when a man hunts to kill. I've never harmed you none."

Coudray was silent, but his bright, keen eyes wandered desperately back and forth from one side of the clearing to another, hunting for a lie that might serve him, but finding nothing. To lie to other men was easy enough, but to lie to this strange fellow was quite a different matter.

"If you ain't gonna talk out," Sandy said with a sudden ferocity, "I'll make you talk. When I find that a grizzly is stalking me through the woods . . . I turn back and I kill that bear if I have to trail him for a month. I've done it, and I'd do it again. If a mountain lion comes sneaking behind me down my trail, I go back and I kill that mountain lion, if I got to follow him right into his cave, in the end. Why should I act any different to you, Coudray? You talk, and you talk quick, or I'll finish you now . . . the same as if you was a bear or a lion. And I'll never have to worry about you afterward. But I'm mighty curious, Coudray. I'm so dog-gone' curious, that I'll let you go. I'll give you your guns, too, before I turn you lose, if you'll tell me why you come out here to hunt for me."

The hope of life took Coudray by the throat. "Sweyn," he said, "I'll tell you the truth and the whole truth, if you'll promise, when I'm through, to tell me how you spotted me in the woods."

"I'll tell you that," Sandy said. "If you'd kept your eyes and your ears open, you would've knowed how I found out where you were. Now you start talkin'."

"They're set and ready for you in the whole of Chorleywood," Coudray said, talking for his life. "They're waiting for you, and they're gonna get you if you don't turn back. All the reasons that they've got, I dunno. But this here gent, this Peter Dunstan, he's mixed up in it, somewhere. What the rest of us know is that Simonides himself has sent around the word that you're to be fixed so's you won't be a bother to anybody . . . and the white mare is to be took away from you. . . ."

"Elena Blanca!" gasped out Sandy Sweyn. "It's for her that they want me dead? For Elena?"

"I dunno. I tell you what I know. I figured that, if they wanted you bumped off, they must have a good reason for it. So I started along and decided that I'd lie out and try to nab you when you come into Chorleywood. Others started along to do the same thing . . . only it was me that had the luck and spotted you with my field glass a long ways off. So I come down to get at you . . . and now, tell me what showed me to you?"

Without a word, Sandy Sweyn handed rifle and revolver across to his prisoner. "You've told me the truth," he said. "I can see that you told me the whole truth. And you're free. But how I found you . . . why, a blue jay told me where you was. That was all there was to it. You must've heard him talking over your head?"

CHAPTER TWENTY-NINE

To the formidable Coudray, it seemed at first that he must be listening to a fairy tale, and not a very interesting one at that. When he searched Sandy's face, he was astonished to be met by the wide-open and frank eye of the truth-teller. Here was a man into whose brain the thought of falsehood had not so much as entered.

Coudray stood up and backed toward the trees. When he saw that there was no hindrance proposed to his exit, he turned and made off at good speed. Many a shiver went down his spine until he was sure that an ample screen of pines had closed in between him and the enemy. He got to the horse that he had left at a distance, and then rode with hard-driven spurs. Where he went, he hardly knew, and he hardly cared, so long as he was carried away from the spot where he had encountered young Sandy Sweyn.

Halfway up the next slope, a voice dashed at him out of a thicket. He turned in the saddle and had a fleeting glimpse of Lawrie, coming through the trees, rifle in hand.

"What's up, Coudray?"

"The devil is up!" Coudray yelled in return, and spurred on his horse more vigorously than ever.

It was enough to root Lawrie to the place. It must be remembered that the reputation of Coudray was a thing founded as firmly as the roots of the hills in Chorleywood.

★　★　★　★　★

Sandy Sweyn had shifted his camp. His mind was in a complete whirl. All that he had been able to gather from the confession of his captured man was that there was danger afloat for him in Chorleywood, that Peter Dunstan was connected in some vague way with that danger. However, since one man had found him here, he decided that he would be on the look-out with the greatest of care.

When he moved there was no trace left, either of his own footsteps or the hoof steps of his two horses, for he took them over a devious way, where he found certain outcroppings of rock that would not show sign of their passing. So, winding up a narrow little ravine, stern with boulders, he came suddenly, at a turn of the cañon, upon the very man of his search—Peter Dunstan.

One instant of doubt burned in the mind of Sandy—and then passed away. When Dunstan came up to him, frankly and happily, shook hands with him, and called him the most wonderful fellow in the world for having captured the mare when so many others had tried and failed, it seemed to simple Sandy that such heartiness could not possibly be linked with dissimulation. He returned the pressure of Dunstan's hand and smiled in turn.

"Aye," he said, "here's the mare. And if you'll turn the dog over to me . . . why, I'll put a rope on her, and you can take her away, Mister Dunstan."

Dunstan nodded, and, cupping both hands at his lips, he called loudly: "Chris! O-o-h, Chris!" Then he listened. He called again, listened, and finally, impatiently he said: "You'll have to do some training of that fool dog, Sandy, because whenever he gets out of my sight, he runs back to the house. . . ."

"That's queer," Sandy said meditatively. "Because he wasn't that sort of a dog when I last seen him. He was the sort of a dog that would cotton onto a man and not leave him, unless he was drove away. But you can't tell how a dog is gonna turn out, any more than you can tell how a boy will turn out. They pick up wrong ways. Maybe this'll fetch him." And raising his voice to thunder, which yet had a mellow and inviting note in it, he sent the name of Chris booming across the trees.

Dunstan, remembering how poor Chris lay dead in the grave on the ranch, felt all his nerves stand on end. What he next remembered was that Simonides's first prediction had been falsified.

"The easiest way," Simonides had said, "is simply to bump off this half-wit. Nobody will care what has become of him. Bury him under some rocks, take the mare, and ride north with her to old Mirandos and his girl. That's the way that we'll manage it. I'll just pass the word around to some of the boys."

Yet here was the mare and here was Sandy. He had not yet been bumped off. However, there was more than one string to the bow of Simonides. In case Sandy was not shot, he was to be brought up to the old prospector's shanty among the upper hills where Simonides himself and a few of his best men lived in such times as these.

"He's gone back to the house," Dunstan suggested with a note of regret in his voice. "But we'll go up that way and get him for you."

"Aye," Sandy said, "but I don't hardly like it. And I'll tell you why, Mister Dunstan. There's danger for me here in Chorley-wood."

"Danger?" Dunstan said with a more emphatic enunciation simply because he felt his very flesh crawl. "Danger? Why, lad, you're mad to say so."

"Listen to what's happened," Sandy said, "and then you'll agree with me."

He told in detail, word for word, all that he had heard and

seen in Chorleywood, and how he had seen the last of Coudray. By the time he finished, Dunstan had mustered his nerve force again.

"I'll tell you how things are," he said. "There are a lot of bad actors in this neck of the woods. A lot of crooked fellows, Sandy. Regular law breakers. Besides, there are some of a good sort who are fiddling around at one thing or another. Some of them have come here to do some prospecting, like a friend of mine whose shack I'm going to take you to. Some of them come here to get the good shooting . . . like myself. I came up here with Chris for a vacation . . . to get into the woods, you know . . . because I never dreamed that you could possibly catch the mare and come back so soon."

"Vacation," Sandy echoed, opening his eyes with wonder at the rancher. "I never guessed that you was interested in things like that. But the mare wasn't much trouble. She's been used wrong. That's about all that you could say about her. Soon as she got with somebody that understood her, she tamed right down. You see?" He whistled, and the white beauty danced up to him and snuffed at the hand that he held out to her. "Here's sixty feet of rope," he said. "When you take her, keep her on this, and give her time to play herself out, if she gets rambunctious."

The very soul of Dunstan ached to get his hands on a rope that was tied to the neck of Elena Blanca. "Show me what you mean, Sandy," he said.

Obediently Sandy tossed the noose over the head of the little mare and gave the farther end into the hand of Dunstan. Behold! The instant that the rope had changed from one hand to the other, Elena Blanca tossed her head and sprang back, bringing the rope taut with a jerk. Had not Dunstan looped it over the pommel of his saddle, it would have been snatched out of his hands. Even as it was, the shock of Elena Blanca's weight made the big horse, caught unawares, stagger. In another moment, there was a fighting, plunging, bucking streak of knotted lightning at the end of the rope, and the hands of the rancher were full.

The voice of Sandy rang—and the little white mare ran suddenly to the big, blue roan and crowded against it, her nostrils expanded like transparent crimson silk, her body trembling with her fear and her hate.

"You see," Sandy said, "it'll take a little time. Go along, girl. There's no danger. Steady, honey. We'll come out straight as a string. He ain't gonna ride you."

It seemed to the bewildered Dunstan that the beautiful creature actually understood the words of Sandy. She grew quieter; in another moment she submitted to being led by Dunstan up the valley and then through the broken hills toward the shack of Simonides. What a joy was in the heart of big Peter Dunstan, and the hand that held the rope seemed to him to be closing upon the heart of *Señorita* Catalina. The picture in his pocket was turning into real flesh and blood.

So they came to the gap in the woods and to the shack of the Greek. There sat Simonides himself in front of the door, smoking a vile cigarette.

"Here we are!" Dunstan called. "Here's Sandy and Elena. Have you seen the dog around the house, here?"

"Ten minutes ago," said the ready tongue of Simonides, "the pup was playing with that tin can, yonder, but he saw a rabbit and took away after it. . . ."

"Where?" Sandy asked.

"Yonder," Simonides answered. "Between that stump and the big pine. That's where he disappeared. Come in and. . . ."

"I'll get Chris," said Sandy, "and then I'll come back and have a cup of coffee off of you, if you got it to spare. So long."

He started the big, blue roan toward the indicated spot. Poor

White Helen began to fight again—but with the choking noose around her neck and the weight of the big gelding in the scale against her, fate was speaking against her, and she was drawn into the corral.

It was the one structure near the shack that was in a state of good repair. There was reason for it, since Simonides and his men often had some high-hearted horse to confine here. The fence was as tall as it was strong. Elena flashed around it the instant she was loosed from the rope. Then, finding no weak point, she sprang to the center and raised her head in a heart-broken neigh that went shivering far and wide across the forest.

There was silence. Then, out of the distance, came something like an answering echo—the voice of Sandy, calling for Chris through Chorleywood, while Chris lay dead, so many dusty miles away.

Simonides said: "He looks like a simple, young fool. What's the danger in him?"

"He's made Coudray run like a scared dog," Dunstan told him. "That's what he's done already today. And he's coming back, Simonides. When he comes, there'll be trouble . . . and maybe more trouble than you and I can handle."

Simonides smiled, but then, growing more sober, he whistled. Two men sauntered out from the cabin. "I made a point of keeping two of the best fellows in the world on hand," he explained. "There's Lew . . . the little chap . . . and Shack Edwards. Shack might have made himself into a light-heavyweight champion a couple of years ago, but he got mixed up with a little card game one night . . . and the next morning the coppers were after him. Lew weighs about two hundred, though he doesn't look it. Before he found out his talents, he used to waste his time wrestling . . . for pretty big money, at that. Besides, they're pretty much at home with guns, and Lew is a wizard with a knife. I'm not without two hands myself, and we know what you can do, Dunstan . . . particularly when you have to fight for what that mare means to you. Do you still think that we'll have any trouble with this half-wit? What a blank, dead eye he has."

Dunstan took stock of the pair again, and truly it seemed to him that he had never before seen two more formidable men than these, standing side-by-side—Lew, low and broad and powerful, the other, rangy, fast, with shoulders and arms meant for heavy, battering work. Besides, here was his own strength, and Simonides, like a tiger cat. At last, he smiled.

"You have the men, Simonides, and even that idiot won't be able to break through. But tonight, all four of us are going to stand watch on the corral."

"Very well," Simonides said. "We won't go to sleep at our posts. Only . . . what keeps us from telling this Sweyn that the dog must have lost itself in the woods, for that matter?"

"Because if there's a trail, he'll find it. And if he doesn't find it, he'll know that there isn't any trail. Y'understand?"

"Unless he's got the nose of a hunting hound himself, how could he be sure of that?"

"I don't know what he's got. I know what he'll do. By sunset he'll be back here, breathing fire for fair."

CHAPTER THIRTY

He was not back at sunset time, nor when the yellow moon went up like a disembodied flame through the eastern trees, losing itself in the overhanging pall of the clouds that already shut away the stars. The wind blew soft; it was wet with mist. Now and then a rattle of rain fell on the roof of the shed beside the corral. Still the four watchers could see the ghostly figure of the little white mare as she roamed ceaselessly up and down across the corral.

"Suppose that this poor fool did take the mare to Mirandos and try to claim the girl," Simonides said. "I know that Mirandos is a lawkeeper, but he's a proud devil, too. Before he saw his daughter married to a clod like that, he would have a knife stuck between the shoulders of Mister Sweyn. So, Dunstan, you may say that it's for Sweyn's own good to keep the mare away from him. It simply keeps him out of danger."

He laughed—it was a light, heartless, effortless laughter. That laughter showed to Dunstan, like a great cold light, the whole world of crime and those who live in it. Yet, had ever a man committed such a wrong as he was planning to practice against poor Sandy Sweyn, the half-wit?

"Another half hour . . . ," Dunstan insisted.

"Your man has gone to bed," Simonides said in a soft whisper. "He's lost his way and can't come back to us."

"What's that in the shed?" cried the sudden voice of Lew. "Shack, watch yourself!"

194

The ex-prize fighter had been assigned the task of watching the little shed that opened onto the corral.

Then they heard the loud, absurdly, squeaking voice of Shack as he yelled: "Keep back from me, kid . . . I don't want to do you no harm! Then take this!"

There was an instant of shuffling, then the sound of a blow of terrible force. It drove the breath in one gasp out of some man's body, then there was a heavy fall.

"Shack has settled your wild man," Simonides declared.

"No one man could settle him with bare hands," vowed Dunstan. "Listen. . . ."

There was a sudden battering and crashing and rending of boards at the back of the shed.

"He's breaking down the wall of the shed to let the mare out!" shouted Simonides. "Lew! Shack! Get at him . . . guns, boys! Dunstan, come with me . . . and come fast!"

Lew took the shortest course to get at the seat of the trouble. He came like a bulldog, head down, hungry to get those trained hands of his on the man who battered at the wall of the shed in the darkness, yonder. Once he fixed his experienced fingers on the other. . . .

He sprang into the darkness, and found there the shining form of Elena Blanca herself, and beside her the shadow of a man, beating a great gap open. He lurched at Sandy Sweyn and put his arms around the half-wit's body.

There are no words except those of Lew to describe what followed. He told of it long afterward.

"I figgered on squashing the breath out of him. I throwed my arms clean around his body and his arms. Then I give all my strength to the bear hug, and I feel him sort of sink in in the middle. Then he stops sinking in. He turns into Indian rubber, y'understand? He turned into a bunch of ligaments and tendons like them that run up from the back of a horse. He just spread out and his arms, they give a wiggle like a pair of pythons . . . and there he was free with his arms. He turned around in my grip as easy as though it was his girl that was hugging him. And he fixed one hand under my chin and jammed my head back.

"I felt like I had rested my chin by accident on the head of a piston. After that . . . he hit me . . . hard, that's the reason why my jaw is planted sort of lop-sided on my face, y'understand? I didn't feel nothing much. It just paralyzed me. I went numb. Sitting in the electric chair and having the current turned on . . . that would be about like getting the wallop from that Sweyn. They call him the half-wit. I tell you, nobody that was a fool could ever've learned to hit like that."

In short, Lew had leaped into the dark and grappled with his man. Half a second later, he lay senseless upon the ground. By this time, Simonides and Dunstan had rounded the outside of the corral and were making for the shed where the wall was in the act of being battered down.

But that sound of battering ceased. What they next heard was from the farther side of the corral. The gate had been barred and secured with a padlocked chain. What they heard was the scream of hard wood being torn away from rusted nails. A shriek, groan, another shriek, and then a section of the ponderous top rail was flung with a clangor upon the ground.

Back turned Dunstan to get around the side of the shed. Little Simonides, with a stream of odd-sounding curses flowing from his lips, led the way. They leaped around the shed's side and into full view of the corral, in time to see a man's body disappear on the farther side of the fence, through the gap made by the tearing down of the upper rail.

Still the fence was high—impossibly high, so it seemed. Dunstan, as he fired wildly toward the spot where Sandy had sunk toward the ground, felt that they had won the game, after all, and kept the mare.

Simonides was shooting, too, but he had only a vague direction in which to aim. Sandy was prone on the ground, and, in the darkness, he was completely swallowed. Only his voice could guide the bullets as he shouted: "Elena! Here, girl. Here, Elena!"

"She'll never make the fence even with the top rail down," gasped out Simonides.

There went the little mare, a ghostly streak across the black of the corral. She headed fair and true toward the voice of the man she loved. They saw her slim body arch high into the air— and then the clash as her hoofs struck the rail—the shock as she toppled and sprawled flat upon the ground on the farther side

"A broken neck . . . and that's the end of the chase," Dunstan muttered, groaning.

No—she was up and on her feet like an agile little cat. As she struck forward at a gallop, the two who strained their eyes after her saw a great shadow rise from the ground and leap upon her back. There, flattened along her, Sandy drove like an arrow toward the sheltering shadow of the distant trees, where the great blue roan was waiting for him.

Still he was not in safety, for Simonides raised his gun and steadied his aim. His was a hand that never had missed so close a target as this. But the heavy hand of Dunstan struck down the rifle, and the bullet plowed uselessly into the ground.

"You fool!" snarled the outlaw. "I'd have dropped the mare, for sure. And then we could have finished up this Sweyn and taken our own time to do it!"

"Let him go," Dunstan said. "There may be ways of stopping him before he gets to Mirandos, even now. But he's earned his getaway. And I couldn't see the mare murdered. She belongs to Catalina Mirandos, and not to me."

Simonides said: "Did you see Sweyn come up from the ground? I've seen a tiger spring like that out of a shadow and break the neck of a buffalo bull in India. And this Sweyn . . . he *is* a tiger, man."

"Aye," Dunstan averred, "but he'll do no harm to us. There's no malice in him."

"Not before tonight," Simonides said. "He never knew his strength . . . except with beasts. But tonight, we've given him a chance to taste his own power, and I tell you, Dunstan, every wound in my body is aching. He'll be back, sooner or later, and he'll let us know what he thinks of us . . . with those hands of his. Others are going to feel the strength of him, too, Dunstan. You've shown a man that he can play the tiger. From this time on, heaven help the people who stand in his way. He'll be ten devils tied up in one body."

"He can never have the girl. Old Mirandos will see to that," Dunstan said.

"I'm not thinking of the girl," Simonides said. "I'm thinking of the men. I'm thinking of ourselves. If he can buy the girl with Elena Blanca, and then settle down and forget tonight . . . bless him for it, and give him more power."

★ ★ ★ ★ ★

PART III

★ ★ ★ ★ ★

Chapter Thirty-One

In the long run, everything depends upon Dick in this narrative. The strength and the strange wisdom of Sandy Sweyn, the fiery beauty of Catalina Mirandos, the sage gravity of her father, the big shoulders of handsome José Rézan, the resourceful courage of Sheriff Kilmer, the wind-blown grace of Elena Blanca, and even the freckled face and the crooked smile of Peggy Kilmer, could not have brought about the final conclusion of this history, giving it the shaping that it took, without the presence of Dick. It is really necessary to give him a little space in the beginning.

Dick was only five years old, but into those five years he had crowded such a quantity of learning that, in certain ways, he was wiser than the wisest king who ever sat upon a throne. There was in Dick a mild nobility such as others might envy but never imitate, unless their ancestry was clearly traceable, as was Dick's, through a, family tree so long that it fairly filled a volume, branching out to truly colossal proportions. There was courage, too, in Dick, and such devotion to the cause he espoused as the Spartans of old might have striven toward as an ideal.

Dick was a setter—a beautiful, red-coated Irish setter—clad in long and curling silk, with the grace of an angel and the mild eye of a saint. He *was* a saint, this dog. Any bird man will tell you that all good setters have been breathed upon by heavenly virtues before ever they enter this world of thorns. Since Ireland is just a little nearer to heaven than any other country—as several million people will agree—it is natural that the Irish setter should have entered just a little more deeply into sainthood than any other breed.

Dick, lying on the lawn outside the patio of *Señor* Mirandos, maintained his composure with a steadfast eye. One would never have guessed, to see the manner in which he wagged his tail and softened his eye on the approach of the gardener, of the deep sorrow in the soul of the dog.

Yet how many crosses were here. From ranging after birds in old Erin to running the arid trails of the great Western desert of the States is a great difference, indeed. However, Dick would not show these swift emotions as they crossed his mind. As the gardener drew near to him, he abased his head a little and brushed the lawn with the long feather of his wagging tail. Into his eyes came a gentle light of love.

The gardener was a stranger, but that really did not greatly matter. Long ago, while he was still in the awkwardness of puppyhood, Dick had been taught by his lovely mother and had partly learned for himself, that all men are good, gentle, and true. Therefore he greeted them all in the same manner, with only a certain reservation of extra grace for those who he knew and loved.

However, all was not well in the soul of Dick. If he had allowed himself to give over to melancholy, he would have crept into a corner and died of a broken heart. Poor Dick yearned for just a single breath of peat smoke, such as he had known of old.

Here men forgot his name of Dick and called him Ricardo. Men spoke to him in a strange language whose accents were all new to him. He would have been quite at sea, had not his mother taught him from infancy that one can read the faces of men just as clearly as one can hear their spoken words.

Dick lay on the lawn and listened to the humming of the

wind down the valley. That wind brought to him keen scents of
the pine trees; from time to time his delicate nostrils informed
him that birds were on the wing, but no such birds as he had
hunted in green Ireland. He closed his eyes, dropped his head
upon his forepaws, and yearned after older and better days.

Then a high, musical voice called: "Ricardo!" He heard it
twice before he realized that the name was meant for him. Up
he jumped with a guilty start and hurried through the patio to
where his young mistress waited for him in the shade. He approached her with care, head lowered, tail wagging in the most
conciliatory manner. It was true that her voice was wonderfully
sweet, but there was a quirt in her hand. He knew of old that
that quirt could sting. However, he came at her voice, for still
the instinct and the lesson remained firm in his mind that, no
matter how strange and cruel some of their ways might be,
mankind must be right. It was foolish and very sinful to doubt
them. Only children might be shunned, for they did not seem
to know that when one's tail is pulled it causes an exquisite
pain; also, they are most careless about stepping upon sensitive
paws.

"Sit down," the girl said. "Sit down, Ricardo!"

Ricardo sat down at once.

"Don't look at me as though I were going to beat you!" Catalina Mirandos cried, and she slapped the quirt angrily against
her skirt.

A shiver ran through Dick. He gave, in spite of himself, only
a tithe of his attention to the face of the girl. The rest of it was
concentrated upon the lash of the whip, which he knew could
cut so deep. Therefore, he failed to understand when the silver
voice commanded sharply: "Come closer, Ricardo!"

Since that order was given in Spanish, Dick did not budge.

"Come closer! I have never seen such a stupid dog! Come
right over here!"

Poor Dick merely crouched lower to the ground and wagged his conciliatory tail. The quirt whirled in the air. There was an angry shout from the girl, and Dick blinked his eyes shut in supreme dread. The whip did not fall upon him, for accident intervened.

"Catalina!" called the voice of a man. She looked askance at her father, who entered the patio.

He was no great lover of animals, but he was a just man, this Mirandos. He said: "What a devil is in you, Catalina, to make you beat your dog in this way."

"I am only trying to teach him a lesson," she said, more angry than ever, "but the fool will not learn."

"Ah, well," her father said, looking curiously at her, "I often wonder, my dear, if you beat him because you wish to teach him?"

"Why else should I?" she said, and stamped her foot.

"Another reason may be that you like to use your power to make him crouch, poor devil. You wish to feel your power over him just as you wish to feel your power over men. Just as you make men crouch before you and act like cowardly fools, because they want your smiles. Is there not some truth in that?"

Tears of passion sprang into the eyes of the girl. "It is always this way," she said. "You always find the hardest things to call me, the worst interpretation to put upon everything that I do. You are never kind."

"There you are," her father said. "In a temper at the dog because he doesn't understand your language. In a temper with me because you will not listen to what I say."

"Do I not listen?"

"Yes, but you will not try to understand me. Have you ever sat down by yourself, Catalina, and wondered if you could be wrong about anything? Do you not always tell yourself that you are right, and the rest of the world is cold and brutal if it happens to disagree with you?"

"I am going to my room," Catalina said. "I shall not stay here to be abused."

Her father watched her leave, while Dick crawled to his feet and lay down there, looking humbly up to his new master, thanking him with melting eyes for this kind intervention.

When Catalina got to the door into the house, *Señor* Mirandos called: "I think you had better stay here, my dear! I have news in this letter that will interest you."

"I don't want to hear your news," Catalina said. "I only know that you hate me." Her voice choked with self-pity.

"It is about Elena Blanca."

At that, she whirled about and came running back. "Oh," cried Catalina, "what has happened? Has my horse been seen again?"

"The mare is caught," Mirandos said, "and the man who caught her is bringing her here to claim his reward."

"His reward?" Catalina said. "You will reward him, Father, I know. My beautiful Elena!"

"You forget," *Señor* Mirandos said, "you promised a reward yourself. You promised the greatest reward you could give, to any man who could bring back the mare to you."

Catalina leaned a hand against a pillar and blinked her eyes as though a flash of light had dazzled them.

"You promised to marry the lucky fellow," Mirandos said sternly.

"It was a joke!" Catalina gasped out. "It was only a joke, as you know. Who would dare to keep me to such a promise?"

"It is a joke," *Señor* Mirandos said gravely, "that has kept men hunting for your mare for months. It is a joke that has appeared in the newspapers. It is a joke that has caused poor devils to squander thousands of dollars and their time and hope and labor to catch the horse. No, no, Catalina, it is not a joke at all, but a sad reality."

"Ah, ah!" the girl cried. "But you do not mean it! You would not give me to some nameless stranger!"

Her father unfolded a letter. "Listen to this," he said. "It is from Peter Dunstan. You know Peter Dunstan, Catalina?"

"He is the rich rancher," Catalina said eagerly. "It is he, Father?"

"It is not he who caught the mare," her father said dryly. "It is quite another man, my dear. It is Peter Dunstan who writes the letter, however, and here it is." He read aloud:

Dear Señor *Mirandos: This will let you know what you may have heard already—that Elena Blanca has been caught. But it will tell you what, perhaps, you cannot learn from any person quite so well as from me. The man who caught the mare is named Sweyn, and the only Christian name that is known for him is Sandy. To give you your bad news in a lump—Sandy Sweyn is a hopeless half-wit.*

At this, *Señor* Mirandos lowered the letter and smiled grimly upon his daughter.

"No, no," poor Catalina said. "You would never give me to such a creature as that."

"Do not try to tell me what I would do, but listen to me, Catalina."

"I listen, Father. But . . . a half-wit . . . a-dull-eyed, loose-mouthed, stupid. . . ."

"If you had exceptions in mind, you should have made them before you published yourself abroad, my dear. The whole world knows that you have vowed to give yourself to the man who brings the mare to you. And as for me. . . ."

"You are a Mirandos," Catalina said unevenly. "You would never see. . . ."

"Hush," the rancher said. "There is more to follow. You have not heard all the facts that concern this lover of yours."

CHAPTER THIRTY-TWO

He shook out the letter again. Dick, seeing that he was un-
noticed by either of them, slunk gladly away toward the lawn.
He could not quite decide to go out of sight. It might be
considered by that quick-tempered and suspicious mistress of
his that he was committing a fault by slipping from view.
Therefore, the setter lay down at the entrance to the patio, and
with one eye he watched the seductive green coolness of the
lawn, and with the other, he kept in mind the uneasy face of his
mistress.

Señor Mirandos continued:

*I have known this fellow for a long time, and it is only right
that I should give you the advantage of my experience and my
knowledge of him. It is not unknown to you, perhaps, that I
myself have spent a good deal of time and money to capture
Elena Blanca. As a matter of fact, the half-wit was in my
employ when he caught the mare. At the last moment, a freak of
fancy came over him. He stole her away, and now he is going
through the mountains to find your daughter and claim the
reward of her hand.*

"That is theft!" Catalina gasped out, shuddering with fright.
"Something can be done about that. There is a sheriff who. . . ."

"Your promise," the rancher said, "was only to take the mare
from any hand that brought her back, and thereafter to marry
him, as a reward. If he has stolen the mare, does that make any

real difference? No. You did not say that it should be the man
who secured the capture of the mare. You only specified him
who brought her to you. You must remember the facts, my dear,
and you must be limited by them."

He went on with the reading of the letter:

*It occurs to me that you may find it worthwhile to attempt to
stop this man before he can come to your daughter with the
mare and claim that reward of which we know. This would be a
tragedy so terrible that I am as much horrified as you can possibly be.*

*Let me tell you, in the first place, that any attempt to stop the
half-wit would have to be made by more than one man. He is,
as I have said, defective mentally, but he replaces the lack of
real intelligence, to a certain extent, by a species of brute cunning. He is sharp and wide-awake. You may take that for
granted, when he is on the trail, however dull and sleepy he may
appear in a house.*

*You will need more than one man, and you will need numbers
for several reasons. One of these is his enormous strength. In
this, as in a great many respects, he is very deceptive. He looks
to be, say, a fellow of about five feet and nine inches. He appears to be rather broad and plump, and you would put him
down at about a hundred and sixty or seventy pounds, at the
most.*

*As a matter of fact, he is not much under six feet in height, I
believe, and what appears to be plumpness is in reality iron-
hard muscle. I am not a weak man, and I have known many
powerful people, but he is without exception the strongest man I
have ever seen or heard of. I have no hesitation in saying so. I
really believe that there is more brute power in his hands and
arms than in those of any two men!*

Here *Señor* Mirandos looked up from his reading. "It would not do to anger such a fellow, if he were your husband. Do you agree to that, my dear girl?"

Catalina, clasping her delicate hands together in front of her white, sick face, could not make any answer. Her imagination was far too busy in probing the unimaginable horrors of the future.

Her father, after a single keen glance at her, continued:

There are other qualities that make him formidable. He is, as I have said, very deceptive in his appearance, which disarms people who he meets for the first time. He is about two inches, I should say, taller than the usual guess. And I think that he is thirty or forty pounds heavier. His sleek and sleepy appearance gives an impression of stolid immobility, but that is by no means what he possesses. When he is roused to his work—and in the open air and on the trail he is nearly always roused—this man unites to his physical strength an uncanny power of eye and ear. He is so thoroughly in tune with the animal world—of which he is really a part—that nothing escapes him. He draws information, I should almost say, from the very scents on the air, like a hunting wolf. Though I don't want you to take this literally— some of the things that he accomplishes are positively beyond any normal understanding.

In addition to this, let no one think that he is incapable of moving with celerity. Among men, he is like the wolverine. And you know that the wolverine, when it is roused, can fight with the speed of a demon. It is the same with this monster, Sandy Sweyn.

He travels armed, of course, and he handles a gun or a knife really as if it were a part of him—equipped with the same nerves and senses that run in his own flesh. He seems incapable of missing his mark, the more sudden the emergency, the more critical the need, the steadier and surer he is bound to be. There is only one way to gain an advantage over him without a terrible loss. That is through surprise, I should say.

I must say, also, that so far as I am concerned I should not regard this person as a human being, but as a sort of beast that walks upon two legs, and wears the face, the voice, and some of the mannerisms of other men. At heart, he is totally dissimilar to other men.

As for his appearance. I have warned you in part. I must say that his face is not displeasing, except in its stupidity. When he is on a trail, and his face lights, he is positively handsome, though in the house there is sure to be something disgustingly sodden and piggish about him. It is only when he is roused that a flare of light appears in his face. The rest of the time, his wits sleep.

His hair has the color that his nickname suggests, or it is perhaps a little more yellow than actual sand. And he has strangely colored eyes—very close to the shade of the lashes and brows themselves. They give a very odd effect. One often can hardly tell when he is watching one. The emotions never show in those eyes until he had been roused to a frenzy, and then they turn to yellow flame.

I have talked to you about this man at a great deal of length. It may be, as I suppose, that you will decide to stop him on the way. But you will not succeed. He has proved too strong for me, and I am sure that he will prove too strong for you, unless you send out sure marksmen to lie in wait for him, as you would make an ambush for a wild grizzly bear. Believe me, the similarity is not entirely far-fetched!

I remain yours with a thousand good wishes. Instruct me in what I can be of service.

Peter Dunstan

"Let me see!" pleaded the girl. And, taking the letter, she read it through again—letter by letter, printing the awful truth deeper and deeper in her mind. "But it is *not* possible!" Catalina gasped out. "You could never give me to a beast like this."

Her father was very pale, and his face had become quite drawn. He began to walk up and down the patio. As he walked, he talked—not so much to her as to his own soul.

"You have always been a delight to my eyes, Catalina," he said. "I have always been foolishly proud of your beauty. But I have not given you the sort of treatment that a girl should be able to expect from her father."

"You have always been kind . . . you will still be kind," Catalina whispered, sobbing.

"Exactly. I have always been kind. I have been too kind, and a child has a right to expect that its parents will give it such discipline that it will be prepared for the coldness of the rest of the world. A girl who has been raised with love only is not prepared for the facts in the world as she will find it. That is cruel. I have been cruel in just this way, my dear. In the meantime, shall I tell you a little truth?"

"Yes, if you will."

"Very dear as you have been to me, I have been able to see certain faults in you . . . such as cowardice, cruelty, selfishness, and others of that kind."

"You hate me?"

"No, child. I have a great and foolish love for you. I see these faults in you, but still I hope that they are things that will be lived down. I hope that you will change before you come into full womanhood. That is what hope says, rather than what reason speaks. But there are the facts for me to face. On the other hand, there is another thing to which I have given half of my love."

Catalina started erect.

"In that other thing," *Señor* Mirandos said, "I can see no fault. It is pure and perfect, and I shall keep it so at the cost of everything . . . my life and yours. It is my honor, Catalina."

She turned paler than ever, now—and there was a hopeless-ness in her eyes. The honor of her father was an old, familiar foe to her. No matter of what malleable stuff he might be made, when that sense of honor was encroached upon, she reached a wall of granite that threw back her advances.

"Since the honor of this name has been clean in my hands, I must give you a final warning, my child. I shall not raise so much as a little finger of one hand to prevent the approach of this man who has caught the horse. Once he brings her here, I shall see that you marry him, if I have to drag you to the altar and whip the responses from your lips."

As he spoke, it was no longer flesh and blood to which she listened, but an abstraction. Honor, indeed!

He turned away from her on his heel. Catalina watched him go, filled with horror, knowing that to appeal would be the height of folly.

She ran toward the entrance of the patio, as though she hoped that help might be seen coming to her—or as though the flash-ing white body of Elena Blanca might be in view. There was nothing except the windy hillside. She quirted the setter at her feet. "Stupid fool of a dog!" Catalina cried through her teeth. "How can *you* help me?"

CHAPTER THIRTY-THREE

She ran out to the stable. "I want the bay gelding!" the girl cried to Filipo.

"Ah, but, *señorita* . . . he is very wild, and he is very fast. And he has not been ridden during these two weeks."

"That is why I want him, fool! Now hurry, hurry!"

While she waited for the gelding to be caught, she looked down at her clothes. Now that she was in a crisis, she must make her appeal carry the greatest possible force, and she could never do this if she were not looking her best. Back to the house she ran. In her room she scattered all about her and made two hours' work for her maid in five minutes of searching.

At last she had the correct silken scarf, knotted in the proper manner about her waist. She had the proper sombrero on her head, tilted at the smartest angle, with the right feather curling in a crimson streak along its brim. She pirouetted and viewed herself from every side. She needed still something—some touch of color—so she caught up a pair of gaudy emerald earrings and set them in place.

After that, she was content, and with a greater sense of power warming her blood, she raced from the room, still clutching the letter that had brought the fatal warning.

The bay gelding was waiting when she reached the stable. Woe to Filipo if he had taken longer than this to prepare the wild colt. He threw her up to the saddle, for she rode like a boy.

There was need for good riding, here. The bay gelding reared and danced like a very devil, his ears back, foam in his gaping mouth. At length whip and spur rocked him forward. He left the ground with a long leap, and shot off like a greyhound down the valley.

She knew that road well, and it was good that she did, for never did a horse career over it more wildly than the horse of Catalina on this day.

The first mile was done at the first speed of the gelding. After that it began to falter a little from this terrible pace, and the spurs on the heels of the girl turned crimson as she drove them home. Every second seemed an eternity. In the meantime, there was a savage satisfaction in tearing the last ounce of power from the tormented body of the gelding.

She turned in a cloud of dust through the gateway of another ranch, leaped down, threw the reins at the head of the *mozo*, and rushed into the house itself. A house *moza* appeared with a smile that turned into a stare.

"Where is José Rézan?" Catalina cried. "Where is José Rézan? Instantly! Do you hear? Instantly!"

"He is here. Has your father been hurt, *señorita*?"

"José! Bring José to me, instantly!"

The *moza* fled as for life. Presently a door crashed. Then there was a hurrying footfall, and here was big José Rézan, looking, if possible, more handsome and huger than ever. He could hardly speak; he was delighted to see this unexpected visitor. He could only extend his hands toward her, and Catalina thrust into those hands the letter that she still carried with her.

"And my father will do nothing!" Catalina cried. She threw herself into a chair and clasped her hands before her eyes.

As for José, he was in a passion of dread when he saw his idol in such a state of mind. Before he had read two words in the letter, Catalina herself was almost forgotten. He read that dreadful missive through from beginning to end, and then glanced back to make sure of the more vital parts. All was vital; all was terrible to him. He threw himself upon his knees before the girl.

"A half-wit!" Catalina sobbed.

"Catalina, my dearest, have I your permission to try to stop him?"

"Do you have to wait for that?" Catalina asked. "Do you stand here, kneeling and moping, while the half-wit is bringing Elena every instant closer to me? If he brings her in, actually, then it is the end. It is the end! Because my father swears like a madman that, for the sake of honor, he will force me to marry this insane man. He will drag me to the altar with his own hands. Do you hear, José Rézan? And still do you stand there and do nothing?"

José Rézan stood still no longer.

Even Catalina was satisfied by the manner in which he rushed from the house; even she smiled with content when she heard his great voice booming in the distance.

There was a hasty stir of preparation in the house. She was aware, past doors and down corridors, of the running of the *mozos* and *mozas*. She heard the clattering of voices, frantic with haste. Here was a household to her taste. Here the position of José Rézan was not that of mere landowner, but, rather like a feudal lord, he had some claim upon the very lives and souls of his dependents, as it were. Obedience to him was an almost religious duty. Oh, that such an atmosphere could be imported into her father's house.

Presently José Rézan himself, mounted upon a superb cream-colored charger with a glistening silver mane and silver tail, rushed forth past the house, still thrusting his rifle into the long holster that ran along the saddle beneath his knee. Behind him rode a full dozen of hardy young cavaliers and old, men who had devoted all their lives to the service of the family of Rézan, now ready to live or to die for him.

It was a glorious cavalcade, and, as they swept past, each cavalier raised his quirt most gallantly to little Catalina—all saving *Don* José. He bowed low above his saddle and swept his great sombrero toward the ground.

The heart of Catalina was contented. After that moment, it was plain that she had not lived in vain. When she walked out to look after them, her soul was so well within her that she even extended her hand with much graciousness toward Dick. He had followed her flying horse at his best speed, as in duty bound. But not even a greyhound could have kept pace with the matchless burst of the bay thoroughbred as it flew up the road toward the Rézan house. So Dick arrived, faithful but a little tardy, and skulked toward his mistress with head abased.

It only needed that half gesture of kindness to transform him. He passed into an ecstasy at once, frolicking around Catalina until he dared to rear and touch her with his fluffy forepaws, deeply coated with the powdery dust of the road.

"Filthy beast!" Catalina cried through her teeth as she saw her skirt disfigured. She slashed furiously at the setter.

The agile paw of Dick enabled him to escape to a safe distance, but Catalina would never rest with a blow that had missed the mark. Now she shouted: "Ricardo! Come again! At once, fool of a dirty dog!"

Dick slunk back. The hardest lesson of all was to come back for punishment, even when one was conscious of no sin. For that matter, he was never at all sure wherein his guilt lay when he was with this pretty young mistress, but he knew that the whip fell hard and often. He sneaked back to the girl and crouched upon his stomach, whining a little. There, with eyes closed and body shuddering, he accepted not one lash, but three.

"For running away like a coward, when you know that you have done wrong. I have half a mind to send you back to your stupid Ireland, where there is never sunshine!"

If that threat could have been translated so that Dick might have understood. He only knew that the mystery and cruelty of the girl seemed to increase from day to day. When he first came, there had been nothing but smothering caresses. He had been squeezed and petted from one end of the day to the other. There was a special *moza* appointed in the ample household of *Señor* Mirandos, whose duty was to do nothing save to comb and tend and brush and feed the noble dog.

After this, there was a change. Having become familiar, Dick was more than half despised. There was now only one reason why Catalina kept him with her, always—it was because the red silk of Dick's coat and the grace of his carriage made a note of color and beauty against which she appeared to good advantage. It drew eyes toward her, and there was nothing in the world that Catalina liked better than to draw all eyes.

She mounted the bay gelding again and set off toward her home with greater content in her heart. She told herself that it would be very strange if twelve gallant warriors, who knew the whole countryside as they knew a book, could not find this formidable Sandy Sweyn. No matter how dreadful a fighter he might he, they would crush him.

Catalina looked with much complacence upon this. She felt no twinge of horror. It seemed to her that the impertinence of the half-wit in daring to raise his eyes to her deserved punishment.

She minced down the road, enjoying the picture that she presented to the eyes of others, rejoicing in the mirror of flattery that presented her to herself in every eye that she passed.

Here a cloud of dust swirled by her and with a clatter of flying hoofs. Peggy Kilmer, the sheriff's daughter, rattled down the road in front of her, the heels of her mustang tossing up a cloud of dust that showered thickly down upon pretty little Catalina.

Catalina reined in her thoroughbred with an exclamation of supreme disgust. She brushed herself off as well as she could. That was like Peggy Kilmer—to rush about the countryside in this unmaidenly fashion, her hair done into two pigtails, and the pigtails twisted into an ungracious knot at the back of her head, her divided skirt not very much more maidenly than the trousers of an ordinary cowpuncher. Here, for instance, she was galloping off without even a saddle on the back of that ragged mustang—only a blanket strapped on it, and no spurs on her heels as she drummed them against the ribs of the mustang.

No wonder Catalina was disgusted. As she passed the house of the sheriff, presently, where Peggy was dismounting and dragging the bridle and blanket from her horse, Catalina drew rein a little.

"Hello!" yelled Peggy. "How's things, Catalina?"

She quite missed the answer of Catalina, for she had to leap backward to escape the heels that the mustang flung at her head before he darted away toward liberty.

"I hear your pa bought the Gregory Ranch," Peggy said, dropping her hands upon her hips and turning her freckled face toward the Mexican girl.

"He has bought it, yes," Catalina said. "You must come to see it soon."

"Can't do it today. Got the washing to turn out. So long, Catalina. Come in and have a cup of coffee with me some afternoon."

Catalina could barely force a smile. She was shuddering with disgust as she rode on up the way. It seemed to her that the entire female sex was disgraced by the existence of such a creature as Peggy Kilmer.

Dick seemed to be of a different opinion. He stood with his head pressed against the gate, and wagged his tail as he looked toward the little shack of the sheriff.

CHAPTER THIRTY-FOUR

Like hunting wolves sweeping forward in a swift line, the men of José Rézan rode rapidly across the hills. As they rode, they scattered until there was a great gap between man and man, but never a gap so great that the sound of a rifle shot would not have alarmed companions to right or to left. There was only one way by which Sandy Sweyn could make his approach to the dwelling of *Señor* Mirandos. Along that way, which was a deep, broad valley through the mountains, the riders of Rézan were combing every inch of the ground.

While they searched diligently, through the pines before them a slender white mare trotted to the first break in the woods, and, seeing a single horseman in view, she whirled and raced back. Making a short detour, she came to another gap, and here again she saw a rider closing slowly upon the trees.

At that, she whirled and galloped straight back through the trees, until she came upon a great blue roan, a monster mare hardly distinguishable from the shadows of the woods through which she was passing. In the saddle was the lumpish form and the impassive face of Sandy Sweyn, with dull, sand-colored eyes and forehead perpetually wrinkled as in doubt. From that rider Elena Blanca did not sheer away as she had from the two she had sighted before. She pressed in close to the side of the blue roan.

That was sufficient warning for Sandy. He dismounted, and with a word he turned the blue roan into a statue, while he went forward in person to the edge of the wood. There he saw an armed rider coming slowly down the valley, looking often from left to right, scanning all before him with the unmistakable air of the hunter.

Sandy smiled and would have drawn back. As he started to move, he saw horse and rider suddenly go down heavily in the dust. At that he paused, very curious. It was not for the welfare of the man that he cared, but for that of the animal, since every beast was to him as one human is to another.

Apparently the horse had stepped into a hole in the ground, for it rose almost at once and hobbled a little. When the rider mounted the saddle once more, his mount cantered a stride or two and then paused, shaking its head.

The rider had little patience to expend on his horse. He urged it once or twice with his voice—the quirt rose and fell and the spurs thrust deep. Thus stimulated, the pony bounded forward for a stride or two, and then came to a resolute stop and refused to budge.

There is nothing in the world that will madden a cowpuncher more than a balky horse. This rider fell into a fury at once. His spurs were quickly reddening the sides of his mount when he heard a rushing of hoofs down the slope, and, looking up, he saw above him a blue roan mare, moving with gigantic strides. In the saddle was a man who answered in every respect to the description that had been given of Sandy Sweyn.

More than that, in the background ran that delicate beauty among horses—Elena Blanca. There could be no mistaking. That cowpuncher had seen the famous little mare once before, when pretty Catalina Mirandos was in the saddle upon her back, and he had never forgotten. What he thought of first was to reach for his rifle and try a flying shot at the stranger, but he remembered in that crisis the last warning of José Rézan—that this fellow was a desperate and sure fighter. No one should attempt to handle him without help.

Moreover, the stranger did not seem to be approaching with any hostile intent. He called out in a friendly manner as he came, and he waved his hand. So the *vaquero* twisted the end of his mustache and waited, trembling with excitement.

When Sandy Sweyn came up, he dismounted at once and went to the cowpuncher with a smile. "You'll never get that horse forward like that," he said. "Never in the world. It ain't the whip and the spur that he needs. It's a little talking and a little rubbing."

The *vaquero*—in the nick of time to keep himself from bursting into heartiest laughter—remembered that this was a half-wit with whom he had to deal. He nodded gravely.

"Talking and rubbing," he said. "I have seen many strange things done with horses, *señor,* but when they balk I have never seen them persuaded with rubbing and talking. I have heard some grand cursing of them, too, but never anything in the way of language that would get them to move. Nothing but whips . . . or even a fire built under them."

"You'll have a chance to see," Sandy said. "I may be wrong. Will you get off the horse?"

The cowpuncher was glad to oblige, for it chanced that, at this moment, he saw two riders heaving into view, one far to his left and one far to his right. He knew that the men of his master would soon be gathering thickly around them. There was the flashing beauty of the white mare to apprise them, even at a distance, of what was there. If only they could send a signal on to the others, in the distance, and so let them know and gather them in a silent circle, it would go very hard, should Sandy Sweyn escape.

As soon as Sandy had dismounted, he stepped toward the mustang. The latter was now frantic with the pain of whip and spur, and backed off snorting.

"Come to him, Cleo," Sandy said. "Come talk to him, girl. He needs quieting down."

The *vaquero* gaped. He was not a superstitious man. He believed that sundry of the saints had been capable of miracles, but he had never seen one that could not be explained by sleight of hand. This, however, was a very different matter, for he could swear that Sandy made no sign to the great blue mare. Yet, as though she actually understood every word that had been spoken to her, she went instantly to the balking, trembling pony and stood beside it. The mustang leaned heavily against her as if to say: "Stand by me, comrade, and we may yet prove too much for these devils . . . these terrible men."

The blue roan touched noses with that frightened mustang. Whatever message it was that she conveyed to him, Pedro, the *vaquero*, could vow that his bad-headed cutting horse grew calm. He allowed the stranger to approach with open hand. Pedro would take his oath before any jury in the land that this was a matter without precedence in the history of that bronco.

In another moment the mustang allowed the saddle to be stripped from it. It was turning its head and pricking its ears as it skeptically eyed the stranger.

"Magic," Pedro whispered, and he crossed himself.

After that, the hands of the half-wit began to roam swiftly over the body of the bronco. Another moment—and there was a sharp squeal of pain from the horse.

"Here it is!" Sandy said in triumph. "I knew that it was something near the hocks."

"*¡Señor!*" young Pedro cried. "Have a care! That demon of a horse has already put my brother in the hands of the doctor for a full six months. Beware of his heels!"

"His heels?" Sandy said, standing up with a blank eye directly to the rear of the bronco. "Oh, he'll do me no harm. He's feeling happier now." With that, he leaned over and began to massage the great tendons and knotted muscles in the back of the pony's right hind leg. So deeply did his fingertips work that the horse fairly groaned with the pain. Its other heel lifted tentatively from the ground half a dozen times, while Pedro looked on in an agony of half-joyous expectation.

There was no kicking. As Pedro declared afterward, even in its pain the mustang attempted to raise its ears from time to time—sure sign that it knew good was being done in its behalf.

Still Sandy Sweyn talked gently: "He gave that leg a wrench when he went down. If I were you, I tell you that I should not ride him home. I should simply walk, and let him walk behind you. Better still . . . camp out here, tonight, and rub his leg down half a dozen times before morning."

"Walk home . . . camp out all night . . . stay awake to rub him down. Ha, *señor,* do you think that I am taking care of an old mother? This is only a horse, and not a very good one. No, not a very good one at all. He'll take me home tonight or I'll know why, and I'll ask him the question with my spurs. They are sharp enough, if I care to make them talk." He laughed rather savagely.

Sandy Sweyn bowed his head and seemed to be lost in thought. He was so deeply lost in it, indeed, that he did not notice beautiful little Elena Blanca come running from the distance to press close to him, her head thrown high, trembling in every limb. He was so lost in thought that he did not hear the creaking of saddle leather as other riders approached him. If he heard, the sounds passed into his subconscious mind and did not affect his consciousness.

At last he said: "If you ride this here horse, stranger, you're gonna ruin him. If you ride him before tomorrow morning, you will ruin him, sure."

"Put back the saddle on him, then," Pedro said, growing more confidently insolent as he saw the others pressing nearer to him in a thickening circle. "You've done your part and wasted plenty of my time."

"I'll put back the saddle," Sandy said, "but you can't have this horse to ride until tomorrow morning."

"Can't?" cried Pedro. "Can't? Are you threatening me?" He reached for his gun with great speed, but he did not make the draw.

Light winked at the right hip of Sandy, and the long, black body of a Colt glimmered wickedly in the sun as it pointed straight at young Pedro. "You watch yourself, stranger," Sandy said. "I don't aim at no trouble with you, but. . . ." His voice trailed away; he had looked up and found a circle of enemies had been thrown around him.

Chapter Thirty-Five

Sometimes, when more than one gun has secured the drop on him, a desperado, to whom surrender means eventual death at the hands of the law, has been known to risk a move and even to win away to freedom, by diving at the table that supports the lamp, or some other trick that throws the others into confusion. There was never a man since the beginning of time, who could boast that he had defied and escaped from five leveled rifles, twenty or thirty yards away, all with a careful bead drawn upon his heart and head.

Sandy Sweyn stared feebly at these apparitions.

"Where did they come up from, Elena?" he said. "Dog-gone me if it don't look like they had growed up out of the ground in the last couple of minutes."

Elena Blanca sidled closer to him as she heard her name. She had had no doubt, for her part, from the first moment when she saw these strangers approaching. She had distrusted them with all of her heart. To her thinking, there was only one human being who was really worthy of sublime submission and love. That was Sandy Sweyn. All of the rest were traitors and devils, to be avoided like poison.

"All right, Sweyn," José Rézan said. "Just put up your hands, my friend. I want the guns that you carry, and I want your knife. Move fast, Sweyn."

A smile rose to the lips and the vague eyes of Sandy. He lifted his hands above his head.

"If you want money," he said, smiling still, "you'll find that I ain't got none. Money is a thing that I get along without pretty well. But you use a pile of men in your hold-up game, don't you, stranger?"

He looked on with admiration. Half a dozen other riders were now swarming over the edges of the hills, coming at full gallop toward him.

José Rézan saw fit to overlook this speech. "Get to him, Pedro," he said. "And go through him for guns. Be quick, man."

Pedro obeyed with alacrity. The clothes of Sandy were swiftly searched. One revolver and an old hunting knife were all that were found in his possession.

"And now," Rézan said, "back up, Sandy Sweyn, and keep clear of us. Valentino, take the blue mare. Get a rope on Elena Blanca, some of you."

Elena Blanca, too late, seemed to realize that protection for her was not in the power of her companion at this moment. She bolted like a white flash for freedom, but swifter than any horse could dash was the leap of the lariats in the hands of three or four of the *vaqueros*. In a moment she was plunging blindly in a tangle of lariats.

Valentino, making for the blue roan, had a different problem on his hands. A shrill, sharp whistle from Sandy made the big mare leap away, and Valentino lunged hopelessly after her. There she stood, dancing in the distance.

"Watch Sweyn!" Rézan called. "Three of you keep an eye on him. The rest of you . . . except the first two ropes on Elena Blanca . . . scatter and get the blue roan. We have to have her unless we want Sweyn trailing right at our heels. Get your ropes ready."

They scattered obediently, forming rapidly into a great semicircle, whose horns began to stretch out toward a complete encircling of the big mare. Another whistle came from Sweyn, thin and high as the whistle of a kite and repeated with a rapid tremor.

"Stop that fellow's whistling," called Rézan, "or put a bullet through him! Cut in, lads!"

They went at the blue roan with a willful rush, but the whistle had been like a precious warning to her. She wheeled away and flaunted off across the valley at a speed that left the horsemen of José Rézan hopelessly to the rear. In a moment or two she was obviously safe from all pursuit.

Rézan saw that before the others. He called back his men and jerked his rifle to the shoulder. When he glanced down the sights and found the body of the blue mare gathered in their ominous circle, he shook his head and lowered the muzzle again. He was an honest fellow, this Rézan, and perhaps the very worst act of his entire life was this capture of the white mare from the hands of the man who had taken her on the desert. Evil breeds evil, and the heart of Rézan on this day was blacker than ever before. Yet there was not viciousness enough in him to permit the slaughter of this magnificent creature.

It was said by some that, blinding as was the speed of beautiful Elena Blanca, with her legs of an antelope and her slender body, yet so much greater was the strength and the swiftness of the blue roan that it had borne the binding weight of a great range saddle and the impost of a two-hundred-pound master and still retained enough stamina and speed of foot to carry it up to Elena in fair racing over the desert.

Rézan did not believe this wild tale, but he felt that the mare was indeed matchless among desert or mountain horses. He could not shoot her down now. Another plan formed at once in his mind.

Old Valentino—the steadiest and the most formidable of all his *vaqueros*—together with young Pedro, was detailed to remain behind with Sandy as a prisoner, while Rézan galloped swiftly away with the rest of his men to carry the white mare to pretty little Catalina Mirandos.

"Take him over to the shade of the trees," Rézan said. "Give him water when he wants it, and roll a cigarette for him when he wishes to smoke. But see that his hands are tied together, and never take your eyes off him for an instant. I tell you, this man is more dangerous than his dull eye may lead you to think. Watch him till well past noon, and then you may take the rope from his hands and you may ride in. Ride fast, too, for fear lest he should overtake you on the way."

With this he galloped off, and his men followed, with only one thing to lessen the speed of their riding—the refractory conduct of Elena Blanca.

Valentino and Pedro, the height of all respect while their master was with them, altered their attitude somewhat as soon as he was out of sight.

They first fastened the wrists of Sandy behind him. Then they led him toward the grove of trees. They did not take him into the shade. Pedro felt, in some mysterious manner, that he had been disgraced in the eyes of his fellows by the strange manner in which this fellow had secured the drop on him even though he was allowed to make the first move toward his weapon. That union of speed of hand together with such vague blankness of eye composed a perfect mystery. Since Pedro could not solve it, he grew vicious.

"The sun," he said to Valentino, "will make this man less dangerous. Let him cook for a while out there, while we watch him in the shade."

"It may kill him," Valentino said with some caution.

"Well," said Pedro, "do you think that our master will very greatly care about that? Does he really want this man to come in and accuse him of stealing Elena Blanca away from him?"

The logic of this was great enough to beat down the objections of Valentino at once. The pair of them ordered Sandy back into the sun with a wave of their drawn Colts.

There was no objection from Sandy. He settled down against a ragged-edged heap of rocks and sat there with the stolidity of an Indian—not a muscle of his face changing.

Pedro settled back in the shadow of the trees. "We shall see when he begins to moan and beg," he said, and he laughed until his glistening white teeth showed.

There was about seven-eighths Indian in the blood of that Pedro. Valentino had his share of the same cruel spirit. They lay back in the shadow and smoked their cornucopia-shaped cigarettes, letting the ashes fall where they would, as all Mexican gentlemen should do.

If you have ever ridden under the summer sun in the mountains, you know with what a force it descends. If you draw rein for hardly more than a moment, that sun begins to eat in through your coat and your shirt. It will scorch the surface of your skin. To sit motionlessly in that white heat, with the rocks and the sand reflecting it like dull mirrors all around, is more than human nerves can endure.

The face of Sandy turned crimson, then it began to grow pale. Perspiration formed on his forehead and ran down into his eyes, stinging them like fire and turning them bloodshot. Valentino shrugged his shoulders in some sympathy with this agony; Pedro laughed aloud.

"This will teach him," he said, "that only fools have gentlemen for their enemies . . . at least, such gentlemen as José Ré-zan. It will teach a *gringo* dog to raise his eyes to such a lady as Catalina Mirandos. And this *gringo* . . . look at him, Valentino! He is no more than a pig."

If the pig heard, he made no sign. He was working his shoulders steadily, in a patient endeavor to shrug the heat off or to create a little air space between his shirt and his skin. This foolish, patient effort caused a shout of laughter from Pedro, who found it an exquisite amusement. Only, there was this to be noted—while the shoulders of the wretched Sandy were working ever so slightly and restlessly, his arms were moving behind his back still more. His hands and wrists were steadily tugging up and down. With the tips of his fingers he had located a sharp and serrated rock edge just behind him. He was sawing the rope that bound him, patiently up and down against that stone.

CHAPTER THIRTY-SIX

It was well for Sandy that he had been fastened with rope instead of rawhide. With rawhide, as a rule, your true *vaquero* much prefers to work. Made supple with oil, it is braided close and seasoned by weathering and dragging upon the ground. It is tested by using it to wrench a mesquite out of the ground; it is as flexible as the body of a dead snake, and as strong as iron. When it is cast through the air, it whistles like a thrown knife, and it cuts very nearly like a knife when it strikes. With rawhide young Pedro had wished to bind the hands of the prisoner behind him. In that case, all would have been safe for the guards. But it chanced that Valentino had a convenient rope end, and Valentino could imagine no better use for it than this. So it was wrapped tightly about the wrists of Sandy. Indeed, it seemed strong enough to hold a pair of raging horses, let alone a single quiet, patient man.

That patience of Sandy was scrubbing the good rope up and down. The rock teeth would not bite into the fabric at once; each strand had to be frayed and then rubbed thin. Finally it parted, shred by shred.

"I think that he is getting sick, Pedro. Look at his face."

To be sure, it was very pale and haggard, and the lines sank deep.

"He is like a balky horse," Pedro said. "He will not stir or complain. However, I shall see how he is." He stepped forward and, with the loop of his quirt, dropped under the chin of the prisoner, jerked the head of Sandy suddenly and brutally back. His hat fell off, and his eyes looked up into the face of Pedro.

Valentino laughed heartily, consumed with mirth at this prank of his companion.

"His eye has not the look of the eye of a dead fish, as yet," Pedro observed, returning with a smile to the cool of the shadows. "But we will let him cook for a while with his hat off. That may hurry the boiling. That sun has an edge like a knife. It bites through my coat."

Sandy sat without a hat, sweltering in that cruel sun, but never changing a muscle of his face in acknowledgment of the increased torment. It was not torment that he had to crowd back from his eyes and mouth. It was a savage exultation and an expectation of revenge, for now the rope was deeply cut. He worked harder than ever.

"He is fainting, Pedro!" exclaimed Valentino at last. "See how he sways! You see that these white skins were never meant to endure the full sun of the day. See how he sways."

"*Gringo,*" Pedro hissed. "Will you beg for help now? Will you crawl on your hands and your knees, or will you wriggle like a worm, if we let you come into the shade?" He raised the quirt with an angry snarl. "Will you speak, pig?"

He got no answer. Therefore, Pedro lurched a long stride forward, swinging the quirt high. The thought of how that quirt would feel, swishing down upon the scorched shoulders of the prisoner, formed an irresistible temptation to Pedro.

This hurried the process that had been carried on with such patience. He forced Sandy to place the knuckles of his hands together and then to buckle the wrists outward. Under that tremendous strain, the last strands of rope parted with a snap, like a parting cable. The thick arms of Sandy swung far out from his side, free!

Ah, Pedro, however swiftly you have leaped and side-stepped

in your wildest dances, be far faster now, for there is need. Pedro leaped, you may be sure, with a scream of terror, forgetting his raised whip and clawing at the revolver at his belt.

He was pulled down from below. Fingers stronger than the talons of an eagle laid hold upon his ankle and wrenched him to the ground, where his back struck with such force that all the air was knocked at once from his lungs and the revolver shot far away across the sands.

Valentino, filled with amazement and horror, whipped out his own gun and leaped to his feet. As he rose, the *gringo* rose, also, with the helpless body of Pedro in his arms. Where could Valentino shoot, without sinking a bullet into the body of his compatriot?

Pedro danced backward and then to the side, in an ecstasy of terror and of impatience.

"Valentino! Do not fire! Do not fire, Valentino, my friend, my brother! I shall give you my gray colt and my blue silk shirt."

"God teach me what to do," Valentino gasped out. "I shall shoot for his legs, *amigo*. Raise up your feet."

Then a miracle happened. The body of young Pedro shot backward through the air straight at Valentino's head, propelled from the inhumanly strong hands of Sandy Sweyn.

There was no more than time for a partial dodge; one of the wide-flung arms of Pedro struck full across the face of his friend. Valentino was man enough to rally in spite of this handicap. He fired, but still more than half blinded by that unexpected blow, and, before his eyes cleared, the wrist of his gun hand was in a grip that made the bones bend. The Colt dropped from his numbed fingers.

Sandy gathered his captives together, one in either arm. Then he shifted his grip. In his left hand he gathered the long hair of their heads and held them so. With his right, he went leisurely through their pockets. He said nothing as he worked, but he proceeded with care. Nothing escaped him. Not even the brown papers of Valentino's cigarettes. Even these were extracted and tossed into a careful little pile.

Then Sandy stood up. Still holding them by the hair of the head, he dragged them backward to the spot where their horses stood.

"Kill me at once!" Valentino cried. "After such shame, I do not wish to live!"

Sandy only laughed, and that laughter made Pedro scream again. He wrapped his hands around the leg of Sandy.

"¡Señor!" he gasped out. "I swear that I shall be your servant. I shall always. . . ."

"Peace!" cried Valentino. "Peace, cowardly dog, because if we live, I shall slit a throat that shames our whole race. Will you beg . . . after what we have done to him?"

Pedro begged no more; he had fainted in utter anguish of spirit.

In the meantime, from their own saddlebows, two rawhide lariats were detached. With these Sandy tied them, back to back and heel to heel. He secured their heads together by plaiting their long black hair—an ingenious device that pleased Sandy. After that, he tied them to the rocks. Then he stood up and regarded his work.

"So," Sandy said, "you will toast a little, also. Come, Cleo!"

At his call, the blue roan mare, which had lingered not far off all of this time, came sweeping in to him with a joyous whinny.

He leaped into the saddle and regarded the prisoners with another critical stare. The sun was hanging at its hottest pitch, and every instant of their exposure would be a keen agony. Unless they died of panic, before very long the setting sun would throw a shadow from the pines toward them. For that shadow, how eagerly they would wait.

These things were noted by Sandy, and he nodded his head

and smiled to himself. Although he felt in his heart a loathing for all humans that he had ever seen, he could not bring himself to downright laughter.

He turned loose the two mustangs, also. From the back of the lamed horse of Pedro he removed the saddle and the bridle with care. He nodded while he watched it hobbling slowly off, throwing its head as the strain came at each step upon its injured leg. Quiet and the heat of the sun would restore that leg by the next morning, Sandy believed. He turned for a last look at the *vaqueros*. Valentino was silent, as ever, composing himself.

"Water!" screamed Pedro, who had revived. "A little water, kind *Señor* Sweyn! A little water!"

The deadly snarl of Valentino interrupted him. "It is not ten minutes since you half emptied your canteen. Be still, or I shall find a way to kill you sooner than the sun would do that good work."

The voice of Pedro broke into a wild sobbing. Sandy, with a shudder of disgust, turned his back and sent his horse cantering swiftly up the valley in the pursuit of the troop that had carried Elena Blanca away.

He thought of the little white mare and the injustice of the men. As for Catalina Mirandos, he hardly thought of her at all. She was to him a strange mystery. Why men should hunt the little mare for the sake of Elena's swift-footed self was explicable. Why they should wish to hunt her merely for the sake of a woman, he could not understand. He had been filled with only a mild curiosity to look upon the face of Catalina.

CHAPTER THIRTY-SEVEN

In riding up the valley, *Señor* Rézan had not neglected to place final outposts—two reliable men. Where the valley narrowed to a simple gorge they were instructed to wait among the rocks, so that, if Sandy should escape from his guards, they could block his way from these final points of vantage.

When he had established these final marks of safety, Rézan hurried on. Finally he reached the Casa Mirandos. Straight into the patio he rode. Others had seen him coming. They had heard the trampling of the hoofs of his horses. They had looked out and seen the famous beauty of Elena Blanca, and in that single picture they were able to read a story that told them that the long chase was over, at last. The most romantic incident that had ever taken place in those old mountains was now preparing for its last act. They tumbled out and mounted their horses in haste to follow.

It was a happy party. There was hardly a young man in that party who had not striven for the prize or yearned to have good fortune in it. Now that they had failed, and the quest was over, there was not one of them who was not glad that José Rézan had been the lucky man. They all knew that he had loved beautiful Catalina Mirandos longer than any other man. He had, at one time, been the accepted lover of the girl; she had been engaged to him and all but the wedding day had been arranged. What more fitting, then, than that he should return to her in such a triumph as this?

Besides, there was no other man in all the mountains who had half the stately dignity, the fine bearing, and the handsome face of this same Rézan. Just as Catalina exceeded all the women in her beauty, so did José exceed all the men. The babble of talk that went up and down the procession was gay and rapid.

"How did he find her? How did he take her? He was at his house, only this morning, and now he is here with Elena. How did it come that she wandered back here from the desert?"

"We shall tell you the truth," they explained. "It has to be known. She was captured by another man. And that other man was bringing her in . . . when our master met him with us all behind him . . . and we took the mare from the stranger . . . a half-wit with a stupid, dull eye. His name is Sweyn. We left him sitting like a fool in the valley, guarded by our men. Now he is losing the price of all of his work."

"There will be trouble, then, if he comes to make a claim to the sheriff?"

"Oh, there might be trouble, then. But what would they do, except to put a great fine upon *Don* José, perhaps? They cannot take the mare away from Catalina Mirandos again, because all men know that the mare belonged to her and merely had strayed away. Neither can they accuse *Don* José of refusing to pay the worth of the mare. What is money to him? Is he not rich? Does not this marriage mean everything to him? When the sheriff comes to him, he will simply say . . . 'Let the man Sweyn put a value upon the horse that he says that I took from him, and then I shall pay him his money in full and a bit more.' That is how the business must turn out."

The procession passed toward the house of Mirandos. When they arrived at the patio, *Don* José would have kept the others back, but there was a great roar from all their voices.

"We will have Catalina Mirandos come down to the patio. Where is she? Let her come. *Señor* Mirandos, bring down your daughter to the patio."

Señor Mirandos would have been glad to escape from such a necessity. He would have sent Catalina closely to her room, to stay there until the mob was gone, for he was not one to enjoy having his daughter stared upon.

But how could he control her? The chance of being looked at was so charming to Catalina that the roses blossomed at once in her cheeks. She was at her glass only long enough to crowd a red rose into the shadows of her hair. Then she was flying down the stairs and dodging past the sedate form of her father. Yet when she slipped out onto the patio, it was with the shrinking step of a deer frightened by the hunter from its covert. The color that vanity and haste had put in her cheeks appeared the blush of maiden modesty. Oh, wise Catalina! So well did she manage it that a veritable shout went up from the crowd, not only from her Mexican compatriots, but from the true Americans, also, who had ridden up to join in the formal triumph of José Rézan.

Then she saw Elena Blanca and started forward with a glad cry. You would have thought that Elena was really something more than a mere peg upon which the notoriety of Catalina Mirandos had been hung. The men grinned in pleasant understanding. It was, of course, the general idea that Catalina was so terribly fond of the mare, and the white mare was so terribly fond of her, that when that beautiful companionship was interrupted Catalina could not help but offer any reward in the world to the lucky man who could bring back the mare to her.

Elena Blanca, like the little devil that she was, now threw a monkey wrench into the idyll by beginning to rear, paw the air, and prance around when she saw her mistress, acting as though her one passionate desire was to smash the fair Catalina to a pulp. Catalina had no idea of letting herself come too close to the white devil.

"See what they have done to her! They have made her into a savage beast!" Catalina cried out, with tears in her eyes—she always had tears at her command. She clasped her hands together.

As for the men, they were busy controlling that little white flash of a mare. There was only one pair of eyes that remained fixed upon Catalina. Glancing down toward the rear of the crowd, she encountered the quizzical smile of Peggy Kilmer, the sheriff's daughter. The flush deepened upon the cheek of Catalina.

She knew that Peggy understood. What men could never understand, the quick glance of a woman could unravel. Catalina knew that her mystery was open as the day to the glance of this girl. She sighed, turned a little away, and wished that the freckled face of Peggy Kilmer were any place in the world other than here.

Now came tall José Rézan and stood before her, looking stupidly guilty and ill at ease. She drew Rézan with her into the house of her father. The crowd gave its last shout as they disappeared together.

Inside, they encountered the wicked-tongued *Señor* Mirandos himself. He said: "So she is taking the bear to escape from the lion. Is that it, José?"

His daughter made answer with an ugly look, and then she drew José on to the living room and sat him down beside the great open window.

"José, my José," she said, "what a hero you are. And how did you manage to do it?"

"We met him and took Elena from him by force," Rézan said, "and that was all that there was to it."

"And he was not so terrible, then, as a fighter? There was no one really hurt?"

It might have seemed, to a discriminating eye, that there was a shade of disappointment in the eye of the girl as her lover answered: "No one was hurt. He looked merely simple. One could see that he was a half-wit. He looked like a man only half awake."

"But how could he have captured Elena, if he has only half of a normal man's wits?"

"Because he rides the fastest mare that I ever saw, and the strongest. We tried to catch her . . . to keep him from following us. She simply laughed at us. I have never seen such speed."

"Then he will follow?" exclaimed the girl. "Oh, José, be careful. You are all mine, now, and you must take the greatest care of yourself!"

Rézan could not help smiling, remembering the rope that bound Sandy Sweyn and his two guards posted in the valley. "There is no fear," he said. "You shall not see him here. He will not follow."

"And yet," Catalina said, "I can hardly believe that he may not find a way . . . if he had wits enough to capture Elena, you know."

In one thing more Rézan felt himself enormously lucky. When he pressed for the wedding day, Catalina was willing to discard a long preparation. It might be tomorrow, she said, and the face of Rézan lighted with a consummate joy.

As the day was turning toward the dusk he rose to depart. Before he reached the door of Casa Mirandos there was a rattle of hoof beats outside in the patio, then a babbling of voices at the door. The door opened. A man staggered in before them, his face drawn, his head tied in a crimson rag.

"Carlos!" Rézan cried. "What has happened?"

"Sandy Sweyn!" gasped out the other. "He has broken through us."

Rézan pushed him into a chair and brushed the chattering servants from the room.

"It is one of the two whom I left to guard the head of the valley and keep back Sweyn," he explained to the girl. "Now we must find out what has happened."

CHAPTER THIRTY-EIGHT

As for Catalina, exclamations of pity and of distress poured from her lips. As she hurried to bring wine, warm water, and to make a clean bandage for the head of this Carlos, it seemed to that hardy *vaquero* that she was an angel of mercy, sent from heaven to relieve the woes of man. In the eye of the girl there was a profound satisfaction.

Sandy Sweyn, seeing that he was a half-wit and a fool, of course, should not be permitted to claim the reward that she had offered to him who brought back the little white mare. At the same time, she was consumed with curiosity about him.

Of all the cavaliers who had ridden forth to perform this great feat, it had remained to this mysterious Sandy Sweyn to conquer. It seemed hardly right that he should be caught like a foolish bird in a net at the very moment when he had almost brought the horse back to her. It seemed very wrong, indeed.

Now it appeared that the foolish goose of a man was a bit of an eagle, also. The net that had held him had been broken through, and, as he burst to liberty, here was one mark of his talons. Her eyes kindled like that of a kindred bird of prey.

Carlos, comforted with wine and a soft bandage, could speak once more.

"Mateo and I watched from among the rocks in the very places where you put us, *señor*. We did not sleep, I can tell you. We did not think that Sweyn could break away from two such men as our friends, Pedro and Valentino. Is not Valentino a great fighter? However, we watched well, if only because the *señor* had entrusted this duty to us."

"I want no more compliments," Rézan said tersely. "Let me hear what happened."

It was Mateo who, looking down the valley, caught sight of the blue roan mare and her rider coming with incredible speed up the rise of the ground. Mateo called a soft warning; he moved to get into a better position, to command the direction from which Sandy Sweyn was riding. The two *vaqueros* came to a brief and clear understanding. Since this man had been able, in spite of his limited wits, to elude the bonds and the guns of their companions, Valentino and Pedro, since Valentino was a known man of prowess with weapons, Mateo and Carlos had decided that it would be far better if they made no attempt to destroy this fellow after a parley, but to shoot as soon as he had ridden into pointblank range. They prepared their guns and watched the stranger dip out of sight for the last time before rising up into the danger of their weapons—he and his blue roan. However, he did not rise at once.

"I am a patient man," Carlos said. "But the moments began to seem long. I have sat to wait for a rabbit to come out of its covert. I have outwaited even a snake in its hole. But as we sat there to keep watch among the rocks, a lair of crows kept scolding at us from a blasted pine tree nearby. Their voices seemed to be calling attention to us. I made a sign to Mateo that I would go forward a little to see what I could see. Mateo agreed.

"So I slipped away . . . a snake could not have made less noise, I swear to you, *señor*. You would have found no fault with me, if you could have seen with what care I went about this work. I pushed my rifle slowly before me. Not even the ear of an owl could have detected me. I came, after much labor, to an edge of the rocks, and when I looked down, I saw the blue roan mare . . . and her saddle was empty. At that, I guessed that

Señor Sweyn, having seen the narrow passage between the rocks ahead of him, may have guessed that there was a danger there, and so he had gone ahead to examine the place.

"When I made up my mind to this, I turned at once, and I went back toward my friend, Mateo, as fast as I could. All was silent, for the crows were making noise no longer. When I came to the place, suddenly there was a great form of a man leaping up and at me from the crevice where only Mateo had been crouching before. I tried to fire my rifle at him, but there was no time. He held a rock in his hand, and he threw it. That made the wound that you see along the side of my head. I fell into a darkness. When I wakened, I crawled to Mateo, and I found him lying, breathing, but very sick. There was a canteen filled with water beside him. And there was a little flask of whiskey. The *Señor* Sweyn, had left these things for him.

"I asked poor Mateo what had happened. He said that a little after I had started, just as the crows stopped their chattering, something leaped on him from behind. A hand was pressed over his mouth that kept him from crying out . . . another arm passed around his body and crushed him until he felt his ribs giving way. He heard a voice behind him saying that, if he remained quiet and made no sound, all would be well with him. If he attempted to give a warning, he would be shot instantly.

"Poor Mateo. There was no need of giving him such warnings. He was too sick to pay any attention to anything in the world except himself. His ribs had been broken by that terrible bear hug. He could barely whisper to me, even so long after it had happened. He said that there was such a power in the arm of that man that he could not believe a human being had done it. It was really as though a terrible machine were crushing him, and he heard his ribs pop like pipe stems.

"After that, I gave him a little of the whiskey, and I dragged him under the shadow of the old pine tree out of the sun. He screamed when I lifted him, but I could not leave him to be baked there. Then I took my horse and galloped him as fast as I could make it all the way to your house. When they told me that you were here, I spurred hard to get to you. I have told you everything, *señor*. There is nothing left out. Will you believe me?"

"I believe you," Rézan said. "There is only one thing. It is nonsense to say that he might have looked ahead and judged from the narrowness of the rocks, there, that the place was guarded. How was he to tell? There were a hundred other places that I might have guarded. No, no, Carlos, you have told everything except the most important thing of all . . . the thing in which you were to blame. Confess to me that just as this Sandy Sweyn was coming close to you, either you or Mateo stood up and showed yourself foolishly or else you made a noise that warned him."

Carlos grew pale with protestation. He threw his arms high above his head. "I swear to you, *señor,* as I hope for heaven hereafter, that we did not stir. We could not have shown ourselves."

"Humph!" Rézan exclaimed, unimpressed. "How could you see him so clearly without giving him a chance to see you?"

"Because, *señor,* each of us had chosen a place where there was only a narrow chink between two rocks, and, looking down through those chinks, there was not half an inch of our faces to be seen. That half inch was covered with black shadow. No, *señor,* if you will come back with me to the place where we were hidden, I shall point out the very spot. Believe me that I do not lie."

"Consider this, my friend," Rézan said, frowning, "there is a mystery in the story as you tell it. There is a great mystery. You swear that you could not be seen and that you made no noise?"

"No, *señor.* Neither of us stirred. Even if we had, the noise that the cursed chattering of the crows made would have covered us. Even so, we did not stir. We knew that this man had found a way to break from Pedro and Valentino. We knew that they had as great an advantage over him as we had in our secret places. Therefore, we were determined to throw away no chances, and, believe me, we did not. No, *señor*, we did not show ourselves, and we did not make any noise."

"Your horses, then?"

"Our horses were half a mile away. I myself took them and tethered them there."

José Rézan shook his head. "I want to believe you, Carlos," he said. "I know that you are honest, and I think that you are trying to tell me what you believe to be the truth. But there is something left out of your story. In some way Sandy Sweyn received a warning that there was danger waiting for him up there among those rocks, and, after he had received that warning, he dismounted and stole ahead on foot with the greatest caution to see what the danger could be. Your own surety was, of course, what ruined the two of you . . . that and your foolish maneuver forward to see what had happened to him. The great question that remains is . . . how did he get his warning?"

"I have a wild thought," Catalina interrupted, her eye flaming.

"And you, my dear?" Rézan said, smiling fondly on her.

"He heard the chattering of the crows. Do not the crows act like wicked little spies? He heard the chattering of the crows from the pine tree, and he knew by the pitch of their voices that they were not chattering at another animal but at men. Tell me, José . . . is not that possible?"

Rézan smiled at Carlos, and Carlos smiled at José with the superiority of man to man, looking above the head of a mere foolish woman.

"Ah, well, my dear," Rézan said, "we suppose that *all* things are possible. And perhaps, after all, this Sandy Sweyn knows the language of the birds."

He could not help breaking into laughter, and Carlos choked himself respectfully to keep from joining.

"That is not what I meant," Catalina said, filled with fire. "And you may learn that this Sandy Sweyn is not such a fool as you all think."

Chapter Thirty-Nine

What she had said remained keen in the mind of pretty Catalina all through the evening, and when she went up to her
room that night, there were only two things of crowning
importance that remained in her imagination. Neither of them
had to do with José Rézan and the fact that she had most
impulsively promised to marry José on the following day. Nor
was it her concern at the anger and contempt of her father
when *Señor* Mirandos had learned of the hasty decision of his
child.

Rézan had so often been in her life, and out again, that she
was used to him; she was also used to the anger of *Señor* Mirandos himself. There were two new features in her history that
seared her thoughts.

The first of these was the keen glance with which Peggy
Kilmer had looked straight through her armor of elaborate af-
fectations to the truth about herself. It was a new and almost an
unheard of thing for Catalina to feel that any human being had
looked in upon the shadowy inside of her existence, with all its
turmoil and noisy shallows. She hated Peggy Kilmer for having
seen so many things so well. She hated the freckle-faced girl for
the superior power that enabled her to smile at what she saw in
Catalina. We chiefly rage, not at those who attack us in passion,
but at those who glance aside at us in scorn. She vowed chiefly
that she would be avenged upon Peggy Kilmer, for knowing too
much. However, Peggy was not even the major half of her

thoughts. There was another person looming larger and larger. That was Sandy Sweyn. Surely his actions on this day had hardly been like the actions of a half-wit. He had twice handled two fighting men as though they were silly children.

The report of what had happened to Valentino and Pedro had come in before the dark. They had brought in Pedro, raging with fever and sickness of mind. He would recover his wits, the doctor said, if he had plenty of time to rest and good nursing and fine food. It was the shock of that long exposure to the sun that had unsettled him. It was the dread of what might happen, rather than the pain of what actually had happened, that had undone him. However, he would soon be well again.

Valentino had nothing to say, except that, when the name of Sandy Sweyn was mentioned, he smiled to himself and showed all his gleaming teeth.

"You will be eager to have a chance at him again, Valentino," Rézan offered, "and I shall see that you have the very first opportunity."

"No, no, *señor.* I have been in the fire once. I do not wish to be burned again."

"What, Valentino? Will you let the other men who have always looked up to you as a greater fighter without fear . . . will you now let them see that you are really afraid of this half-wit?"

"Half-wit?" repeated Valentino. "Well, I would change all of my brains for his half-wit, as you call it. No, I want nothing more to do with him. If he comes near to me again, I shall put my hands into the air and say . . . 'Hello, friend. Do not shoot. Valentino is only a weak little child, and he will do you no harm.' That is what I shall say to him. No, I want no more chances at Sandy Sweyn. I have had my one big chance, and that was entirely too much."

With this astonishing speech of resignation, Valentino shrugged his sunburned shoulders and rolled another cigarette.

Thereafter, he walked forth among the other *vaqueros.*

"You have met one who was too much for you?" said one of his friends with a rather malicious grin.

"Does not every wise hawk run away from an eagle?" Valentino responded calmly. "Nevertheless, no hawk fears a foolish crow like you."

Which was sufficient to establish that the spirit of this Valentino was as high as ever.

All these reports had been carried to Rézan as a matter of course, and he had been forced to retell all of them to Catalina. He did not wish to, but he could not help it. She would not rest until she had dragged from him every detail, little by little.

"It is because I tremble for you, love," Catalina said. "When I think of this dreadful man roving around through the mountains, do I not tremble for you? Tell me everything."

Rézan told her everything, and with each syllable that she heard the eyes of pretty Catalina burned brighter and brighter. She clasped her hands together and shrank deeper and deeper into her chair. She pressed her hands against her breast and gasped out as she heard each new detail. "Ah, José, what a dreadful, dreadful man. Is there any other like him?"

"Have no fear," José said, smiling. "You must not tremble for me. If he comes across my path, I trust that I shall be able to handle him well enough."

She would close her eyes, overcome with her fear for his sake, as flattered José thought. In reality she was wishing to close out the sight of her lover and take home upon her mind the image of this odd fellow—whose hair was the color of golden sand and whose eyes were the color of his hair, so that you could not always tell when he was looking at you.

Early in the evening, when she developed a dreadful headache, it was only because she wished to go upstairs and lie there in the semi-dark, with only one lamp lighted and the flame turned low. There on her couch, with a mantilla gathered around her flashing shoulders, she lay and brooded and dreamed and smiled, because this was a figure of a man such as the world had never seen before. For its very oddity Catalina could almost have loved him. She loved novelties for their own sake. With eyes half closed, she pondered over this figure, who lay more in a world of dreams than in the world of reality—a half-wit with the strength of a giant and with a craft in fighting that turned even such sturdy *vaqueros* into mere puppets and children.

What roused her from her ponderings was a mere whisper of sound at the farther casement, on the other side of the room. Catalina looked up in time to see the figure of a man swinging through the open window and dropping lightly to the floor—so lightly that, in spite of his bulk, his feet made no sound whatever as they struck.

It brought Catalina instantly to her feet. It was characteristic of her that in ordinary times she chose to be excessively feminine, while in a crisis she was as cool as a young tigress. She sprang back toward the door, and she laid a hand upon the knob of it, ready to flash away to safety at the first movement of the stranger. She lingered for an instant, and from her dress she plucked forth a little Italian stiletto, delicate and deadly, shaped to a long needle point. In spite of her soft beauty, this Catalina was a true daughter of the desert, practiced in its ways.

She knew him instantly by the descriptions that others had given to her of him. She knew him by the deceptive appearance of softness and the real power that underlay it. She knew him by the deft quiet in which he had climbed the smooth side of the house and swung into her room. No leopard could have been more dexterous in the hunting of his prey. She knew him, above all, by the dull and handsome features—that unlighted eye, the color of sand—that seemed blurred and lost under lashes of the same tone.

Staring at her beauty, the eyes of Sandy opened a trifle, and there began slowly in their deeps a tremor of golden fire that waxed and waxed until, at last, it was flaming at her.

It seemed to Catalina Mirandos that he stood straighter, his head raised, and a faint smile of joy stirred his mouth. What a fire was this she had lit in him. The beautiful form of Dick slipped in from the outer room, sensing trouble though there had been no sound even to reach his sensitive ears. He sprang in front of his mistress like a true hero, ready to do his duty. When he faced the stranger, a little tremor ran through Dick, and presently he crouched on the floor and was staring up with wonder at Sandy Sweyn, beginning to brush the floor with his silken tail.

Danger in this man? Catalina was no fool, and she knew that where her Ricardo could love so quickly there must indeed be something lovable. She, looking wide-eyed upon the stranger, began to see what those qualities might be—endless strength, endless simplicity, endless trust, endless power to worship. She knew that as she was, at this moment, seeing Sandy Sweyn, no other person had ever seen him. She had been able to strike a great fire that hitherto had never flamed, and that might never go out. It was an exquisite flattery, so subtle that it was beyond words.

When he spoke it was as directly as a child. "I came to bring back Elena Blanca, but they stole her from me. Then I wanted to see you, so I came here. You are not afraid of me?"

"I am not afraid," Catalina said.

She saw the silken softness of her voice send a tremor through him. He passed across his eyes that hand that had beaten down so many men this day.

"I've been walking in a dream," Sandy said. "But now I'm awake. I never knew that a woman could be like you, Catalina. May I come closer?"

She was too excited to answer. Perhaps it looked like fear to Sandy; to the girl it was really only the thrilling joy of her power that moved her, and wonder at this strange creature that had come to her hand. She saw him move a step nearer, and another. He stood just before her, and now his eyes plunged deep in her great black eyes.

Dick stood up, but the stranger had no eye for him. He made a vague gesture toward her, and Catalina shrank a little. Yet she did not step back. All that he touched was her hand, and he raised it to his cheek, to his lips.

Then he stood straight before her again, and her hand had fallen away. It was unlike all that other men had ever done in her presence. It was a strange mixture of the worship of a child and the love of a man. There was such joy in him that he was almost laughing.

"I listened at the window below," he said. "I know that *Don* José is to marry you tomorrow. Tell me, Catalina, do you love him?"

She had no words. A sort of trembling weakness spread through her body and rose to her throat and closed it.

"Ah," Sandy said, "I knew that you did not. Forget him, then, because he does not exist."

He stepped back to the window. One gesture swung him out. He turned to give himself a last look of her, with the expression of one drinking the wine of the gods. Then he was gone. Only then Catalina realized that she had not spoken a word since his entrance, except: "I am not afraid."

It was not much to say, yet she felt that she had conquered a new world. She ran hastily to the window to stare after him, but he was gone in the blackness beneath. Not so much as a whisper came back to her.

Dick, standing at the casement, also, with his paws resting on the edge of it, looked down, too, and whined as though his heart were breaking to be out.

CHAPTER FORTY

Those who listened through opened doors and windows heard a man ride, singing, down the valley that night. There was never a voice so great and so ringing, they thought. They hurried outdoors, but all that they saw was a vague figure, under the dim moon, riding down the road. Even when they stood in the open, they could not distinguish the words of that song or the language of the singing. The tune itself seemed to be a merely inarticulate overflowing of joy.

When the rider came to the house of Sheriff Kilmer, the wind blew tidings of food to him. The sheriff had returned late this night from a long ride, and his daughter had barely set the meal before him on the table. An instant later there was a knock at the kitchen door, and Peggy Kilmer opened that door on a man with wild yellow eyes and long, thick sandy hair.

"I'm hungry," said the stranger. "Will you feed me?"

The black cat leaped up from the warmth behind the stove and ran into a far corner of the room, where it cowered in the sheltering blackness.

Peggy Kilmer had never been afraid of men, any more than had little Catalina Mirandos, but from a different reason by far. Catalina knew that they were helpless in the power of her smile. Peggy Kilmer considered that they were all her brothers.

Nevertheless, she was afraid now. Never had the night showed to her such a person as this. Yet her duty was clear before her. In the mountains, when food is asked for, it must be given even by a miser. She was very glad that her father was here with her, sitting at the kitchen table with his supper spread before him. She cast at him a single glance that was enough to show him that here was something extraordinary. The sheriff leaned forward a little and loosened the revolver in his holster.

What he saw, as the stranger stepped through the doorway, made him come to his feet. "You're Sandy Sweyn," Kilmer said.

The stranger turned on him with such a sudden lightness of body that the sheriff started again. When he met the yellow light in those eyes, he caught his breath.

"I'm Sandy Sweyn," said the stranger. "Who are you?"

"Kilmer is my name. I'm the sheriff of the county, Sweyn."

"Good," Sandy said. "Have you got chuck here for an extra hand, partner? I've never ate with a man-size sheriff before."

He laughed in an odd, joyous way that made Sheriff Kilmer, for an instant, suspect that his guest had been drinking.

"Sit down," he said, "but before you sit down, I have to say that I have an idea that I ought to put you under arrest, Sweyn. You're accused of having attacked four men today. And one of them is badly hurt. There's no charge against you, and that's why I'm a little in doubt."

"We'll talk it over while I eat," Sandy said.

The sheriff nodded. "Put on another steak in the frying pan, honey," he said to his daughter. "Excuse me a moment, Sweyn. I have to telephone."

As he passed from the room, he heard Sandy Sweyn saying: "Never mind the new steak. I smelled beans as I came in." The stranger went to the stove, and, taking from it the great, blackened bean pot at the back of the fire, he sat down contentedly with a huge iron spoon.

At the telephone, behind closed doors, the sheriff was speaking rapidly and softly. "Is this you, Rézan? I have news for you. Sandy Sweyn is in my house. He stopped to ask for his dinner.

Now, Rézan, never mind exclaiming. What I want to know is if you are preferring any charge against this man?"

"No," Rézan said instantly. "He's more likely to prefer a charge against me. You understand, don't you, Sheriff?"

"I understand," the sheriff said. "You stole a horse from him, and he raised the devil with four of your men. One of them is still out of his wits, and another is dangerously hurt. I don't know where the balance lies, but I suspect that it lies against Sweyn. You don't want to do anything?"

"Not a thing."

"Then I make one suggestion."

"What's that, Sheriff?"

"Keep a gun under your pillow when you sleep tonight. I've never seen such a queer-acting fellow, and he may be up to mischief."

"I'll take your advice, Sheriff, and thank you."

"One thing more. Can you tell me why people call this man a half-wit?"

"Why, Sheriff, there was never any doubt as to the reason for that. He's different from other people. And his dull eye, if nothing else. . . ."

"Dull eye?" the sheriff repeated. "I've never seen a bright one, then. But I've sent you a warning, Rézan."

"A thousand thanks. I'll be on my guard. But I wish nothing but good luck to this fellow. Has he made a charge against me?"

"Not a word, but it may come later."

The sheriff returned to his kitchen, and there he found Sandy Sweyn deep in the contents of the bean pot, talking to Peggy Kilmer at the same time. As for his Peggy, he had never seen her so flushed or so pretty, sitting in the window, swinging her heels. In the instant that her father had been away, she seemed to have pocketed all of her fear of this stranger.

"Look, Dad," she said. "Old Tabby has found a friend. Never

knew her to *look* at a man before."

The sheriff could hardly believe his eyes. Black Tabby sat upon the broad shoulder of Sandy Sweyn, her tail wrapped around her forepaws, purring in blissful content. Every movement of the spoon she regarded with much interest, as though this were a sort of food that even she could enjoy.

The sheriff was in awe when he sat down. In years of effort he had never secured the confidence of that mysterious cat. No wonder, then, that the heart of his daughter had been touched.

"But," Peggy went on, as though her father were not there at all, "if you live all alone in the woods most of the time, what do you do for company? I should think that you would die of loneliness."

"Oh," Sandy Sweyn said, "I never lack for company. You see?" He whistled, and instantly, through the open kitchen door, the head of a magnificent blue roan was thrust. She whinnied no louder than a whisper and pricked her ears at her master. "You see," Sandy said, "that I have company."

"I see. But very queer company, most people would call it. And only your horse?"

"There's a bear," Sandy said, "that drops in on me in the summer. And we often hunt together. There is more fun in going fishing with a bear than with a dozen men, I suppose."

She started to laugh, but when she saw that he was in earnest, it did not occur to her to doubt. The sheriff himself felt no question in his mind. To the man with those blazing eyes and that inward joy all things seemed possible.

"But tonight," Sandy said, "I've got a different slant on things. I've waked up to the fact that there's something besides animals in the world. Girls, for instance. I never really saw them before." He looked straight at Peggy Kilmer and laughed—not an insulting laugh, but as though he were flooded with such happiness that it had to find some expression. A flare of color went up the cheeks of Peggy—and she looked rather guiltily and impatiently at her father, for all the world she wished him out of the way. The sheriff was amazed. It was not in the cards for his daughter to pay more than the most casual attention to young gentlemen—except to include them as sort of second-hand brothers.

Sandy was enlarging on the point. "Look at her," he said. "I've tried out men and found that most of them are hounds. But the girls are different. There's something in her that no man could ever have. Will you see the color in her cheeks, Sheriff, and how her eyes sparkle? Why, I tell you that it makes me happy only to look at her."

The sheriff started to frown. Suddenly it dawned upon him that this was not brazen boldness, but merely a true naïveté such as no other man in the world possessed. Peggy herself seemed to know the honesty of the stranger—certainly her blush was not one of displeasure.

The iron spoon grated on the bottom of the iron pot. The steaming cup of coffee was poured at a single gulp down the capable throat of Sandy. He stood up and laid Tabby on the floor.

"¡*Adiós!*" Sandy said then, standing at the doorway and smiling back at them. He turned to the girl. "I'd like a lot to come back, sometime, and talk to you again, if I can."

"Sure," Peggy Kilmer answered. "There's nothing to keep you from it, I suppose."

"Because," Sandy said, "if I was to talk to you a little longer, I think that I might be able to find out why it is you make me so happy. You understand? ¡*Adiós!*"

He was gone into the night.

The sheriff stared after him in complete bewilderment. "Look at that confounded cat," he said. "It's following Sweyn, or trying to."

There was no answer from his daughter. When he stared at

her, he saw that she was peering far off at things that he could not see and that, he guessed, he never could entirely understand. The dream was in her eyes. Her fingers twisted idly together. A faint smile touched her lips.

"I never saw another fellow like him," said the sheriff.

"Nor I," Peggy said.

"Fresh talking, but not really brassy. No manners, either, and yet he didn't seem to need 'em."

"Manners?" Peggy said. "What was wrong with them?"

"What was wrong?" gasped out the sheriff. "Why, honey, he didn't take his hat off for a minute while he was in the house."

"I didn't notice," she admitted.

"And how much did he thank us as he left?"

It seemed that Peggy was slipping back into her dream again, and she made no answer. Presently she stood up from the low window sill and left the kitchen, and the sheriff, frowning into his cup as he stirred the sugar into the coffee, realized that Peggy was a woman, after all. Soon she must leave him.

It was a lonely supper for him. When he went into the front of the house to smoke his pipe and read his paper—a week old—a glance through the door of his daughter's room, which was a little ajar, showed her sitting in front of her mirror, untwisting the stiff pigtails of her hair. With busy comb and brush she was transforming them into a soft and shining fluff of brown.

The sheriff sat down to his pipe, but he forgot to light it. There was a day not far hence when his life must be lived in a boarding house, while Peggy went elsewhere to shed happiness like a light.

CHAPTER FORTY-ONE

In the house of José Rézan, he was as good as his promise to the sheriff. He searched his mind to pick out the men best qualified to serve him. First, he selected two stout and watchful *vaqueros* and bade them keep constantly roving about his house. To sharpen their watchfulness, he murmured one word only: "Sweyn." That was enough.

Then he remembered two men who were both dreaded and despised by his *vaqueros,* two surly giants, black of brow and dark of face, who had recently come down from the mountains and taken employment with him, tending his flocks of sheep. He had sold his sheep. Now they waited for the purchase of his new flock; they waited in sullen silence, speaking to no man, communicating even to one another by signs only, most of the time.

Vicente and Lorenzo stood, thick of neck and with crooked wrists from much hard labor that they had done in their lives. In such hands as these, gun or knife would be out of place. Such hands were not meant for adroitness and agility, but to crush with the seizure. Such hands were made to break and to rend. They were like the paws of bears.

He put a stout cudgel in the hand of either man. "Now," Rézan said, "here is the corridor in front of my room. The window of my room is barred, and no man can come through it. I expect that an attempt may be made upon my life tonight. Tomorrow I am to be married, and such great happiness, my friends, seems almost too much for me to look forward to. Therefore, I put my life in your hands, and I give you a great trust."

They heard him without a sound, and they went to the end of the halls, where they were concealed in the thickness of the dropping shadows. Rézan knew that there would be no danger; eyes that watched over his flocks by day and night would not close in this greater time of need. He went to his bed and slept like a child, secure that all would be well.

When he wakened, it was to hear a slight groaning sound in his room. He sat upright. Again he heard the groaning, and this time he made out that it came from his window. Presently he recognized that awful sound as the noise of iron bent with a ter- rible force against the stones. Rézan could hardly stir, for a mo- ment. Then, against the stars, he saw the head and shoulders of a man thrust into his chamber. He tried to shout—but the result was a scream, rather than a call for help. He jerked the revolver from beneath his head and fired. Even as he pulled the trigger, he knew that the shot had flown wild from his trembling hand. The next instant, the black form had slipped through the window and dropped to the floor of his room.

In the corridor, outside, there was a stir of great voices. Vicente and Lorenzo knew that danger was there, and they were beating against the door to come to his aid—that door that he had so madly locked the night before, secure in the strength of the iron bars that guarded his window. In a moment, unless his hands could be steadied and unless he could shoot straight, the hands that had bent the iron at his window would be at him, breaking and rending.

Another scream rose from the throat of Rézan as he fired again and again. But his nerves were shattered. Through the dark a form leaped at him like a cat, which springs in and dodges with a swerve as it springs. A hand shot past his gun arm; a frightful grip was laid upon his wrist. Then a blow struck full against his face. He fell with a faint moan and knew no more.

That instant, however, the door of his chamber fell with a crashing. The two giant shepherds were rushing in to the defense of their master. What they found was a confused tangle of shadows upon the floor. Vicente struck, and his master groaned like a dying man beneath the stroke. They threw themselves into the struggle with their bared hands, and therein they made their mistake. With the clubs they could have felled oxen. Under their hands they felt a lightning and an animal power, shifting from their grips. When they strove to sink their fingers into the flesh of this man, it turned instantly to India rubber beneath their touch. Their fingers slipped harmlessly away. Dreadful hands laid hold upon the two brothers.

The house had been roused by this time. The two *vaqueros* from the outside were speeding in. The stout *mozos* had tumbled from their beds and come, knife and gun in hand, in a swarm.

Sandy Sweyn heard the rushing of the many feet. Intent as he was upon the dreadful work that lay before him, he knew enough to understand that this was the limit of his daring. He must turn and strive to get away, if he wished to live.

He rose from three prostrate figures and rushed to the door. There he met a flood of struggling, shouting men, and he dived through them like a hot wedge through butter. He had scooped up one of the clubs of the two brothers, and before the very shadow of his stroke the *mozos* gave way. The tangle of their forms as they strove to flee from him blocked the efforts of more valiant fellows.

Perhaps Sandy would have come unscathed from this strange battle, had it not been that Vicente had risen from the place where he fell. His left arm was broken by the terrific wrenching grip of Sandy, but his right arm was intact. In that arm there was the strength of two. Besides, he was nerved by a frenzy of excitement now. As he plunged for the door, he gathered up the club that he had let fall when he leaped to the help of his fallen master. Armed, he leaped with a shout into the hall. With his broken arm swinging and hanging drunkenly at his side, he rushed forward. His footing was upon fallen men more often than upon the floor.

Sandy heard that shout and guessed at the flying danger behind him. As he turned, his foot slipped. He dropped to one knee, and, before he could rise, the blow was driving at his head. He reared the club as a guard; in his hand it was like a shield. Had there been power enough in the wood, he would have been saved, but the blow of Vicente's club snapped the bludgeon that Sandy raised to meet it, and descended on his head.

What seemed to Vicente himself the greatest miracle of all was that the stranger was able to rise even after this blow. To be sure, its force had been partly checked by the guard that he had raised against it. Even so, there seemed enough sheer weight remaining to have broken the head of any normal man.

Sandy was no normal man; even he was staggered. He rose to his feet and lurched at Vicente, but half of his power was stolen from him, and his head rang with the effects of that blow.

They could close on him now, and close on him they did, like valiant bulldogs pulling down a bear. By the grace of chance no ready knife was sheathed in his body, but he was fairly swathed in stout ropes. By the time his senses had cleared, his arms were almost helpless.

They stood about him, panting and gasping with their efforts. Seeing the great rise and fall of his breast as he breathed himself, it seemed to those awe-stricken men of the Casa Rézan as though the stranger would snap even the strong ropes that bound him.

Some of them guarded him closely with ready weapons. Others went running back to the room of the master and lifted the senseless body of big Lorenzo.

They found Rézan breathing, but senseless. He would not be married on the morrow. That much was sure. A driving blow from the fist of the stranger had smashed his nose as though a horse had trampled upon him. His throat was swollen and purple where the grip of Sandy Sweyn had rested for a moment. So they carried him to his bed and cared for him tenderly.

The telephone was busy, and the sheriff was speaking again at the other end of the line. He only waited until he heard the name of Sweyn. He dropped his receiver and made for the horse that, day and night, was always saddled, ready to receive him. As he ran down the hall, the door of his daughter's room opened, and he saw her pale, strained face in the glow of the lamplight from her room.

"Dad, is it Sandy Sweyn again?" she asked.

"Aye," the sheriff answered, "Sandy Sweyn."

"He has not killed a man?" cried Peggy Kilmer.

He paused for one startled backward glance at her. Plainly she was in an agony of dread. "I don't know," the sheriff muttered. "I don't know. I hope not, honey. I'll be back before long."

Then he rushed away through the night. He knew, now, what he had only guessed in the earlier evening. Sandy Sweyn was something more than a mere chance acquaintance to his daughter. It made his heart sore to think of it. He was an honest man, was the sheriff. He may be forgiven if, as he galloped his horse furiously down the valley, he hoped fervently that the mischief that Sandy Sweyn had done this night might be enough to keep him secure behind prison bars until the madness should have died from the brain of Peggy. If, indeed, it would ever die.

He knew her very well, and he knew that, when once her

heart was made up, it would not soon be pulled down.

The curse, to the mind of the sheriff, was that when at last she looked with favor upon a man, it should have been this wild fellow, this mystery among men—Sandy Sweyn.

CHAPTER FORTY-TWO

When the sheriff arrived, he found six men guarding the bound form of Sandy Sweyn. So far as he could see, there was no sign of any harm done to Sandy himself. His head was high and jaunty, and in the eyes that so many men had called dull there was still burning that brilliant yellow light of life. He greeted the sheriff with a careless and confident smile, and Sheriff Kilmer passed on without saying a word.

He reached the wreckage of the upper hall of the house. He passed on to a room where the two brothers, Vicente and Lorenzo, lay on two beds, silent, controlling their agony with set teeth. He gave them one look, and then went with his guide to the chamber where the master of the house lay, his pale face almost obscured with bandages.

"Something is gone inside of me, Sheriff," he said faintly. "He hit me in the face and in the body, when he came at me. The blow in the face broke my nose. The one in the body turned me numb, and I'm still numb, now. That's the window that he came through. My father had it barred with the iron when he had the feud . . . you remember? . . . with the sheepherders."

The sheriff stepped to the window. The bars had been fastened in place with a thick layer of stout cement. That cement was torn away. One bar remained only drawn to the side, instead of being torn bodily away. It was greatly bent, and the sheriff, using all the force in his wiry body, strove to complete the removal of that single bar. He could stir it a little back and forth, but he could not break it out entirely, neither could be bend it any farther back.

A broad-shouldered *vaquero* stood beside him. "I have tried it, too," he said in an awed whisper. "But I cannot break it out. Consider, *señor*, that this devil, climbing up from the outside, could not have had more than one hand free for pulling at the bars."

Kilmer put his head out and looked down. The wall fell sheer away, a dizzying height, and it seemed to him that there was nothing where a man could plant his feet. He drew back with a little shudder and returned to his prisoner. He examined the ends of Sandy's fingers. One nail was splintered and the very tips of all the other fingers were a little chafed. It was a conclusive proof to Kilmer. By power of hand alone the stranger had drawn himself up that steep wall, with such deadly peril to life and limb that Kilmer hardly dared to conceive.

Still in silence, Sheriff Kilmer substituted for the many ropes a single pair of stout handcuffs. The prisoner was placed in a buckboard, and, with a voluntary guard from among the men of Rézan, he was brought to the jail.

It was a modern jail, built, through the importunities of the sheriff himself, of strong natural stone for walls, with strong steel bars for the block of cells. Into one of these he showed the prisoner. Kilmer sat down outside the bars and loaded his pipe, and he lit it carefully.

"Now, Sweyn," he said, "I'd like to know what devil got into you. How did you come to try to murder three men tonight?"

"Three?" Sandy asked mildly. "No, Sheriff, only one."

"Sandy," the sheriff said, a little moved, "I want you to realize that whatever you tell me here will be repeated in the court before the face of the judge and the jury. Do you understand? Whatever you confess to me now will be used against you. Still, I'd really like to know what was in your mind.

Because you look rough to me, but you don't look like a midnight murderer. Not you."

Sandy shook his head. "I never meant to kill three," he said, "but only one. That one it was my right to kill, of course."

"Of course?" echoed the sheriff. "Man, what gave you a warrant to kill anyone?"

Some of the light departed from the eyes of Sandy, and for a moment the sheriff could understand what people meant who had called him a half-wit.

"What warrant?" Sandy asked. "Why, Sheriff, he was to marry Catalina tomorrow."

"And what the devil has that to do with it?" asked the sheriff.

"Everything," Sandy said, recovering some of his confidence. "Everything of course, because I am the man who will marry her."

The sheriff stared. Then he rose and paced up and down the floor of the alley between the cells. Then he came back and took his place on his stool again. "Go on," he said. "You're to marry little Catalina, then? And does she know about it?"

"I did not speak to her in words. But her eyes said yes, I think."

"You've seen her, eh?"

"Of course."

"Of course? It's the first that I've heard about it, and I think that, if you'd called at the Mirandos house, I should have heard. When did you go there?"

"Just before I came to your house for food."

"And you saw *Señor* Mirandos and his daughter . . . and they didn't let me know that you had been there. This begins to look like a devil of mystery."

"I did not see the *señor*. . . ."

"What? Would the girl see you alone? More mysterious still."

"I climbed up to the window of her room and went in to

speak with her."

"The devil! She didn't call for help?"

"She started to run away, but she changed her mind. We did not talk long, but we said enough, I think."

The sheriff tilted back his head with a long whistle. "I'd never believe it," he said. "And yet . . . I can't disbelieve you. Anything seems possible to you, young fellow. But after you had talked to Catalina, you decided that you would marry her and you went singing down the valley?"

"Yes."

"Intending to kill *Don* José? Don't answer me unless you fully realize that your confession is damned dangerous."

"Of course I intended to kill him."

"Will you tell me why you take it for granted that you had to kill José?"

"That is something that even a child could understand. I have said that he was to marry the girl tomorrow, and I had to stop that marriage."

"Ten thousand devils! And so you would stop it by killing the man?"

"I could not ask Catalina to break her word to him. You will see that, of course."

The sheriff groaned. "This is a mess such as no judge in the world ever tried to unravel before," he said gloomily, shaking his head. "I am glad that I don't have to sit on the bench and pass judgment. Man . . . child . . . fool . . . whatever you are, you deliberately decided to kill this Rézan?"

"I did not intend to harm him, at first," Sandy confessed. "All I wanted was to steal Elena Blanca away again. But I thought that I would see this Catalina first, and after I had seen her, I knew that I wanted her more than I wanted Elena. Now, *Don* José had stolen the mare from me. With that stolen horse, he got the hand of Elena. Also, he tried to keep me from com-

271

ing to her. He posted four men to keep me from it. The first two tried to kill me with the heat of the sun. They tied me in it."

"The devil they did!"

"It is true, however. And the second two tried to kill me with their guns."

"I know . . . I think I know."

"Therefore, certainly it is clear that I have a right to kill José Rézan if I can. He robbed me, and then he tried to murder me."

The sheriff scratched his head. "And the other two that you piled up in the room on top of Rézan?"

"I ask you fairly, Sheriff. Did they have a right to interfere between me and the man that I had a right to kill?"

It seemed so clear to Sandy that he leaned back and smiled in a broad and open confidence at the sheriff.

Sheriff Kilmer gasped. Then he stood up. "Sandy," he said, "maybe I'm violating my oath as the sheriff of this county, but I can't help seeing that you're different from other men. I'm going to forget everything that you've told me. And I'm going to send the best lawyer that I know about to you. Maybe he can do you some good. I don't know of anything else that can. In the meantime, I hope that you sleep well. *Adiós,* Sandy. I'm sorry to see you in this mess. But I've got to tell you this, to begin with. A man who breaks into another man's house in the middle of the night, with intent to rob, is a burglar, and as such he stands in danger of taking a mighty long sentence from the judge. The man who breaks into another man's house, in the middle of the night, to commit a murder on him, is going to get about as long a sentence as the law allows . . . or else be sent for life to some insane asylum. Heaven knows where you'd be better off. Good night, Sandy. I'm sorry for you."

With that the sheriff turned out into the night. He said first to the jailkeeper: "Sam, do you know what we've got in the jail tonight?"

"Sure," Sam answered. "We've got that Sweyn, Sheriff. The half-wit, of course. I know that."

"No, Sam," said the sheriff, "but I'll tell you the truth. We've got a grizzly bear in there. And, if I were you, I wouldn't trust to any weakness of his wits. If I were you, I'd see to it that every half hour of the night I walked down through that alley between the cells with a shotgun in my hands . . . that big, double-barreled shotgun, yonder, loaded with the big slugs. Because, you may have to use it. And if you do have to use it, don't shoot for the legs to stop him. Shoot to kill!"

CHAPTER FORTY-THREE

When the sheriff got to his home, he found what he had expected to find. Peggy was waiting for him. He had left his house really interested only in what reaction Peggy would have to this affair. Although a great part of his interest was back yonder in the cell, in the strangest prisoner that had ever fallen into his hands, still his daughter came first by long odds.

He put up his horse, and went around to Peggy's window, and peered into her room. He found her sitting beside a lamp in which the flame was turned down low. There was a book in her lap, but she could not maintain even a pretense of interest in it. Her face was white, and her vacant eyes were wilted toward the empty blackness of the window beyond which her father was standing.

Sheriff Kilmer came slowly around to the back door and let himself in. It was as bad as he could have feared, possibly. This odd chap had worked into the secret heart of poor Peggy, and now it was Kilmer's determination to get him out, if he could.

He had barely opened the kitchen door and stepped into the house before he heard the slippered feet of Peggy as she came running. "Was there anything wrong, Dad?"

He could hardly force himself to look into that strained face. "When I got to the house of Rézan, I found things in a mess. This Sweyn, that we've seen, had been there. Do you know what he had done?"

Her voice was nothing more than a husky whisper. "Don't

ask me to guess . . . only tell me, quickly . . . no dead man?"

"No one dead," said the sheriff, "but just about as bad, I can tell you."

Peggy had slipped against the wall and leaned there with eyes half closed, breathing slowly and deeply. "Oh, I'm thankful for that."

Certainly there was no shame in her. She did not care in the least if her father should guess how the stranger had moved her heart. The sheriff was not in a mood for talking about such tender subjects. If it were possible to raise horror in the heart of the girl, he intended to try his hand at it.

"I'll tell you what that man did . . . not a man, a gorilla . . . he got to the house of Rézan and climbed up the wall clear to the top story . . . holding onto the crevices by the tips of his fingers only."

"Aye," Peggy said, a faint fire coming to her eyes. "I knew that he could do a thing like that. There's the strength of a giant in him. I could tell that by the first glance."

The sheriff bit his lip. "There he tore out the iron bars that the old *don* put up at the time of the feud with the sheepmen."

"With his bare hands?"

"His bare hands."

"Wonderful!"

"Wonderful? Then he swung himself into that room, and I tell you that he dropped to the floor and ran at *Don* José."

"Was *Don* José asleep while the bars were being torn from his window?"

"No, he was awake and shooting."

"Ah, good heavens!"

"But Sweyn got him by the throat and. . . ."

"Sandy was not hurt, then?"

"Confound it, Peggy, you really act like an idiot. Have you no sympathy for poor Rézan?"

"Of course . . . of course. But what happened then?"

"Two more men that Rézan had wisely posted in the hall of his house came running in and tried to handle this Sweyn. He smashed them almost to bits, and it took the whole household to beat Sweyn down and tie him. I got him then, and put him in the jail. Confound me if the madman doesn't talk as if it were the most natural thing in the world."

"And wasn't it?" asked the girl.

"What!" cried her father.

"Why, Dad, he had tried to have his men destroy. . . ."

"Confound it, Peggy, you talk like. . . . Well, now I have to tell you the rest of the story . . . the reason why he really wanted to kill Rézan."

He had hoped that he would not have to use this weapon against her. He had hoped that the picture of Sweyn, like a long-armed gorilla, climbing the wall of the house, and tearing his way in to murder a man, would have been enough to revolt her. Apparently she was not touched.

"It was because the marriage of *Don* José and little Catalina was set for tomorrow."

Now he had touched her, to be sure. The color that had been surging back into her cheeks, making her pretty face almost beautiful, now was being swept away, again, at a stroke.

"Because of that?" Peggy murmured, looking suddenly down at the floor.

"You'll never believe it, Peggy. But this wild man had climbed to the room of Catalina . . . seen her . . . gone mad with the love of her. . . ."

Peggy reached for the wall, found it, and steadied herself against it. "And then?" gasped out poor Peggy.

"Finally the madman decided that the only thing that was left for him to do, was simply to murder this Rézan, so that the girl, if you'll believe me, would not have the trouble of breaking her word to José Rézan. Yes, sir, he considers that Rézan is his by right . . . and with Rézan dead, he, Sandy Sweyn, will marry the Mexican beauty. Isn't it enough to make you laugh?"

"Yes," Peggy said faintly. "Enough to make one laugh . . . but . . . it's pretty late. I'm going to bed." She went slowly off toward her room.

The sheriff closed his teeth upon his pipe so hard that the stem splintered in a dozen shards under the pressure. Then, stealing down the hall, he leaned his ear at the door of his daughter's room. For a moment, he heard nothing, and then there was a muffled pulse of sound, hardly louder than the beating of his own heart. Poor Peggy was inside there, almost sobbing her heart out, he knew.

The sheriff went to his room and paced up and down, full of anxiety. He knew that Peggy was deeply in love with this strange fellow from the wilderness, who charmed animals with his voice and eye, and stirred the hearts of impressionable girls with a glance. He was determined to keep the wild man behind the bars so long as he honestly could do it.

He went back to the jail at once, and there he found Sam, the keeper, just finishing his rounds. Sam was very glad of company.

"Just sits and looks at me," Sam stated, "and never closes his eyes, so far as I can see. Never even winks them. I offered him a cigarette, but he laughed and said that he wasn't smoking. There he sits still on his bunk, and when I come in with the lantern, the first thing that I see is the yaller light of his eyes. When I go out with the lantern, the last thing that I see is still the yaller in the same eyes. It's the spookiest job that I ever had in my life, and, by the looks of this fellow, I'd say that he wasn't no half-wit, but a lot more like a fellow that knowed that before morning some of his pals would come along and crack this jail like a walnut and take him out with them. Which is one way of saying that I ain't having a very pleasant night here, old-timer."

The sheriff grinned. "Watch him like he was your right hand, Sam," he said. "Now bring me all the keys . . . those to his handcuffs and his cell door . . . set an extra pair of irons on his legs, and bring me the key to that, while you're about it."

Sam obeyed, and, when the keys had been brought, the sheriff pocketed them with a grunt of satisfaction. He returned at once to his house. There he found Peggy, fully dressed, waiting in the kitchen. She came to him with a gasp.

"Was there another telephone message, Dad?" she asked him. "Has something gone wrong again?"

"Nothing has gone wrong. I was simply making a little surer of our friend, Sweyn."

"What has he done now?"

"In the jail? Nothing, and I don't intend that he will do anything. I have the keys in my vest pocket that unlock his irons, honey, and, no matter what happens, I'm sure of keeping him safe till the morning, now."

"But could he in any way have escaped?"

"How can I tell what friends he has that might break in to him?" asked the sheriff. "No, Peggy, I want you to go back to bed. Sweyn is in that jail for keeps."

He set the example by going to his room. There he lay awake until he heard Peggy stirring about in her own chamber, and finally he closed his eyes. He wakened once, a little later, with a start, and reached to make sure that his coat and vest were still hanging on the chair at the side of his bed. Then he turned over and fell asleep in real earnest, as one who had performed a hard day's work successfully.

In the morning he wakened and listened for a moment, surprised by the silence, for in the kitchen there was generally the stir of Peggy, at this hour, busy about her task of preparing his breakfast. There was no sound now.

He rose, feeling that the evening before had been too hard on her, and deciding that he would let her sleep as long as she might. He reached for his coat, to feel the familiar jangling of the keys. To his horror, there was no responsive sound. He felt hastily in the pockets—the keys were gone!

CHAPTER FORTY-FOUR

The keys were gone, and not by chance. In the black hour that precedes the rising of the sun, a figure skulked close to the wall of the jail, until it came to the little rear door, set strongly into the wall, and secured by an outward tangle of strong iron bars.

It was Peggy Kilmer. From beneath her cloak she produced, now, a number of keys, tried two or three, and finally fitted one to the lock. It opened easily, noiselessly for Sheriff Kilmer was not one to allow the locks at his jail to grow rusty. So she drew the door wide, and a whistling gust of wind rushed into the interior of the jail. Closing the door hastily behind her, she leaned for a moment against the wall, faint with fear, listening to the beating of her heart.

The whistling burst of wind had not caused alarm, apparently, within the jail. There was no sound of voice or footfall. When the silence had continued for a moment, she began a stealthy progress toward the nest of cells.

She had not taken half a dozen steps when a door at the farther side of the big apartment opened suddenly, and a shaft of yellow light struck her full in the face. Terror made her collapse. She dropped to the floor, and waited, unnerved, for discovery. It did not follow.

Sam carried his lantern into the place for his final tour of inspection, stepping along with a weary stride. The swinging lantern that he carried threw waves of barred shadows up the walls and flooded onto the white ceiling. At the coil of Sandy

Sweyn, he paused and held the lantern high.

"Still awake, eh?" Sam asked. "Still waiting?"

There was no answer. Peggy, looking through the forest of crossed and intercrossed bars before her, could see the prisoner sitting erect, his arms folded, with a flame in his yellow eyes as he smiled at the guard.

"Well," Sam said, "in half an hour more there'll be sunrise light, and that's the end of your hopes, young feller. Keep that fact in your mind, will you.? And . . . if I was you, I'd go to sleep. You must be plumb tuckered out."

Sam turned away, and his hobnail shoes gritted upon the concrete floor as he left the room. The heavy door closed with a ponderous sigh behind him and showed, at last, only a thin rim of light outlining the rectangle of the door.

Peggy crept to her feet and hurried softly to the cell. There was a night light in the jail—a single smoking lamp—that burned in a far corner, making the cells and the steel bars seem ten times their normal size. By that light, it seemed to the girl that it was a monster rather than a man who was waiting there in the cell.

She had studied the keys before. One was for the door; this for the leg irons. When the irons were loosened, and fell away heavily into her trembling hands, she looked up, and saw the faint glimmer of those yellow eyes above her. Still Sandy had not spoken. She fitted the last key of all into the handcuffs, and now the man was free to do as he pleased. He did not rise.

"Hurry," whispered Peggy Kilmer at last. "The irons are off. The door is open. I left my own horse outside, and I think that he'll carry your weight . . . for a ways. Here's an ammunition belt and a Colt. Don't use it unless you have to, Sandy Sweyn."

He would not take the proffered weapon, but reached out and took her face between both his hands. "What'll they be doing to you, Peggy, when they find out that you've turned me loose?"

"I don't know," Peggy admitted, "and I don't care. They'll never find out, if I can get back, quickly enough."

"I got a feeling," Sandy said, closing his eyes in intense thought, "that maybe it would be best if I was to stay here and see this thing right through. Better than letting a girl save me from the jail."

"Don't you understand? It's not a question of fairness. They'll put you in prison for years and years. I've heard my father talk. They'll coop you up in the darkness, Sandy. Maybe they'll never let you out. They can do queer things if they want to."

"But you see," Sandy said earnestly, "I had to do it. I had to try to kill that José Rézan, didn't I? It was the only way, wasn't it?"

"I don't know . . . I don't know. But hurry, Sandy. Sam may come back any minute. And if he comes . . . if he comes and finds me here. . . ."

"You're right," Sandy said. "If the sheriff wouldn't believe that I'm right, and Rézan is wrong, would any judge believe it, either?"

"No," Peggy said, "no judge would be as easy on you as my dear old dad."

"I believe you, and I'm going with you, Peggy."

He glided beside her from the jail, and she turned the key in the lock. All seemed blackest night still.

Sandy raised his head and took a breath. "The dawn'll be up in another minute," he observed. "D'you smell the morning coming? Aye, there's the rim of it beginning."

It seemed impossible to detect the change. Only, the eastern mountains were a little blacker than the western, and the eastern stars were turning pale, while the western stars still shone bright. It was the faint beginning of the dawn.

"I've got to hurry," Peggy Kilmer gasped. "Good bye, Sandy. Take good care of that mustang."

"I don't need your horse," Sandy said. "My own must be somewhere around here, waiting for me."

"Your own? Waiting for you?"

"Don't tell me that they caught her."

"Caught her? Not that I know of."

"Then she would follow them along like a dog, when they brought me away from Rézan's house, and she would have stayed just out of sight behind them until she seen them bring me into this place. Then she would stay around and wait, because that's her way. Come over that next hill, and I'll try to call her."

They crossed the low, wooded ridge, side-by-side, with the slippery pine needles under their feet, and the pure sweetness of the pine trees in their nostrils.

Where the trees hung like a veil around them, she heard Sandy Sweyn whistling, long and shrill, like the whistle of a bird. It did not jar against the ear of the night. It melted into it, and she could only judge of its strength and carrying power by the echo that presently came faintly flying back to them from across the little valley.

In the blackness, they waited, and while they stood, a rosy pencil streaked the horizon line in the east, just above the hills as they joined the sky. Presently a distant rhythm was felt rather than heard, and then came the unmistakable noise of a galloping horse.

"It's Cleo," Sandy confirmed with a sigh of relief. "I knew she wouldn't fail to come to me."

Here was the blue roan. She came like a winged thing out from the shadows of the trees and plunged at her master. Now he stood with one arm thrown over her head.

"What I don't make out, though," Sandy said, "is how you

could do this for me, or why you should do it?"

"A woman doesn't have to have reasons for everything," said Peggy.

"That doesn't go," Sandy said. "I can see through that. I've got one more thing to do, and then I'm coming back to see you. May I come?"

"I can't keep you away. I'm not a whole posse," Peggy said, laughing. "But before you go, you'll give me one promise?"

"I'll give you a hundred."

"That you'll not use that gun against another man, unless your back is against the wall, Sandy."

"It's a good deal to ask," Sandy said. "What if they hunt me?"

"You can keep away from them, if you want to. You know that you can."

"Tell me this. Is Rézan to marry Catalina tomorrow?"

"No, of course not. He'll spend a week in bed, they say. Or maybe a month. He's badly hurt where you struck him in the body."

"Then," Sandy said, "I'll promise to do no harm with this gun for a month."

Peggy gasped. "But you do promise, Sandy?"

"On my honor."

"Then . . . so long."

"So long, Peggy. You'll be late home. The sun is pushing a lot higher."

She realized that, as she swung into the saddle on the mustang that she had intended should carry Sandy away to freedom. When she came to the next hill and looked back, there was plenty of light to show her Sandy Sweyn still standing at the side of Cleo. He took off his hat and waved to her. Then she was swinging away on the straight road toward her father's house.

As she galloped the mustang fiercely on, hoping against hope that she might arrive before her father's wakening time, she realized that Sandy Sweyn had given her no thanks for the help that she had brought to him on this night. However, manners were not what one expected from him, or the usual way of doing anything.

The east grew rosier and rosier with flooding light. When she came in sight of the house, her heart sank, for she saw the smoke rising slowly from the kitchen chimney, and sloping in a long, white column across the valley. She did what one would have expected from Peggy Kilmer. She went straight up to the kitchen door, and there she threw herself from the saddle. The door opened at the same moment, and there stood the sheriff before her.

There was no torrent of questions or guesses or reproaches from his lips. There was merely: " 'Morning, Peggy. Where the devil is the sharp butcher knife? I can't get the bacon cut with that other infernal thing."

She brought the sharp butcher knife, and she sliced the bacon, waiting in a tremor for the trial to begin. As she poured his coffee and finally sat opposite him at the table, watching him eat, she began to realize that there would be no crisis. Her father simply sat with a pale face, and lips compressed with an iron determination.

By that she could guess how deeply she had cut him. It had been a necessary act from her viewpoint; from his it was a betrayal.

She endured it until she could stand the pain no longer. Then she stood up and placed the keys on the table. "He's gone away on the roan mare, Dad," she said at last. "I don't know where. I only know . . . that I wish that I were a man, and a stranger, so that you could treat me the way that I deserve."

The sheriff did not so much as look up. He kept his glance fixed upon his coffee cup, into which he was stirring the sugar industriously.

CHAPTER FORTY-FIVE

The whole valley learned the news before the morning was an hour older. The sheriff sent the tidings far and wide, sitting at his telephone and ringing number after number. He talked to the judge, first of all. His honor listened to the story with many most illegal curses.

"What's in the girl's idiot head?" asked the judge. "Has she lost her mind about a half-wit, Kilmer?"

"I'm not guessing," the sheriff said sadly. "I'm telling what she did, and not why she did it. The question is . . . what should we do with her? She's broken the law, Your Honor. She's broken it bad."

"Leave her be," said the judge. "When a fool girl gets sentimental, there's no use in trying to discipline her back into her senses. No use in the world. Cheer up, Kilmer. This will turn out for the best. By the way, who's laying the charges against Sandy Sweyn? We ought to know that."

"Why, José Rézan, of course . . . I suppose," the sheriff answered. "I'll get a statement from him at once."

A youngster on a fast horse had brought to the house of Rézan a little pink envelope addressed in the handwriting that meant more than all others to José Rézan. He tore it open eagerly. In place of a message of sad and loving condolence, he read within:

José, José, do you know that they are hunting Señor *Sweyn up and down the valley today? And for what crime? For having attacked you and your men in your own house. Where he, poor simple man, thought that he had a right to go to seek redress after you had robbed him of Elena Blanca. I am told that you are the only person who can lay a charge against* Señor *Sweyn. I know that that charge will not be pressed. There is too much generosity in you.*

Let the boy know when you are well enough to receive a visit from your devoted Catalina.

Poor José read this letter again and again. It made him excessively ill at ease, but there was certainly a shred of justice in what Catalina said. What shocked him, indeed, was simply the vein of chivalry that appeared to have developed in her at this late moment. Chivalry in Catalina, of all the people in the world.

However, there was not much time remaining to ponder upon this note, for now the sheriff was announced to him. When Kilmer entered, he spoke as though he had just been looking over Rézan's shoulder to read that same letter.

"Rézan," he said, "I want you to swear out a formal warrant before I start rampaging up and down the valley to find this Sandy Sweyn who's made a monkey out of us all."

"How in the name of all that is wonderful," Rézan asked, "could he have escaped? They say that the door to his cell was found unlocked, as well as the rear door to the jail."

"How he got away is interesting, but not important," said the sheriff. "What is to the point now, is getting him back. I need a posse to help me with that rascal, and I need your warrant before I open a case against the fellow. Can you write enough to sign your name?"

"Enough to sign it a hundred times," answered José Rézan. "But I'll never write it under a warrant to arrest this Sweyn. And the reason, Sheriff, is simply that I got what I more or less deserved. I tried to impose on a poor half-wit, and the poor half-wit that I had robbed turned around and nearly wrecked me and my home."

"The whole world has gone mad with its talk on the side of Sandy Sweyn. I begin to think that crime pays. It's a moral virtue . . . to hear you madmen talk about Sandy."

"Sheriff," Rézan said, closing his eyes and shaking his bandaged head, "I do not complain. Hunt up another witness. I'll not serve against Sweyn."

That news spread instantly abroad. The sheriff was not one to allow head-hunters to proceed with their work when they did not have law and order behind them. Since the work of law and order had been checked by the odd inconstancy of José Rézan, the sheriff sent out riders to call back his hunters. They came, and they came without tidings of the hunted. One thought that he had seen a blue roan shadow moving through the trees here; another thought that he had seen a bluish horse galloping down a hollow—but all was on the testimony of fleeting glimpses of which they could not be sure. So it was that Sandy Sweyn went unscathed, after such a career of wildness as the valley had never seen before.

As that day wore toward a close, a dozen armed men guarded every inch of the ground around José Rézan's house. Around the corral where Elena Blanca was kept, *Señor* Mirandos had posted more warriors. It was commonly felt that if the wild man chose to strike again, it would be in one of the two places, although Mirandos was rather startled by a telephone message from the sheriff, saying: "While you're on your guard, keep an eye on your daughter tonight, Mirandos."

"A thousand thanks," Mirandos said.

When he hung up the telephone, he smiled to himself. The rest of the world might regard his Catalina as a shrinking flower and a tender bud, but he, who knew her for these many years, felt that she was the last person in the world to need any cherishing from any person, even from her father. He paid no heed to establishing any guard over his daughter.

Little Catalina was left strictly alone. She had spent the entire day in her room. She was smiling and gay in the morning, when she heard of the escape of the prisoner. But as the day wore on, the miracle that she had expected did not develop. No Sandy Sweyn came to her, and toward night she grew into a towering passion.

Something had to bear the brunt of it when 9:00 p.m. arrived, and no wild lover had appeared at either window. When poor Dick stood up and stretched himself with a yawn, she flew into a mad, unreasoning passion, snatched up a whip, cut him twice with it, and as he fled with a howl, she threw the whip after him, and stamped with all the passion in her furious little body.

Poor Dick! He would never know that in this moment he had accomplished his destiny and one more good service to the world than any other of his kind in many and many a year. At that moment, as the whip was raised and cut against his tender hide, a shadowy head had risen at the casement of the bedroom. Two blazing, yellow eyes watched the scene, then the head slowly disappeared.

Catalina rushed into her inner chamber to be utterly alone with her disappointment, but Dick, cowering in the corner, suddenly came to life, and hurried toward the casement, whining softly.

To another girl, that evening brought no eager expectations. Peggy Kilmer felt that she had abdicated in behalf of her rival. There was not the slightest doubt in her mind that Sandy Sweyn was mad with love of Catalina. How could Peggy guess that a dog, a mere dog, might come between?

In the soft black of the night, Peggy sat in the hammock outside the sheriff's house and watched the stars that shimmered through the trees above her. She stroked old Tabby, who lay purring in her lap. Purring in her lap one minute, but with a snarl and a gasp, here was Tabby scooting up the trunk of the first tree and spitting from the branches, while a dog whined underneath, eager-eyed.

"Heavens above," Peggy Kilmer said. "It's Dick . . . it's Catalina's dog."

We will sometimes speak our thoughts aloud, when we feel ourselves most securely alone, and Peggy spoke hers aloud on this night. A deep voice answered her at once from the thick of the black night beneath the tree.

"Aye, it's Catalina's dog. I went looking for a girl, and I only came away with a dog. Sit down here, Peggy. I'm gonna tell you why."

Sit down by the side of a strange youngster like Sandy Sweyn? She had not time or chance to make up her own mind. For Sandy scooped her lightly into the hollow of his arm, and there they sat in the hammock, side-by-side.

"I went up the valley to the Mirandos' house," Sandy said, "looking to find Catalina, because that pretty face of hers has been living here behind my eyes for the last day, you understand?"

"I understand," Peggy replied faintly.

"When I got there, I worked my way up to her window, as I'd done before, and as I got there, I was just in time to see her take a whip and flog this dog . . . flog him for nothing at all. Why, Peggy, when I watched it, it turned things into a red blur. I wanted to take her by the throat. I waited till she was out of the room, and then I scooped up Dick and brought him down here. What I want to know is, do you think that a delicate dog like this could follow me the way I live, in the woods, without

291

getting sick?"

"I think he could . . . I know he could," Peggy said with more animation.

"Well," Sandy Sweyn said, "you think you would trust a dog to me, then?"

"I would, Sandy."

"Then there's one thing more, Peg. There were two faces in my mind. One very pretty, and one very freckled. One of them has gone out, tonight, and I'll never see it again. That leaves the freckled one, Peg. And that leaves one question more that I've got to ask. If you'd trust a dog to me, Peg, d'you think that one day you would trust yourself?"

"I . . . ," gasped out Peggy. "I. . . . How can I tell?"

"Who but you could?"

"Dad, and he's yonder in the house."

"The sheriff!" Sandy Sweyn cried.

"Aye," Peggy said with a strange note in her voice, "and I think that he's sort of expecting you to call."

"I'll do it," Sandy Sweyn avowed. "The sheriff is a white man, and I'll do it. Dick, you come along and back me up."

He started slowly toward the lit window of the house, with the setter close against his heels.

ABOUT THE AUTHOR

Max Brand is the best-known pen name of Frederick Faust, creator of Dr. Kildare, Destry, and many other fictional characters popular with readers and viewers worldwide. Faust wrote for a variety of audiences in many genres. His enormous output, totaling approximately thirty million words or the equivalent of five hundred thirty ordinary books, covered nearly every field: crime, fantasy, historical romance, espionage, Westerns, science fiction, adventure, animal stories, love, war, and fashionable society, big business and big medicine. Eighty motion pictures have been based on his work along with many radio and television programs. For good measure he also published four volumes of poetry. Perhaps no other author has reached more people in more different ways. Born in Seattle in 1892, orphaned early, Faust grew up in the rural San Joaquin Valley of California. At Berkeley he became a student rebel and one-man literary movement, contributing prodigiously to all campus publications. Denied a degree because of unconventional conduct, he embarked on a series of adventures culminating in New York City where, after a period of near starvation, he received simultaneous recognition as a serious poet and successful author of fiction. Later, he traveled widely, making his home in New York, then in Florence, and finally in Los Angeles. Once the United States entered the Second World War, Faust abandoned his lucrative writing career and his work as a screenwriter to serve as a war correspondent with the infantry in Italy, despite his fifty-one years and a bad heart. He was killed during a night attack on a hilltop village held by the German army. New books based on magazine serials or unpublished manuscripts or restored versions continue to appear so that, alive or dead, he has averaged a new book every four months for seventy-five years. Beyond this, some work by him is newly reprinted every week of every year in one or another format somewhere in the world. A great deal more about this author and his work can be found in *The Max Brand Companion* (Greenwood Press, 1997) edited by Jon Tuska and Vicki Piekarski. His next Five Star Western will be *The Tracker*. His Web site is www.MaxBrandOnline.com.